Murder at the Harvey House

A Beatrice Adams Mystery

Murder at the Harvey House

A Beatrice Adams Mystery

Ari Ryder

Poison Apple Publishing

Interior Design by Ashley M. Pringle.

Library of Congress Cataloging-in-Publication Data is available upon request.

ISBN: 978-0-578-78917-0

Printed in the U.S.A.

To my family, extended and immediate,
for putting up with my writerly quirks
and never discouraging them.

TABLE OF CONTENTS

CHAPTER ONE

A CORPSE MISLAID

Train was the absolute best way to travel, of that Beatrice Adams had a high opinion. She stood on the rear balcony of the lounge car, laughing giddily as her red curls blew madly about her face in the wind. At twenty-five, she was a slender, seemly creature full of life and exuberance, favoring adventure to the dull slavery of everyday existence. Her full lips were painted the brightest red, a perfect contrast to her blue sailor dress and cream heels. She clutched the railing with a white-gloved hand and an infectious grin.

"This is incredible!" she cried above the clacking of the wheels, beaming at the smitten steward standing at the door. He looked as though his eyes might fall out of his head if he stared a moment longer.

Beatrice, the daughter of a film director and famous actress, was far too used to the stares and gaping mouths to mind his expression. Such looks had followed her down red carpets and into lavish parties ever since she could walk. She turned to her fair-haired cousin, Eleanore, who stood uncomfortably beside her.

"What do you think, Ellie? Doesn't this just blow your wig off?"

"Doesn't it just?" Eleanore replied with a forced smile, a hand trying to tame her billowing curls. Her olive-green dress flapped in the wind like a flag, and she was clearly trying to pretend it didn't bother her. "Say, any chance we could go back to the passenger car?"

Beatrice laughed. "Don't be such a drag, darling! You need to learn to have a little fun."

"And you needn't be such a live wire," Eleanore retorted.

Beatrice tutted and waved a hand as if being a live wire was her life's ambition and Eleanore was being silly.

"Please, Bea," Eleanore begged.

Beatrice tore her gaze from the desert scenery rushing past. She knew she was pushing her luck. Anything even remotely daring had always made her younger cousin nervous. "Oh, all right," she conceded, adding with a playful smirk, "Spoilsport."

The young steward, still starry-eyed, stepped aside as Beatrice and Eleanore returned inside the wood-paneled lounge car. He bolted the door behind them, staring as Beatrice took Eleanore's hand and headed for the door to pass between cars.

"Put your tongue back in your mouth, boy," said a portly man sitting in an armchair nearby with a cigar in hand.

The steward shook himself back to his senses and returned to his duties as the girls, stifling giggles, passed from the lounge car into the sleeper car beyond. The hall narrowed here, and they had to walk single file to pass a few other passengers. They maintained their gait through the bright red and silver dining car with its two rows of white clothed tables, which were currently devoid of place settings. Eleanore visibly eased once they reached the passenger car.

"When you said vacation, I imagined something a little more relaxing," she mused.

Beatrice dropped her cousin's hand with a musical chuckle. "Just because your father is a lawyer doesn't mean you can't be unruly every now and then," she teased.

"Maybe I like societal norms," Eleanore defended.

They shortly reclaimed their seats, and Beatrice fixed her cousin with a smirk. "Well I don't. They hardly allow one to get into trouble."

"Says the private detective," Eleanore countered.

Beatrice smiled in self-satisfaction. "Phooey. I've only had one *official* case."

"One case that caught a killer and shut down the dirtiest juice joint in Los Angeles," Eleanore pointed out. "Your picture was in the paper."

"My picture is always in the paper."

"Sure." Eleanore shrugged. "As Virginia Adams's daughter. Face it, doll. You're finally famous on your own."

Beatrice grinned at her cousin. "Nearly."

Despite the recent stock market crisis, 1930 had never looked so good. Hollywood was heating up, speakeasies were everywhere, and she, Beatrice Adams, was finally getting her own piece of the action far from the spotlight of Virginia Adams and Thomas Hughes. It was more than any girl of her status could ask for, and besides, she'd already made business cards.

"Well," Beatrice went on, "this week I'm just your cousin, and we're going to have a swell time of glad rags and no calamities."

"And how!" Eleanore agreed spiritedly. "Say, why did you pick this place anyway?"

"Mary Coulter designed it, and I like her work," Beatrice replied. "Besides, who doesn't love a good trip on the Santa Fe? Just look at that scenery, will you!" She gestured to the desert mountains and plains rushing past the windows. "They say the Fred Harvey Company has really outdone itself this time, and it's only been open a month."

"I guess we'll find out, won't we?" Eleanore mused.

"Mm, won't we," hummed Beatrice, her gaze lost in the Arizona countryside whipping by.

The companions fell into a contemplative silence after that, and the train rattled on toward Winslow, their final destination. Beatrice was thrilled her cousin had agreed to come along on such short notice. Traveling alone was never half as much fun as having an accomplice to share it with, and while Eleanore was less adventurous than her older cousin, she was no stranger to a good time. They'd been attached at the hip since childhood, neither having any siblings to speak of other than Beatrice's younger half-brother, whom she rarely saw. Though Beatrice's parents had never married, they'd maintained a friendly relationship, both contributing to Beatrice's upbringing. This had allowed Beatrice to get to know her father's side of the family, Eleanore included, and Beatrice was grateful for it. A cousin was just as good as any sister.

Beatrice soon took up a book—*The Right Way to Do Wrong: An Exposé of Successful Criminals* by Harry Houdini—and Eleanore nodded off with her cheek in her hand. The sun steadily dipped below the horizon, giving ownership of the sky over to the stars, which glittered like beacons of hope in the night. Beatrice stared at them in wonder, picking out familiar constellations. She couldn't see half this many stars in Los Angeles. Eleanore, still asleep, missed them entirely. A blanket of clouds had covered them by the time she stirred, lit up now and again by a streak of lightning. To Beatrice it was a beautiful light show, but Eleanore eyed the distant storm with apprehension. It was near eight in the evening when the train finally lurched to a stop at Winslow station. Beatrice and Eleanore grabbed their handbags and carry-ons before joining the conga line heading for the exit. The steward stood on the platform below, politely handing ladies out of the train as each descended the steps. He was again smitten by Beatrice's appearance as if cupid had hit him with a volley of arrows.

"Thanks ever so," Beatrice said warmly when he helped her onto the platform.

The steward seemed to have lost his voice, tipping his hat in reply.

Eleanore's thanks was a bit more bashful, and he added a wide smile as he tipped his hat to her.

"You ladies take care now," he spoke at last.

"We will," Beatrice promised with gusto.

As they walked on, Eleanore's gaze was drawn to the station itself, which wasn't a station at all, but rather their hotel right there on the tracks.

"Leaping lizards," she murmured. "It's gorgeous!"

"Isn't it just?" Beatrice enthused.

A wide walk hugged by a sprawling lawn led from the tracks to the rear of the hotel, which rose to the height of two stories, built in the southwestern pueblo style. A red terra-cotta-tiled awning covered the walk along the side of the hotel, creating a sort of veranda where guests could sit on wooden benches and watch the trains or the activities on the lawn. Stone paths wound around the hotel, leading into courtyards with rich desert plant life and herb gardens. It was like something out of an old western film, and the hotel stood like a beautiful Spanish mission where weary travelers could take refuge from the perils of the desert. Beatrice took her cousin's arm as they ambled through it all, heading for the hotel's station entrance.

"What's the name of this place again?" Eleanore asked when they passed through the double doors into the hotel lobby.

"La Posada," Beatrice supplied. "It means resting place."

The interior of the hotel was even more charismatic than the exterior. Tile floors of the deepest umber complemented the bright oranges and yellows of the walls, all decorated with southwestern art and subtle hints of turquoise. It was a vibrant, colorful environment with gorgeous brickwork and eye-catching tile mosaics that made Beatrice's heart soar with a need for adventure. Even Eleanore couldn't help but marvel.

As they approached the front desk, they were met with a warm smile by a man in a pristine suit and tie. His thinning hair was slicked back with oil rather than pomade, and he sported a pencil mustache that was groomed to perfection.

"Good evening," he said. "I am Mr. Morrow, the hotel manager and your host for the duration of your stay. Are you checking in?"

"Yes, sir!" Beatrice beamed. "The reservation is under Adams."

Mr. Morrow turned to his ledger and ran his fountain pen down the list of names. "Ah. Here we are. Miss Beatrice Adams."

"That's me."

Mr. Morrow adjusted his tie with the air of one about to deliver bad news. "Unfortunately, Miss Adams, the suite we had reserved for you is having a few electrical problems at this time. We can place you in a temporary room while the suite is being amended?" he suggested hopefully.

Beatrice cast him a disarming smile. "That'd be swell."

The manager visibly eased, clearly used to higher-class guests who were unreasonable. "Excellent! I have just the room. It has a lovely view of the garden."

He jotted a few things down in his ledger and pulled a key from one of the slots behind him.

"Here we are." He handed Beatrice the key. "Second floor. I'll have a bellhop deliver your trunks from the baggage car. I hope you and your companion enjoy your stay with us."

She grinned, all ruby lips and white teeth. "Thanks. Say, is the dining room open?"

"But of course. It's just through there." He indicated the archway behind him.

Beatrice turned to her cousin. "I'm famished. How about a little something before we head up, hmm?"

"Fine by me," Eleanore agreed. Though they'd eaten on the train, it'd been a good three hours since then.

Beatrice waved farewell to Mr. Morrow and headed, arm in arm with Eleanore, for the dining room. It was sprawling with patio tiles on the floor, colorful murals on the wall, and a long white-tiled counter with stools for lone diners. There were already several people seated about the delightful tables being served by the famous Harvey Girls in their traditional black dresses and starched white aprons. Beatrice chose a table where she could observe the room at her leisure and plopped herself in a chair, setting her handbag on the table and her carry-on beside her seat. Eleanore did the same.

"It's too bad we can't order wine," Beatrice mused as she perused the menu on the table.

Eleanore looked appalled. "You shouldn't say such things, Bea," she insisted in hushed tones. "You never know who could be listening."

"Oh, horsefeathers," Beatrice laughed. "You've had plenty to drink at my mother's."

Eleanore glanced about, then leaned closer to whisper, "It's not against the law to drink liquor you had in your home before 1920."

"You're under the assumption that my mother obeys the law when it comes to our wine cellar," Beatrice teased.

Their conversation was cut short by a dark-haired Harvey Girl with a grim expression. She poured water into their glasses without so much as a word and trudged off moodily. Beatrice stared after her, surprised. Before she could comment on the matter, another Harvey Girl walked up with a pleasant smile.

"Don't mind Mary," she said apologetically. "What can I get you ladies?"

"I think I'll have the corn chowder," Beatrice decided. "Is she all right?"

"She's just grumpy. It was meant to be her night off. She had a date with this fella to go see one of those talkies, but one of the other girls didn't show for her shift, so Mary had to stay. Can't be one girl down when the train comes in."

"I suppose that'd make anyone sour," Beatrice reasoned. "What was your name?"

"Oh, I'm Alice!" the girl replied, embarrassed that she'd forgotten to introduce herself first.

"Beatrice. And this is my cousin, Eleanore."

Eleanore gave a wee wave of her hand and rested her chin on it.

"Nice to meet you," Alice said pleasantly. "What would you like, Miss Eleanore?"

"Oh, just Eleanore, please," said Eleanore with a good-natured smile. "I'll have the chowder as well, and some biscuits if you have them."

"Coming right up," Alice assured, and she turned to put the order in.

"Poor Mary," reflected Beatrice, her electric blue eyes sweeping the room.

"I can't blame her for being sore," Eleanore agreed.

"Nor can I."

A traveling salesman sat not two tables away, flirting with the Harvey Girl who refilled his soda. Beyond him sat a pair of flappers—twins by the looks of it—with close-cropped black hair and shiny dresses. Beatrice could only imagine where they were traveling to. A few tables from there sat an agreeable young man with clean-cut brown hair and expressive, kind eyes. He nursed a coffee, the empty dishes around him speaking of his finished meal. His suit was casual but pristine. He was clearly a professional man.

It was only when the gentleman looked up and caught her eye that Beatrice realized she'd let her stare linger too long. Rather than averting her gaze in embarrassment, which Eleanore surely would have done, Beatrice flashed him a vibrant, red-lipped smile. Enchanted, the man smiled back. Only then did Beatrice turn away.

"You're a terrible flirt," accused Eleanore.

"Says you!" Beatrice rebuffed.

Another roll of thunder sounded, this time much closer. Alice returned with their soups and carefully set them on the table, placing the biscuits between them.

"Thank you, darling," said Beatrice. "Say, that's some storm on the way, huh?"

Alice nodded. "June's the start of monsoon season around here. The lightning is pretty bad, but it's really the flooding you've got to worry about."

"Fantastic," Eleanore grumbled, digging into her soup.

"Relax," Beatrice encouraged as Alice dismissed herself. "Everything will be jake. You'll see!"

Eleanore seemed less than convinced, but she was predisposed to see the glass half empty. To Beatrice, the world was simply full of wonder—a view that presently worked in her favor. The handsome gentleman she'd smiled at stopped by on his way out of the dining hall.

"You ladies just arrived?" he asked, fiddling with the fedora in his hands.

"Sure are," Beatrice answered. "Came in on the evening train. What about yourself, Mister . . . ?"

"Riley," he supplied. "Harry Riley."

"Beatrice Adams," Beatrice introduced, offering a gloved hand. "And this is my cousin, Eleanore Hughes."

Harry shook their hands in turn. "Pleasure."

Eleanore turned back to her soup the moment he'd relinquished her hand, but Beatrice had all but forgotten hers.

"What brings you to Winslow, Mr. Riley?" Beatrice asked conversationally. "Business or pleasure?"

"Business," he replied. "I'm on my way to Los Angeles to fill a post at the hospital."

"Swell! That's where we're from!" exclaimed Beatrice, her eyes sparkling. "So, you're a doctor?"

"That's right."

Eleanore rolled her eyes, and Beatrice sent a swift kick to her shin that nearly made Eleanore spit up her soup.

"You okay?" Harry asked with concern.

"Everything's aces," Eleanore uttered, dabbing her pink mouth with a napkin.

"You should look us up some time," Beatrice suggested, already digging through her purse for a business card. It was embossed and glimmered in the light when she handed it over. "Then you can say you've one acquaintance in Los Angeles. It's an easy city to get lost in."

"I'd like that, Miss Adams," he said, giving a million-dollar smile. "I'd like that very much."

It was only then that he bothered to glance at the card. "Say, a private detective! How exactly does a lady get into that profession?"

"With class and style, Mr. Riley," Beatrice intoned with her own winning smile.

Harry chuckled and tucked her card in his breast pocket. "I don't doubt it, Miss Adams," he said warmly. "I'll let you ladies get back to your soup. Have a good night."

He replaced his hat to his head and departed.

"Goodnight!" Beatrice called after him.

When she turned back to her soup, Eleanore wore a look of extreme incredulity.

"What?" demanded Beatrice. "I'm allowed to be ridiculous. It's part of my charm!"

"Yeah?" Eleanore patronized. "And what happened to Patrick?"

Beatrice waved a hand. "Oh, Patrick is . . . Patrick."

A smirk crossed Eleanore's lips, and she quirked an accusing eyebrow. "Entirely attractive and overly controlling?"

A slow, innocent smile painted Beatrice's cherry lips. "At least I let him think as much."

The girls shared a laugh over that, and the conversation quickly changed topics ranging from Clark Gable's dreamy eyes to whether that new James Cagney fellow would finally make it in the movies. Beatrice had bumped shoulders with him last time she'd visited her father at the studio. He seemed a pleasurable enough fellow, and he and his wife would certainly add a sparkle to Hollywood parties.

Dessert came, and then coffee. A long day of travel began to take its toll, and Beatrice found herself looking forward to a fresh bed and a good night's sleep. She charged the bill to the room with a final smile and a hearty thanks tossed Alice's way, then took up her things. Eleanore did the same, and they made their way down the long, windowed hall, up the curved tile steps, and to the room indicated on their key—just to the right of the staircase and two doors down. Beatrice opened the wooden door and switched on the lights.

"Oh, how charming!" she remarked as she walked inside.

The room was small, much smaller than the suite she'd booked, but rather than being cross over it, Beatrice could only find splendor in the two full beds and the southwestern decor. The bedspreads were a vibrant red to match the handwoven rug hanging on the wall. A desk sat in the corner near the window with a clock that read nine fifteen, and a quick peek in the bathroom revealed more tile mosaics and a gorgeous turquoise mirror. The departure from Art Deco was a breath of fresh air despite how much Beatrice loved extravagance. Their luggage had been delivered, already perched at the end of each bed.

"See, darling," Beatrice said with delight, sitting on the end of her bed to remove her heels. "All jake!"

A light rain pattered against the window, steadily picking up until it sounded like machine gun fire against the panes.

Eleanore smiled, her eyes apologetic. "I know, honey. I'm sorry. I'm just sorta tired, you know?"

Beatrice stretched out on her bed while Eleanore began the dubious task of opening her trunks to hang up her clothes. Lightning flashed, accompanied by rolling thunder and a howling wind. Beatrice smiled to herself. She loved a good storm. It didn't rain enough in California for her liking.

"You know, you can do that in the morning," Beatrice pointed out. She only planned on pulling out her nightdress before collapsing in bed with her book.

"I don't want my things to get wrinkled," Eleanore said simply as she pulled out a stunning red dress. She moved to hang it up in the closet.

When she opened the door, a body fell at her feet with a horrifying *thud*. Eleanore screamed, thunder crashed, and the lights went out.

CHAPTER TWO

Beatrice Adams, Private Investigator

Beatrice was on her feet in an instant, digging through her handbag for a small flashlight she kept handy for just such occasions. Eleanore had covered her mouth to quiet her scream, but Beatrice could still hear her sniveling. At last, Beatrice's gloved hand closed over the metal tube and pulled it from her bag, switching it on. The narrow beam of yellow light first found Eleanore's terrified face. Eleanore squinted away from it, her back to the wall, seemingly paralyzed.

Unlike her cousin, Beatrice was little frightened by corpses, and she turned her beam next to the body that had been mercilessly stuffed in their closet, approaching with care. It was a young woman, one of the Harvey Girls judging by the uniform. Beatrice would bet her favorite pair of shoes it was the girl who'd never showed for work. She knelt by the body and slipped off a glove to check the poor girl's pulse at her wrist—nothing. Her skin was cold to the touch too.

Somberly, Beatrice wiggled her glove back on. "I think we'd better . . . call the police," she uttered, the beam of her light catching the corpse's neck.

"You think?" Eleanore repeated in disbelief. "A body fell out of our closet, and you *think* we should call the police?"

"Don't go into a panic," said Beatrice, distracted. She leaned closer to examine the bruising on the dead girl's neck. She'd clearly been strangled and discarded. This was no accident. It was murder.

A knock on the door made both women jump. Eleanore shrieked. Mr. Morrow's voice called from the other side. "Miss Adams? Is everything all right? One of the bellhops heard screaming."

Beatrice breathed easy on recognizing the manager's voice, and she moved fluidly to open the door. Mr. Morrow stood in the hall with a candlestick in hand, the flickering light casting eerie shadows around the darkened hall. A bellhop stood behind him, presumably the one who'd heard Eleanore's scream.

"I'm afraid we have a *slight* problem," said Beatrice.

She stepped aside to give a fuller view of the room. Her flashlight beam fell on the body, and Mr. Morrow's countenance dropped.

"Good gravy!" the bellhop exclaimed. "That's Holly!"

Mr. Morrow, now ash white, was at a loss for words. He stared at the body as if it might reanimate and come after him next. A multitude of questions flooded Beatrice's mind as he processed, but she knew well that *when* those questions were asked was just as important as *how*. She turned instead to the bellhop.

"Say, my cousin's had a nasty shock," she said. "Could you take her down for some tea?"

"Y-yeah. Sure," he stuttered, still in a shock himself at the sight of his fellow employee sprawled on the floor.

"Here . . . take my light, Tommy," Mr. Morrow offered, finally finding his voice.

Tommy accepted the candle and gestured for Eleanore to follow him.

"I'm not leaving you on your own," Eleanore complained to her cousin.

"I'll be fine, Ellie. Unless you want to continue staring at a body, I suggest you go with Tommy."

It took a moment's stare-down, but Eleanore finally relented and allowed Tommy to lead her into the hall and toward a cup of moxie-restoring tea. Beatrice turned her attention to Mr. Morrow, whose eyes were fixated firmly away from the dead girl.

"I know this must be a sock in the teeth," she sympathized, "but can you think of anyone that she didn't get along with? Anyone who may have hurt her?"

"Hurt her?" repeated Mr. Morrow incredulously. "You're not suggesting—"

"Murder, Mr. Morrow?" she finished for him. "I'm not suggesting it at all. Holly was definitely bumped off."

"Good Lord," he uttered, wringing his hands. "And during opening month. . . ."

Beatrice decided not to mention that the hotel had passed its opening month and was technically now in full swing. Mr. Morrow already seemed a man near unraveling, and Beatrice knew she had to act fast before she was barred from investigating.

"How soon can you phone the police?" she asked.

"The phone lines are down," he said nervously. "And the storm blew a fuse."

A crash of thunder bellowed as if the storm itself were laughing at them.

"Time is of the essence, Mr. Morrow," Beatrice urged. "I don't mean to alarm you, but the killer may still be here. We have to act fast."

"Act fast? What exactly do you intend to do?"

"I'm a private investigator," she said simply. "I plan to investigate. Or would you rather be trapped here in the dark with a murderer on the loose and no phones to call the police?"

Mr. Morrow looked confused, and Beatrice knew that look well. She'd seen it a hundred times over. It was usually accompanied with a round of annoying queries. *Aren't you related to that actress? I thought you were in films? What's a dame doing investigating?* She fixed her gorgeous face in as serious an expression as she could muster.

"I'm not playing you for a sap, Mr. Morrow," she said. "I can handle this. Unless you'd like to go down in history as the hotel manager who let a murderer get away. . . ."

"Oh, all right," he conceded, trying with all his might not to look at Holly's corpse. "What do you need me to do?"

"I need Dr. Riley," she requested, trying not to get too excited. "And I may need to question the staff. If you could gather everyone downstairs, that would be a help. How full is the hotel tonight?"

Mr. Morrow nodded, looking on the verge of a breakdown. "Not even at half capacity. Many of our guests left on the evening train."

"Thank you," Beatrice replied, feeling a little sorry for him. She was sure murdered guests hadn't been a part of his hospitality training.

Certain that she had all the information he could presently give, Beatrice sent Mr. Morrow on his way with a new candle from the decorative side table drawer in the hall. He departed with the speed of one who thought the devil was after him, leaving Beatrice alone with the body. Her eyes traveled to the poor girl at her feet.

"Holly, what happened to you?" she murmured.

Beatrice knelt once again to examine the body without interruption, noting how crinkled and torn the girl's uniform was. She examined Holly's dainty fingers with a closer inspection of the light. Holly clearly had a regular manicure to keep her hands fresh and Harvey Girl approved. Several of her nails were chipped, however, and the smallest sliver of skin and dried blood was trapped under the nails of Holly's right hand.

"You surely put up a fight, didn't you?" Beatrice whispered somberly.

On further inspection of the body, she found a note tucked in Holly's apron pocket. It was typewritten, omitting any hope of identifying the handwriting. It read:

Meet me in the boiler room at midnight to discuss payment.

But payment for what? Of one thing Beatrice was certain—Holly was lured to her death, and whomever wrote that note must surely be the killer. Beatrice mentally put a trip to the boiler room on her to-do list as she slipped the paper into her handbag.

A gentle knock sounded at the door, and Harry poked his head inside, candle in one hand and medical bag in the other.

"Mr. Morrow said you wanted to see me?" he spoke, eyes landing on the body. "And here I was hoping the news of a corpse was your way of getting me alone," he teased.

"Oh, please." She smiled. "I'm much too straightforward for that." She indicated the body with a sweep of her hand. "Any insight you can give me would be lovely."

"I'll do what I can," he promised as he knelt beside her. He set the candle aside and pulled a pair of medical gloves from his bag, carefully covering each digit before he set to work.

Beatrice watched with interest as he examined Holly's neck and rotated her head side to side. It didn't move quite right.

"Her neck's broken," Harry observed. "Judging by the bruising and crushed windpipe, though, I'd say it broke after she died. Maybe falling from the closet."

"Or on her way *to* it," murmured Beatrice.

Harry went on to investigate the body, like Beatrice, taking note of Holly's nails. He felt gingerly for any other injuries, the raging storm outside the only noise. Holly's bruising, coloration, and general temperature were taken into account. Beatrice sat by in patient silence, wondering why someone would murder a Harvey Girl. They were meant to be pillars of modesty and innocence.

"What's the diagnosis?" asked Beatrice when he'd finished.

Harry pulled off his gloves and tossed them in his bag. "Cause of death was definitely asphyxiation by strangulation. Given the severity and width of the bruising, I'd say your killer is a fella with strong hands. The marks are too far apart to be a lady."

"That narrows down the suspects," Beatrice mused. "Anything else?"

Harry nodded. "I'm no expert on . . . dead patients," he said delicately, "but I don't think this was recent. She's cold, and she's started to stiffen. I'd say she was killed well over six hours ago."

"Giving our killer plenty of time to run," sighed Beatrice.

"Maybe," Harry agreed, "and maybe not."

He met her eye.

"You sure you want to get tangled up in this? It's a real messy business."

"Try and stop me," she dared with a grin, standing. "Can you write a report to give the police when they arrive?"

Harry too got to his feet, smiling at her attractive display of moxie. "You betcha."

"Aces," Beatrice beamed. Her eyes traveled to the dead girl. "We should seal this room . . . put her on the bed. Lend a girl a hand?"

"Shouldn't we leave her for the police?" Harry observed.

"Oh, she wasn't killed here anyway," said Beatrice with a wave of her hand. "Besides, we can't just . . . leave her on the floor. It feels wrong."

Harry shrugged in silent agreement, and the pair of them moved to either side of Holly's body. He took her shoulders, leaving Holly's feet for Beatrice. On the count of three, they lifted Holly onto the nearest bed, which unfortunately happened to be Eleanore's. Beatrice decided against mentioning it to her excitable cousin. It was, after all, Eleanore's first body.

"Thanks," Beatrice puffed out, catching her breath. Holly wasn't exceptionally heavy, but dead weight was still dead weight.

"It's no trouble," Harry assured her. "What happens now?"

"Now we lock this room," Beatrice said, scooping up her purse. She'd nearly crossed the threshold when Harry's voice stopped her in her tracks.

"Don't you need shoes?"

Beatrice paused and glanced down at her stocking-covered feet. "Oh, fiddlesticks," she cursed, turning back for the heels she'd abandoned.

Harry chuckled as she scooped them up, and together, all their things acquired, they made their way into the hall where Beatrice stepped back into her shoes. She locked the door and tested the handle to be sure it was secure, musing to herself that a body couldn't very well get up and wander off, but there was a first time for everything. She stowed her flashlight in favor of Harry's candle, and together they made their way down the curved stairs and down the long hall toward the lobby. The vibrant halls seemed more foreboding in the dark with a storm wailing outside like a banshee on the moors, and Beatrice was secretly glad of Harry's company.

CHAPTER TWO

"Some night, huh?" said Harry.

"Yeah," Beatrice agreed. "Some night."

When they made it to the lobby, they found every member of the hotel staff gathered around, accompanied by a few of the guests who'd still been awake. Candles sat in every nook and cranny, spreading warm light through the room as if the lobby were a bona fide safe haven. The hubbub died immediately when Beatrice and Harry entered. Mr. Morrow had, no doubt, let a few details of Holly's current state slip. Eleanore sat quietly in a corner nursing her tea, and from the guilty look on her face, Beatrice surmised that any further information gleaned had spilled from her cousin's excitable lips.

The bellhop who'd escorted Eleanore downstairs was the first to break the awkward silence.

"Miss Hughes says you're a detective."

"I am," replied Beatrice.

"Then . . . you know what happened to her? To Holly?"

Every eye in the room fixed expectantly on Beatrice. At least a dozen Harvey Girls, three bellhops, three porters, the kitchen staff, Mr. Morrow, the salesman, the flapper twins, and an older couple Beatrice had yet to meet. Harry was the only person not gawking at Beatrice like a frightened deer.

"I don't know everything," she said carefully, her eyes flicking over each face in turn, looking for a sign of guilt among the oglers. "But I do know . . . that Holly was murdered."

The usual outcry of gasps and murmured prayers followed. Beatrice allowed them to die down before going on.

"What's more, I think the killer is still with us," she said boldly. "And I intend to find them . . . unless they'd like to save us all some trouble and fess up now."

Not one person met her eye, afraid of being suspected. Beatrice was little surprised. Murderers rarely fessed up without a little help. She let her dare hang for a few uncomfortable moments, then spun to face the hotel manager.

"Mr. Morrow?" she said.

Reluctantly, he stepped forward, dabbing his perspiring brow with a handkerchief. "Yes, Miss Adams?"

"Is there anywhere I might conduct a few preliminary interviews? A girl does like her privacy, after all."

"Well . . . you could use my office," he answered halfheartedly.

"Wonderful!" She whirled on Eleanore. "Come along, darling. You're so good at taking notes."

"But I—oh, all right," Eleanore grumbled, setting her tea on the nearest end table. Beatrice could tell she wanted no part in this business, which was usually Eleanore's reaction to all of Beatrice's schemes unless they involved shopping or a luxurious spa.

"Do you need me to hang about?" Harry asked.

"Oh, no," Beatrice assured, a gentle hand on his arm. "You've done enough, Mr. Riley. If you could get that report ready for the boys in blue, that'd be aces."

"Sure," he replied, almost sounding disappointed.

Mr. Morrow called across the lobby to an older, responsible-looking Harvey Girl. "Miss Bishop, if you would please direct everyone to the dining hall and put on some more tea."

Miss Bishop nodded and herded the other girls along to help. Mary alone glanced back at Beatrice, her expression suspicious. The salesman complained the whole way out of the lobby about dying of boredom before any dame could solve a murder.

Beatrice once again captured Mr. Morrow's attention. "I'd like to chat with you first, if I may. It is your hotel, after all. You know it best."

"Yes . . . all right," he conceded, gesturing in the direction of his office as he scooped up a candle.

Beatrice and Eleanore followed, Harry watching them go.

Inside his quaint office, Mr. Morrow lit more candles, revealing the cramped space to be stuffed to the brim but quite organized. It was hardly bigger than a broom closet with a set of filing cabinets and a bookcase behind his mahogany desk. Being an interior room, not a single window lined his office. The storm was effectively silenced the moment they closed the door.

"Do you have a pen and paper?" asked Eleanore.

Mr. Morrow nodded and pulled both from his top desk drawer,

saying to Beatrice as he handed them over, "You're not intending to interview the whole hotel, are you?"

Beatrice nearly laughed. "Oh, no."

She sat in one of the two chairs in front of his desk. Eleanore sat in the other, writing the date and Mr. Morrow's name on the paper he'd provided in neat, spiraling letters.

"I'll only ask the essential," Beatrice went on, "but it's hard to weed out the essential without some direction."

"Ah, yes. A fair point," said Mr. Morrow. He finally sat in his own chair.

Beatrice rested her hands in her lap. "Mr. Morrow, when did you last see Holly?"

"Let's see. . . ." Mr. Morrow's eyes considered the ceiling as if the answer were written there in invisible ink. "Yesterday evening around eight o'clock. She was resetting the dining room for breakfast. The girls all have a ten o'clock curfew, you see, so we close the dining room at nine to give them ample time to clean up."

Eleanore took studious notes.

"And how did she seem?" asked Beatrice.

"Well, she was . . . now that you mention it, she did seem a bit distracted."

"How so?"

"Forgetting orders, spilling drinks, dropping dishes—she was usually a very careful girl."

"Did anyone confront her?"

"Sally Bishop," came his reply.

Beatrice's mind went to the woman he'd called to in the lobby.

"She's the house mother," he explained. "Keeps all the girls in check and sorts out any misdemeanors. They're all quite close with one another."

"Did Miss Bishop say anything about their conversation to you?"

"Only that Miss Albright—Holly, that is—was homesick and that she'd be fine by morning."

Homesick indeed, thought Beatrice. It was a convenient excuse when one considered the year-long contract Harvey Girls signed, but Beatrice didn't buy it for a second. It sounded an awful lot like an excuse to her.

"How long had Holly been working for the Fred Harvey Company?" asked Beatrice.

"I'm not entirely sure," Mr. Morrow answered earnestly. "She came to us from another Harvey House down the line. Many of the girls did. I believe she'd worked half of her contract at least."

"Is there anyone else Holly was close to? Anyone who would have seen her after you left for the night?"

"Miss Bishop, of course. And there's her roommate, Sarah Acre. This is her first Harvey House, and I believe she and Miss Albright were quite close."

"Do you think you could fetch Miss Acre for us?" Beatrice requested with a charming smile.

Mr. Morrow was stunned by her quick line of inquiry. "That's it, then?"

"For now," Beatrice promised. "I like to find my corner pieces before I tackle a good puzzle."

"Yes, well . . . in that case, I won't be long."

He rose fluidly and, with a minute bow, departed the room.

The moment Mr. Morrow was gone, Beatrice hopped up and started poking around, opening drawers and sifting through papers atop the desk.

"What are you doing?" Eleanore hissed. "We don't have a warrant!"

Beatrice chortled in mild amusement. "Private investigators don't have the luxury of warrants, silly. And if we wait for the police, the killer might scram. Do you want that?"

"No, but—"

"Then hush."

Eleanore fell silent, but not without an annoyed huff. Nothing more was said on the matter.

Other than deducing that Mr. Morrow's first name was Henry, Beatrice came up empty, interrupted all too soon by the approaching footsteps of the office owner. She scrambled back to her seat, doing her best to look the epitome of innocence. Eleanore shook her head.

Mr. Morrow entered then, followed by a young girl of twenty with ash-brown hair and eyes puffy from a good cry. It was evident she'd cared for Holly, and Beatrice's heart bled. Losing a friend was hard enough without the added element of murder.

"Take a seat," Mr. Morrow said, tone gentle but firm.

Sarah sat, timid and closed off, in Mr. Morrow's chair. He stood like a sentry behind her.

"I'm sorry to ask this of you, Miss Acre," Beatrice empathized. "I wouldn't trouble you if it weren't of the utmost importance."

Sarah nodded feebly.

"Is . . . is it true what you said?" she sniffed. "That the killer might still be here?"

"I'm afraid so."

"Then . . . how can I help?"

Sarah sat up a little taller, her face suddenly stone. Her youth and small stature were instantly diminished by the determination in her eyes Beatrice couldn't help cracking a smile, seeing a sliver of her younger self in Sarah.

"I just want to jabber for a few minutes. See what we can dig up. Think you can manage that?"

Sarah nodded, this time more confidently.

Eleanore added a new section to her notes with Sarah's name and general description.

"Swell," Beatrice bubbled, trying her best to keep the mood light despite the dismal proceedings. "According to Mr. Morrow, you lived with Holly. What sort of roommate was she?"

"Oh, she was a regular wife," Sarah said affectionately. "You know, keeping the place organized and such. I felt kinda bad, her being stuck with me. I'm not exactly easy to live with."

"Why's that?" wondered Beatrice.

"Well, I'm not very tidy, see," Sarah admitted. "My mother hoped a year as a Harvey Girl would help all that and improve my prospects, but I just don't have a knack for organization."

"Intelligent people rarely do," Beatrice mused.

Sarah flushed.

"What can you tell me about yesterday? How was Holly?"

"Nervous," Sarah described, eyes glazed in thought. "When I asked her why, she said it was nothing, but I knew she was lying. All day long, she was in a mood. Around mid-day, just after we'd served lunch, her attitude changed . . . like she was . . . determined. She disappeared for half an hour after that. I don't know where, but when she came back, she was worse than before. Dropping things and running into other girls. Holly was always more put together than that. Say!" An idea dawned. "You don't think she met her killer then, do you?"

"I think it's a safe bet," Beatrice agreed.

"Jiminy!" Sarah exclaimed. "I should have followed her! I should have—" Beatrice's hand rested on Sarah's, and the girl quieted.

"It's not your fault, honey," Beatrice comforted. "And even if you'd followed, who's to say you wouldn't have been offed too?"

Sarah nodded, holding back a sob.

Beatrice patted her hand, then sat back in her seat. Eleanore circled a note she'd made about Holly's missing half hour.

"When Holly was gone, did you notice anyone else who might have been missing?" asked Beatrice.

"No," Sarah answered, thinking on it a little harder. "Not anyone that shouldn't'a been anyway. The fellas had all gone out for a smoke, and the guests are always coming and going."

"Not that we're accusing any of the guests," Mr. Morrow jumped in nervously.

Beatrice flicked her gaze to Mr. Morrow as if the fly on the wall had suddenly started buzzing too loudly.

"Everyone is a suspect until ruled out, Mr. Morrow," she said simply. "Even you."

Mr. Morrow fell silent at this, and Beatrice was pleased.

"On to the evening," Beatrice continued, attention back on Sarah. "When you and Holly returned to your housing, how did she behave then?"

"She was still anxious," Sarah answered, "but not like before. There was a sort of . . . determination there again, like she'd made whatever decision she'd been juggling all day."

"Did you talk to her about it?"

Sarah shook her head. "I was beat. We work ten-hour days, you know. So, I just poured myself a glass of water and went to bed. When I woke up in the morning, she was gone. In fact . . ."

Sarah paused, glancing to Mr. Morrow, clearly afraid to go on.

"You can tell me anything, Sarah," Beatrice encouraged. "I won't hold it against you, and I won't let him, either."

"Well," Sarah began, wringing her hands. "It's just that . . . when I woke up, it looked like her bed hadn't been slept in at all. She must have broken curfew and slipped out. I told everyone she wasn't feeling well because . . . well, I was terrified she'd gone out with some fella, and I didn't want her to get sacked. Oh, this is all my fault!"

All at once, the sobbing started. Beatrice was impressed. Given Sarah's puffy eyes, she'd expected the whole of the interview to be laced with tears.

Mr. Morrow offered Sarah his handkerchief, and she blew her nose.

"It's not your fault," Beatrice reiterated. "Did you hear anything last night? Maybe her leaving the room?"

"No," Sarah sniffed, reigning herself in. "Which is strange. The slightest noise usually wakes me right up, but last night I was out like a light."

She seemed on the verge of losing herself to the sobs building in her chest.

Beatrice gave a sympathetic smile. "You've been a big help. Why don't you see Miss Bishop about another cup of tea?"

Sarah's eyes turned to Mr. Morrow. He gave a subtle nod and coaxed Sarah out of her chair, guiding her from the room with one of the many candles.

"Poor dear," Beatrice murmured when they'd gone.

"Yeah," agreed Eleanore. "If someone killed you, I'd be in hysterics."

A surprised grin crossed Beatrice's face. "Would you?"

"Oh, stuff it!" Eleanore jibed, hiding a smile. "You're family!"

"That doesn't mean you have to like me," teased Beatrice.

"Sometimes I don't."

They grinned at one another, enjoying a brief respite from the grim task at hand. Beatrice returned their attention to the case.

"Well, how are our corner pieces looking?"

Eleanore consulted her notes, angelic features twisted in deep thought. "Messy," she replied. "Holly was surely killed in the dead of night, though. But when and where?"

Beatrice beamed like a Cheshire that had cornered a particularly juicy mouse. "I have a few ideas about that."

"Such as?" pressed Eleanore.

Beatrice pulled the note from Holly's pocket out of her handbag and showed it to her cousin. Eleanore's eyebrow's shot up.

"Gee whiz," she said. "The boiler room? Can't we wait for the lights?"

A particularly loud crash of thunder penetrated the quiet as if the storm agreed with Eleanore and wanted desperately to make it known.

Beatrice patted her cousin's knee. "Don't be such a bunny. I have a less exciting job for you."

Eleanore sighed in relief.

Beatrice stood decidedly, returning the note to her bag. "But first, tea!"

Mr. Morrow returned then, a hopeful look in his eyes. "Are we through, Miss Adams?" he asked.

"For now," she replied. "I'd like to take a look at Holly's room later, if I may."

"Of course," he agreed, tone suggesting he'd do anything to have this business over and done with.

Beatrice's eyes lingered on his desk once more. "Say, is that the only typewriter here?"

"No. There is one in the library for guests and another in the dorm parlor for the girls to use in their off time. Why do you ask?"

Beatrice shrugged innocently, picking up one of the two remaining candles in the room. "No reason. Come on, Ellie. Let's go see what Miss Bishop has put together."

Eleanore followed her cousin into the hall and leaned in close to whisper, "Why do I get the feeling we're not just going for the tea?"

"Because we aren't," Beatrice admitted. "We're going to mingle. I have more suspects to meet, and you're going to help me."

Eleanore groaned at that. "Why do you always get me into such trouble."

Beatrice chortled. "Because, darling, you're so good at getting us back out of it."

CHAPTER THREE
A Strange Tea Party

The hotel dining room could easily have been mistaken for a wake with the multitude of candles spread about to light it. Beatrice mused to herself that it was a capital place for a ghost to hide and an even better one for a murderer. Where better to hide than in plain sight? And from the looks of things, she had a lot of digging to do. The murder of Holly Albright had all but shattered the rules of social status. Guests mingled with the hotel staff all about the room, forming new social circles in the name of survival and comfort. They were all so engrossed in gossip that no one noticed Beatrice and Eleanore enter the room.

"What do you want me to do?" Eleanore whispered.

Beatrice, knowing her cousin's strengths and weaknesses well, smiled in the direction of the flapper twins. "Grab a tea and go jabber with those two," she instructed.

Eleanore nodded and moved toward the table laden with tea things. If there was one thing Eleanore could be credited with, it was her exceptional socialite skills. Beatrice had only recently begun putting said skills to use. It was Eleanore who'd talked Beatrice up to the investigator following the trail of Tony Baker's murder, the first real case Beatrice had cracked. She'd even provided an in with the clumsy but adept forensic analyst Daniel Green, who had a crush on Eleanore that was larger than the Pacific Ocean. The case had earned Detective Raglan a promotion, which in turn gave Beatrice more access to LAPD resources, and it was all made possible by Eleanore's gift of gab.

Beatrice watched in self-satisfaction as Eleanore expertly inserted herself into the twins' conversation, their smiles and open postures indicating their acceptance of her cousin. Her mole planted, Beatrice made her way to the tea table. Miss Bishop stood behind it, tall and solemn. Her smile was forced as she offered Beatrice a cup. Beatrice smiled in sympathy. "You don't have to pretend," she murmured. "It's okay to be sad, you know."

Miss Bishop's countenance dropped. She slowly lowered the empty cup and saucer to the table. "Forgive me," she begged, almost whispering.

"Whatever for?" asked Beatrice. "Being human?"

Miss Bishop smiled somberly. "I guess."

"Fred Harvey won't roll in his grave if you take one night off," Beatrice assured her, coming around the table and pulling a teacup toward herself.

Miss Bishop's eyes widened. "What are you doing?"

Beatrice beamed as she poured piping hot tea from the kettle into the cup. "Making you tea."

Miss Bishop was flabbergasted. "But I—it just isn't right. It isn't what's done. It—"

"Darling," Beatrice cut her off, eyes sincerely boring a hole through Miss Bishop's armor. "A girl is dead. Your only duty is to yourself, and you won't get through this by pretending everything is jake. So," she handed the cup to Miss Bishop and began pouring her own, "let's sit and talk it out, hmm?"

As Beatrice hoped, a little kindness went a long way. Miss Bishop's facade melted into a more human model, and that was far easier to work with. After adding a bit of cream and sugar to her tea, Beatrice guided Miss Bishop to a table away from the gossip and chatter of the rest of the room.

"It must be hard," Beatrice began once they'd both taken a seat, "being the house mother through all this."

"It's no picnic," Miss Bishop agreed. Her eyes glistened, but she soldiered on without a tear shed.

"Did you know Holly well?"

Miss Bishop shrugged. "About as well as the other girls. We've all been here a little over a month. I enforce the rules, so I'm not always the favorite."

"Have you had any problems?" asked Beatrice. "Girls breaking curfew? Arguments? Things like that?"

"Not much. Though Mary and Holly didn't get along. Not sure why, exactly. You'd have to ask Mary."

"What about the other girls? Did they get along with Holly?"

"Oh, sure! Everyone loved Holly. She was spirited, organized—a real gas, honestly. She would have made a good house mother . . . one day."

The reality of Holly's stolen future crashed down on Miss Bishop like a tidal wave, and the tears began to pour. "Oh, I'm sorry."

"Nonsense!" Beatrice exclaimed, patting the poor woman's hand. "If you need to cry, by golly, you cry! I'd be worried if you didn't."

Miss Bishop nodded in thanks and dabbed her face with a nearby cloth napkin, trying in vain to recompose herself. Beatrice took the interlude to glance toward her gossip-happy cousin. Eleanore was laughing at something one of the twins had said, and Beatrice had to suppress a smile. She turned her attention back to Miss Bishop and reclaimed her hand. There were several other questions she'd like to ask, but they were a little more intrusive and thusly had to be asked with discretion and care.

"Miss Bishop," she began.

"Call me Sally."

"Sally," Beatrice corrected with a smile. "I know it's probably the last thing you want to talk about—"

"You want to know about the chat I had with Holly."

Beatrice was taken by surprise.

"Mr. Morrow said you might ask," Miss Bishop explained.

Beatrice couldn't decide if Mr. Morrow's warning was fishy or simply the behavior of an unraveling hotel manager. "I'm just trying to get a clearer picture," she said.

"Sure."

"Did Holly tell you she was homesick?"

Miss Bishop pursed her lip. "Not exactly."

"What *exactly* did she say?"

Miss Bishop glanced about to ensure no one was listening in, then leaned closer to murmur, "She said she was having . . . lady troubles, you know?"

"Well enough," uttered Beatrice.

"She said they were worse than usual, and could she take a break. I said sure."

"How long was she gone?"

"Maybe . . . half an hour at most?"

"Do you know where she went?"

"I assumed she went back to her room," Miss Bishop admitted. "Now I'm not so sure."

"Sarah mentioned the boys going out for a smoke about that time?"

"That's right. The station porters and bellhops often go for smokes together."

"How many are there?" asked Beatrice.

"Six in full on a normal day. Three bellhops. Three porters."

Beatrice made a mental note, then asked, "Any chance I could get into Holly's room while the other girls are cleaning up? She might have left something behind that could tell me where she went."

Miss Bishop shrugged. "If you think it'll help. I can get you a key."

"That'd be aces." Beatrice gave a warm, ruby-lipped smile, sensing she'd gleaned all she could from this line of inquiry. "Thanks ever so. I should catch up with my cousin before she thinks I abandoned her."

Miss Bishop gave nothing but a meek nod in reply, and Beatrice almost felt bad for leaving the poor woman. Searching for words of comfort and coming up empty, however, Beatrice took up her tea and made a beeline for Eleanore. Halfway there, someone grabbed her wrist, and it took all her strength not to cry out. She whirled to find an older woman gripping her wrist in an iron vise.

"Hang on there, sugar," the woman said colorfully. "Let me get a good look at you."

"Say, that's some grip you've got there, lady," Beatrice hinted, her patience slipping with every second.

"Martha," the woman's husband warned.

"Oh, sorry, dear! Sorry!" Martha chuckled and released Beatrice's arm.

Beatrice shook out her appendage, peering hard at Martha's rosy cheeks and glassy eyes. "Are you sauced, honey?"

"Isn't everyone?" she guffawed. "Bit of gin in one's tea always takes the edge off."

Beatrice's eyebrows shot up. "I should say so."

"You're the detective, aren't you?"

"Sure as shootin'."

"Splendid! Splendid! A lady detective, and about time too! Martha Vickeridge. And this is my husband, Dennis."

"How d'you do?" Dennis greeted, shaking Beatrice's offered hand.

Beatrice chortled in mild amusement. "Very well, all things considered."

They were an older couple somewhere in their seventies. By their baubles and doodads, Beatrice reasoned they had to be old money. None of what they wore was new, but it was all high quality and expensive.

"What was your name again, sugar?" demanded Martha. "You look very familiar."

"Beatrice Adams."

"You don't say! *The* Beatrice Adams? Virginia Adams's daughter? Oh, I loved her pictures! She hasn't worked much since those talkies came out, poor dear."

Beatrice took a measured breath but smiled nonetheless. "That's me, honey, but I'd appreciate it if we kept that between us girls, huh?"

"Why, of course!" Martha laughed. She was in no way discreet. Beatrice thought an elephant had a better chance of getting away with murder than this loud, ill-mannered fossil.

"We're celebrating our forty-fifth anniversary," Martha went on. "I must say, murder is a new one."

"I'll just bet it is," mused Beatrice.

Dennis was quiet, and Beatrice noted an expression of patience on his brow. She imagined it was a common occurrence for his wife to jabber on.

Beatrice made a few more minutes of polite, albeit empty, conversation before she managed to peel away from Mrs. Vickeridge.

"Heavens to Betsy," she grumbled under her breath as she made her way to the far wall. She signaled across the room for Eleanore to meet her.

While she waited, Beatrice leaned against the wall and observed the room. Her tea was cold by now, but she hardly cared. It was more a prop than a relaxer. Beatrice preferred champagne to tea.

The porters and bellhops were all sat around a table, the only difference in uniform being color. The station porters wore maroon while the bellhops sported white. Otherwise the buttons, collars and trousers were the same. A few of the Harvey Girls mingled with the gentlemen for comfort. Harry was chatting mildly with the salesman a few tables over.

Good, Beatrice thought. She could ask him for information later since Harry seemed so willing to help. Allies were important in any investigation, and Beatrice had a feeling the salesman would speak more freely to Harry than to herself.

Eleanore presently joined her, also sporting a cup of barely touched tea.

"Whatcha got for me, skipper?" asked Beatrice, proud of her little spy.

"Their names are Essie and Tunie Hartman," Eleanore divulged. "They're on their way to Los Angeles to crash a few parties."

"Some things never change," sighed Beatrice. "What else?"

"They want your autograph."

Beatrice jerked like she'd been slapped with a wet fish. She peered in annoyance toward the twins, and one of them waved.

"So much for being famous on my own," she muttered.

"Oh, put a sock in it," murmured Eleanore. "You never minded before. You shouldn't now. Either way, you get through locked doors, right?"

Amusement and surprise colored Beatrice's countenance, and she beamed at her cousin. "Ellie Hughes, I do believe that may be the most impassioned thing you've ever said," she teased.

"Says you," Eleanore retorted, trying and failing to hide a smile behind a carefully timed sip of tea.

Beatrice let her eyes wander the room again, lingering once more on the bellhops and porters. "What about the fella who was at the door with Mr. Morrow? Anything there?"

"Who? Tommy?" Eleanore said. "Oh, he's on the level. I think he was sweet on Holly, though. Poor guy."

"Poor guy indeed," Beatrice agreed, spotting Tommy's fair hair in the sea of maroon and white. While all the others seemed put out, Tommy was clearly having a harder time of it. In fact, he looked rather like someone who needed to chat.

"Say," Beatrice whispered, "think you could lure him over here?"

"Sure."

Eleanore turned to catch Tommy's eye. Before she succeeded, the grandfather clock in the lobby chimed eleven o'clock, and Mr. Morrow took the center of the room.

"Ladies and gentlemen. Yes . . . thank you," he stuttered as the hubbub died down. "Given the lateness of the hour and the evening's dire business, I suggest we all turn in for the night."

"Hooey," Beatrice swore, folding her arms. She had no intention of going to bed until this case was solved. Not that they had a room to retire to at any rate. Theirs was currently occupied by a cadaver.

"There are plenty of extra candles for any who need them and, of course, I can't keep you from the common areas, but I'd like to allow the staff to tidy up and retire."

At this, all the Harvey Girls took their cue and convened with Miss Bishop by the tea table. Beatrice knew it'd been foolish to hope she could keep everyone in the same place all night. She had a clearer picture than before, at least, and plenty of gentleman to fill the suspect list, but there were still far too many unanswered questions for Beatrice's liking.

"Why do I have the feeling neither of you is about to turn in?" murmured Harry as he approached them.

"Probably the stiff taking a nap in Eleanore's bed," mused Beatrice.

"What?" Eleanore nearly shrieked.

All at once, Beatrice realized what she'd let slip.

"Relax, honey. Everything is aces," Beatrice said cheerfully, but there was no recovering from that. Eleanore's color had suddenly gone very pale.

"Honestly," Beatrice hissed. "You need a staunch supply of moxie, and no mistake."

"What's the plan?" Harry asked Beatrice.

"You've done more than enough, Mr. Riley," Beatrice reiterated.

"No way am I letting you ladies wander the halls with a killer on the loose. I'm comin' along."

Beatrice locked stares with his hazel hues, her gaze just as stubborn. She could see he wouldn't budge.

"Fine," she huffed. "You can tag along with Eleanore."

"Where am I going?" Eleanore wondered.

Beatrice pulled the typewritten note from her handbag and discreetly passed it to her cousin. "Do you remember where Mr. Morrow said those typewriters were?"

Eleanore nodded. "I wrote it down."

"Good," murmured Beatrice. "I want you to type that note *exactly* on each one. Make sure you note which came from which typewriter. If you come across a locked door . . . well . . . remember what I taught you when we used to play Harry Houdini on rainy afternoons?"

"Picking locks?" Eleanore looked horrified. "But—"

"Ellie, this is serious," Beatrice said sharply. "I need to know which typewriter that note was written on."

Eleanore sighed and gave a nod that she'd do it.

"Where are you off to?" asked Harry.

Beatrice was already heading toward Miss Bishop. "I have my own adventure to tackle," she called over her shoulder with a wink. "Meet me back in the lobby."

The storm was now in full swing, obnoxiously loud and steadily worsening. Even if anyone had planned to sleep it out, there'd be no slumbering through it. Deep thunder shook the very foundation of the hotel as Beatrice got a key and instructions from Miss Bishop. It was the kind of storm that struck fear into the hearts of those trapped beneath it, and even though the hour was late, Beatrice knew it would draw people together, and if her luck held, draw certain people out.

Harry and Eleanore had already departed on the task she'd assigned when Beatrice turned for the darkened halls. As she slipped out her flashlight and switched it on, she was instantly struck by the chilling sensation of being alone. Alone but not afraid. She ventured into the gloom, her flashlight cutting at the darkness like a sword, determined. The killer was out there somewhere, and she intended to find them.

CHAPTER FOUR
A GHOST IN THE HALL

The hallways of the La Posada seemed to stretch and grow as Eleanore and Harry traversed them by candlelight. The hotel that had been so charming on arrival was now an eerie haunted house. Holly's ghost could be hiding around any corner—or worse, another body. That, at least, was the path of Eleanore's thoughts as her sparkling eyes flicked back and forth along the corridor. Something moved to her left, and she gasped.

It was her shadow.

Eleanore clutched her chest and took a moment to breathe. Harry's eyes fixed on her with the utmost concern.

"Say, you're all nerves, aren't you?" he sympathized.

"You don't say," Eleanore muttered, letting her hand drop.

They ambled forward, voices kept at a whisper in case other guests might be sleeping.

"I take it you don't like adventure as much as your cousin?" Harry asked.

Eleanore stifled a laugh. "Bea and I have a different definition of adventure. She's always getting me into trouble."

"Yeah? Such as?"

"Well," Eleanore began, "when we were kids, she wanted to poke around the old Applegate mansion It was sort of a local legend, meant to be haunted, and she wanted to go ghost hunting."

Harry chuckled. "Of course she did."

"Naturally, she dragged me along. It was all cobwebs and dust, and I'd worn my favorite shoes. Turned out we weren't the only ones interested in the ghost stories. We stumbled on some bank robbers using the place as a hideout."

"Get outta here!" Harry said.

"It's true!"

"What'd you do?"

"Bea had this clever idea to make the 'ghosts,'" she drew air quotes, "scare them off. We rigged up a few traps and called the cops. I've never seen anyone jump so willingly into a squad car."

Harry laughed, and Eleanore smiled. Talking, it seemed, was a great distraction from the shifting shadows. Harry was an easy person to get on with. He was gentle and soft-spoken, and standing next to his towering six feet made Eleanore feel a little safer. She knew, of course, that being smitten with her cousin was part of his motivation to help, but there was something in the genuine nature of his laughter that made her trust him. He was a good egg.

When they reached the library, the storm shook the hotel again as if warning them off the case. Eleanore jumped, but she managed not to slip back into hysterics. If Harry had been startled by the thunder, he didn't show it. He held their candle aloft, and the pair of them took in the small guest library. It was smaller than a parlor, was lined with bookshelves, and housed two armchairs for reading. A glossy Remington typewriter sat on a desk at the rear of the small space, primed and always ready for use, should guests need to write letters or business documents. Eleanore, who was an excellent typist owing to secretarial work for her father, pulled a sheet of paper from the drawer and set up the machine. Harry watched curiously as she pulled the killer's note from her handbag and smoothed it over the desk.

"Could you bring the light a little closer?" she requested.

Harry moved his arm so the light illuminated the paper and keys more fully.

"Thanks," said Eleanore.

"You betcha."

Without further interruption, Eleanore's manicured fingers flew over the keys, copying the note to perfection. The hammering of each stroke echoed like a gunshot throughout the library, accompanied only by the sound of pounding rain on the window and the occasional rumble of thunder. When she'd finished, Eleanore pulled out the pen she'd borrowed from Mr. Morrow and wrote "*Library*" in the upper corner of the new note.

"How's this supposed to catch a killer?" wondered Harry.

"Typewriters leave fingerprints," Eleanore explained. "Look."

She sat the letter she'd just typed next to the one from the murderer. "The M key on the typewriter the killer used is heavy," she said, pointing out all the letter Ms in the original letter. "See how dark each character is?"

Harry nodded.

"But on this one," Eleanore moved to the note she'd just typed, "the Ms are light and slightly crooked. It wasn't this typewriter."

Harry was impressed. "That's some scheme."

"I've typed up a lot of case reports for my father," Eleanore replied, beaming. "You'd be surprised what the smallest evidence can do."

"Copper?"

She shook her head. "Lawyer."

"I was beginning to wonder how you got into this racket," he teased.

Eleanore folded both notes and put everything back in her handbag. "Mostly my cousin's dragging," she joked. "She never has let me sit on the sidelines."

They made their way back into the hall, Harry cupping a hand around the candle's flame to keep it from going out, and started toward Mr. Morrow's office.

"You don't sound too terribly upset about it," mused Harry.

Eleanore was struck by his words as if they hadn't occurred to her before. "No," she realized aloud. "I suppose I'm not. If it weren't for Bea, I imagine my life would be pretty boring."

"She get into it because of your pop too?" asked Harry.

"No," Eleanore answered, averting her gaze.

Harry paused before asking, "What happened?"

Eleanore didn't answer right away, wrestling with her conscience. She wasn't sure if it was really her story to tell, but she also saw no harm in telling it. Harry seemed an honest enough listener.

"She . . . witnessed a murder," Eleanore murmured. "When she was twelve."

"Really?"

Eleanore nodded. Now that she'd begun, the words poured from her mouth as if she were competing for first prize against the town gossip. "She was on a film set with her mother. Beatrice never liked to sit still for long, so she set to wandering while Aunt Ginny was filming. Mickey Ryan was shooting on the set next door."

"Didn't he die of a heart attack?"

"That's the *official* story."

It took a moment for Harry to grasp her meaning, but it soon struck, and he gaped at her. "No . . . you don't mean—but that's crazy!"

"Absolutely bananas," agreed Eleanore, "but I know my cousin, Mr. Riley. Beatrice isn't the sort to lie for attention. She saw someone slip something into Ryan's coffee. When she told the police, they didn't believe her. The man she claimed to have seen didn't exist, as far as they were concerned, and the autopsy report confirmed he'd had a heart attack. They couldn't find anything to suggest foul play, and anyway, they didn't look very hard. Beatrice has been obsessed with solving murders ever since."

"Gee whiz," muttered Harry.

"Isn't is just awful?"

Harry nodded. "Does she ever work other types of cases?" he wondered.

"Oh, sure," Eleanore shrugged, "but she takes the murders to heart the most. I think she feels like Ryan was her fault somehow. But don't tell her I said anything!"

"Hey, I'm no blabbermouth," he promised.

She grinned. "Good."

Beatrice would skin her alive for spilling secrets, but there was something about Harry Riley that Eleanore liked. Not for herself, of course—he was clearly smitten with her cousin—but for Beatrice. Eleanore and Beatrice were more than family; they were the best of friends, which meant that whomever Beatrice courted was a potential friend as well. Eleanore couldn't say she hated the idea of a cousin-in-law she could be friends with, if Beatrice ever got rid of Patrick, that is. Thus was the nature of Eleanore's meddlesome thoughts when they reached Mr. Morrow's office. Harry thrust his hand in her path, effectively stopping her and jarring her from her reverie. She followed his eyes to the door. The lock was broken, and the door sat ajar.

"I'll go first," Harry said, and Eleanore nodded, her previous fear reappearing as she remembered the danger they were actually in.

Harry edged forward, candle in his off hand, his strong hand formed into a fist, ready to strike if anything went awry. Eleanore watched him disappear into the office, suddenly chastising herself for worrying about such things as her cousin's sporadic dating habits when they had a job to do. She waited in the hall, holding her breath. Harry poked his head out.

"All clear," he whispered.

Eleanore entered the office behind him. It looked the same as it had before: cramped but tidy. Her eyes roamed instinctively to the desk—the empty desk.

"The typewriter," she uttered. "It's gone!"

There was something about darkened hallways and rolling thunder that brought Beatrice Adams to life. While Harry and Eleanore were off on a jaunt to collect the requested typewriter pages, Beatrice had retreated into the bowels of the hotel in search of Holly's room. She often found that retracing the victim's steps painted the clearest picture, and she wanted to get a good look around the dorms before the girls returned. Snooping, authorized or not, tended to stir up a hornet's nest.

The shadows seemed to watch Beatrice as she navigated by the narrow beam of her flashlight, soon turning down the hall Miss Bishop had described. A quick slip through the Staff Only door, and Beatrice presently found herself in the living quarters of the Harvey Girls. It was all dark shapes and strange lumps apart from the bits caught now and then in the glow of her flashlight. Beatrice could just make out a couch, arm chairs, and a writing desk. A beaten-up typewriter sat on it, and Beatrice wondered if her cousin had checked it yet.

She crept on, following the crude instructions whispered previously by Sally Bishop. She ambled down a hall of doors, flashlight highlighting the door numbers in passing until she found number six. Beatrice shivered. While most had unlucky thirteen, her unlucky number was six. It seemed it'd been Holly's unlucky number too.

Beatrice pulled out the key Miss Bishop had slipped her and opened the door. It creaked ominously to a well-timed crack of lightning as she edged it open. The interior of the room was small and simple. Two twin beds were separated by a nightstand, on which sat a lamp, a half-drunk glass of water, and a pitcher. Judging by which bed the water was closest to, Beatrice deduced the bed on the right to be Sarah's.

She turned her light to the double-sided, mirrored dresser. If dorm tradition held, the drawers would coincide with the side of the room each girl had claimed as her own. Beatrice set to opening Holly's drawers, shoving aside delicates without a care. She uncovered a small red box labeled Veronal.

"Oh, Holly," Beatrice whispered. "You didn't."

She crossed the room and set her flashlight on the nightstand, carefully slipping off a glove. As Veronal was odorless, she didn't bother to sniff Sarah's glass when she raised it but instead tilted it with care until she managed to touch a bare finger to the water. She dabbed her digit on the tip of her tongue, met with the familiar bitter taste she expected. Beatrice's mother kept a steady supply of Veronal in the house, and there was no mistaking the tart flavor. Holly had drugged her roommate. But why? And how had Sarah not tasted it?

Beatrice returned the glass to the nightstand, slipped her glove back on, and reclaimed her flashlight, turning the beam next to Holly's immaculate bed. There was nothing at first glance to suggest Holly's movements, but a quick turning out of the covers and the pillowcases shortly revealed a diary. Beatrice held the small red book with a somber reverence. There was a sort of code among women, a sacred trust. Diaries were off limits. In a murder investigation, however, Beatrice knew key bits of information were often hidden within a victim's personal life. Propriety had to be thrown out the window.

Resolutely, Beatrice laid the book open on the bed, turning the pages with one hand and holding her flashlight aloft with the other. She skimmed to Holly's last entry, dated the day before her death:

A new day, a new train, and new guests. It's been a real riot working at this place. It's taken some getting used to, but I've found a real friend in Sarah. She's learning the ropes like a champ. I'm so proud.

I saw someone today. Someone in the new arrivals. I think I've seen him before, but I can't remember where. It's eating at me like an itch I can't scratch. I think he was at my other Harvey House once. All the faces run together after a while. I guess I'll sort it out eventually. I better go. Miss Bishop is hollering for lights out.

Beatrice perused the entry again and again, combing for anything she may have missed. Had Holly's killer come in on the train? Or was this a coincidence?

"You shouldn't be in here!"

Beatrice shrieked and dropped both flashlight and diary. Mary stood in the doorway, face set in sharp relief by the candle in her hand. She almost looked like a ghost herself.

"Jeepers," breathed Beatrice, hand on her chest. "You surely know how to give a girl a heart attack."

"What are you doing in here?" Mary demanded, not bothering with an apology.

Beatrice snatched up her flashlight. "Retracing Holly's steps. Shouldn't you be helping the others?"

"Sarah asked me to fetch her some aspirin. I was doing just that when I saw her door open." Mary's voice was sharp as a tack, and her eyes were twice as glacial.

Beatrice stood a little taller and cocked her head to the side. "I was told you didn't get along with Holly. Why do you care if I go through her things?"

Mary blanched. "You always dig up people's garbage when you poke around?"

"Nature of the job. Why'd you hate her so much, anyhow? Everyone else seemed to have hearts in their eyes where Holly was concerned."

Mary scoffed. "None of your beeswax, Detective Know-It-All. Now scram before I tell Mr. Morrow you were in here without supervision."

Beatrice set her hand stubbornly on her hip. "You tell me now, doll-face, or I can find out the hard way. A girl is dead. How do I know it wasn't you?"

If there was one thing Beatrice could always count on, it was people getting defensive. Mary pounced like a lioness.

"Why would I kill Holly?" she spat. "Sure, she's a sweetheart stealer, but I never touched her! She even got in my way by dying, the scag!"

Beatrice recalled Mary's canceled cinema date and wondered which sweetheart Holly was meant to have stolen.

"You moved on pretty fast for someone who was heartbroken over a lost lover," Beatrice mused. "Or is the fella you had a date with the same one she's meant to have stolen?"

"Life goes on," Mary said coldly.

"Not for Holly."

"And boo-hoo for her."

Beatrice could see this conversation was over. Mary was determined to be difficult, and Beatrice didn't sense any other pressure points to press.

"The aspirin is on the dresser," Beatrice said, departing out the door.

Once back in the main hall, Beatrice took a moment to collect herself and mull over what she'd just learned. Mary clearly wanted the attention of someone whom Holly had stolen away. A lover scorned was usually motive for murder, but other than that, Mary didn't fit the profile. Though her bark was loud and obnoxious, Mary was by no means a large woman. Holly could easily have thrown Mary off if Mary had tried to strangle her. Even still, Beatrice found Mary's supposed aspirin search fishy. Was she really looking for medicine? Or had she been hoping to hide something before Beatrice could find it?

A crash of lightning and thunder ripped Beatrice from her thoughts, and she realized she was standing exposed in the hallway. She pulled her shoulders back and ventured down the hall for the boiler room. The typed note had said to meet there at midnight, and per Mr. Morrow, the Harvey Girls had a ten o'clock curfew. If Holly's bed hadn't been slept in, there was an entire two-hour window unaccounted for, and Beatrice needed to fill it in. She had no idea what she hoped to find in all this gloom, but mysteries were rarely ever solved by sitting still.

When Beatrice reached the hall where the boiler room waited, she understood her cousin's apprehension to poke around in the dark. There were no windows here, and thusly the darkness was all consuming. It nearly swallowed Beatrice on all sides despite the glow of her light. Eleanore would have been all nerves. Beatrice edged forward confidently, eyes fixed on the boiler room door. The handle turned with ease when she reached it, and she descended the concrete steps with care.

The room beyond was, in many ways, the heart of the hotel. Several boilers lined the large room, each connected to a different part of the hotel. Various sizes of metal piping crisscrossed overhead and disappeared into the walls like giant snakes slithering back into their holes. If ever a monster were to materialize, it would have been then. Beatrice swallowed back her imagination and tiptoed on, turning her flashlight every which way, searching for signs of Holly's struggle.

The room seemed endless, and without proper lighting it was almost a fool's errand to look for clues. With a sigh, Beatrice performed a circle with her light. The narrow beam crossed brick patch to boiler, brick patch to boiler, brick patch to—she paused. Something else had landed in her flashlight's path. Something she recognized immediately. The fuse box. A mad grin crossed her lips, the sort she usually gave when she had a brilliant idea. She'd helped Owens, the family butler, change fuses more than once back home. If she could find the spare fuses, the hotel would have power again in no time, and her investigation would no longer be hampered by the dark.

Beatrice approached the fuse box and pried it open with purpose, scanning the little glass bulbs with her flashlight in search of the blown ones. Her brow furrowed. Not a single fuse was blown, and several were missing altogether.

"The storm didn't blow a fuse," she realized aloud. "They were stolen."

Suddenly hands were around her throat, and Beatrice couldn't breathe. She bucked and kicked, clawing desperately at the meathooks around her fragile neck, but they didn't budge. Spots formed in front of her eyes, and Beatrice had a terrible thought: if she died, who would solve her murder?

CHAPTER FIVE

The Mysterious M

If I could just . . . loosen his . . . grip, Beatrice thought to herself. She gripped her assailant's hands and kicked off the wall, throwing them both backward. The attacker tripped over something in the floor, something hard and loud. They both went down, a detriment for Beatrice. Her strangler quickly took the higher ground, pinning her to the floor by her throat. Fear struck Beatrice, and she no longer had to guess at how Holly had felt before her life was ended.

"Don't leave me alone!" Eleanore's voice echoed from the hall.

Something clattered to the floor, and another dark shape tackled the one trying to kill Beatrice, successfully throwing him off. Beatrice choked, gasping for breath, willing the spots in her eyes to go away. They were like millions of paparazzi flashbulbs hounding her after a scandal. She squinted through the gloom, her vision steadily normalizing, and tried to make out the two goons now duking it out a few paces away. It was pointless. The two of them were nothing but hulking shadows trying to tear each other apart. One of them finally managed to land a good punch on the other, knocking him hard into one of the boilers. As the downed boxer struggled to right himself, the shadow that had knocked him down bolted clumsily for the door.

Beatrice was in a daze. She had no idea which had fled and which remained. As the present contender approached her, she feared she might have traded one murderer for another.

"You okay?" the shadow asked, now standing above her.

Relief flooded Beatrice like a good cup of coffee after a sleepless night. "Mr. Riley?" she murmured, her voice hoarse.

Though she could hardly see him, Beatrice was certain he smiled. "Call me Harry," he offered. They were well beyond formalities now. "C'mon, doll. Let's get you upstairs."

"My light," she groaned. She stubbornly avoided his helpful hand and crawled toward the luminance emanating from beneath the nearest boiler, shortly reclaiming the small metal tube. "I never go anywhere without my flashlight," she said. It sounded like she'd smoked an entire pack of cigarettes in one sitting.

"Try not to talk, honey," Harry urged gently.

Now that her light once again flooded the room, she could see her assailant had tripped over a toolbox and sent the tools clattering over the floor. It was a lucky thing he had; otherwise Beatrice would be another cold case left unsolved. It was luckier still that Harry and Eleanore had been passing by at just the right moment.

"Easy does it," Harry said as he placed a careful hand under her arm and hoisted Beatrice to her feet. Something small glittered on the floor, caught momentarily in the beam of her flashlight.

"Wha's that?" she slurred. Perhaps she should heed his advice. It hurt to talk.

Harry followed Beatrice's gaze and bent down, scooping up the small bauble with ease. He held it under her light.

"It's a button," he said, turning it betwixt his fingers.

"Jeepers," whispered Beatrice. "It must have popped off in the struggle." It wasn't much, but it was a lead, and she'd take any lead she could get.

Harry fleetly pocketed the evidence, worried gaze sweeping over her. "You okay to walk?"

"Little dizzy," she murmured, "but'm fine."

She tried to march forward on her own, but at the first sign of swaying, Harry draped her arm over his shoulders and supported her weight.

"Buy me a drink first, mister," she wheezed.

Harry smiled. "I'll owe you one. No more talking, all right. Doctor's orders."

Beatrice nodded, though another witty remark sat temptingly on the tip of her tongue.

Together they left the boiler room behind, soon coming upon a shaken Eleanore at the end of the hall.

"Who was that?" she demanded, taking in her cousin's deteriorated state. "What happened?"

"Just someone trying to kill me," said Beatrice as if this were an everyday occurrence.

"I said no talking," Harry cut in. "Are you always this stubborn?"

"Always," Beatrice replied.

Harry blinked at her, trying and failing to come up with an adequate response. He gave up and turned instead to Eleanore. "Did you get a good look at the fella?"

Eleanore shook her head. "It's too dark. He went that way, though."

She pointed toward the bowels of the hotel. The assailant could be anywhere by now.

Harry sighed and adjusted Beatrice's arm around his shoulders. "Right, then. I left my medical bag in the dining room. I say we swing by, get a few candles, then regroup back in my room since yours is . . . well . . ."

Eleanore grimaced at the reminder of a dead body in her bed.

Beatrice nodded in agreement to Harry's plan. A short sit-down to think things through would give her time to regather herself and decide what to do next. Danger was something Beatrice usually didn't think of until she was in the thick of it. In hindsight, splitting up may not have been the best idea. They truly had no clue what sort of killer they were dealing with, though if Beatrice had to guess after what had just occurred, she'd say the killer was a desperate one. Desperate would mean mistakes, but the three of them would have to walk with careful footing. Desperate also meant the killer was willing to do anything to get out.

The trio ambled for the dining room, Beatrice still relying on Harry for support. The storm raged outside. Rain sounded as bullets against the windows, and if the wind picked up anymore, Beatrice thought it might blow the whole hotel over. The dining room was lit by two lonely candles when they entered, leaving plenty of shadow for a stalker to hide in. Harry left Beatrice leaning against a table while he made for his bag, which was thankfully still resting behind the planter where he'd left it during the odd tea party. Eleanore snatched up a few extra candles from a box in the back, and they headed into the dark corridor once more. The shadows seemed increasingly ominous after the monstrosity that had just melted out of them. Faceless and nameless, the murderer might as well have been some hideous creature from a Mary Shelly novel. *And just as strong*, Beatrice thought to herself.

She was glad when they reached the safety of Harry's first floor room and immediately bolted the door.

"There's matches in the side table," Harry informed Eleanore as he helped Beatrice into the only chair in the room.

It took him a moment to pry Beatrice's flashlight from her stubborn fingers, but she soon released it, feeling as if Harry had confiscated her only weapon. Warm light flooded the room when Eleanore lit the first candle and placed it on the end table. The shadows were instantly chased away, and the whole party eased. Harry switched off Beatrice's light and sat it on the desk behind her.

"How do you feel?" he asked, gingerly running his fingers over her neck in search of further injury. "Dizzy? Lightheaded?"

She nodded, wincing a little at his touch.

"Anything else?" he pressed.

Beatrice delicately shook her head.

Harry extracted a small medical light from his bag and shined it into each of her eyes, checking her dilation. Both responded normally.

"Well," he said, clicking off the light and tossing it back in his bag, "the good news is you'll live."

"And the bad?" Beatrice croaked with a grimace.

"You might sound like a frog for a while," he teased with a charming smile.

Beatrice scowled, which drew a chuckle from the doctor. He moved for his trunk. Eleanore lit the last candle with a breath of relief and set it on the dresser.

"Are we done playing cops and robbers now?" she asked her cousin hopefully.

Again, Beatrice shook her head, gradually coming back into her own.

"I was afraid you'd say that," Eleanore grumbled as she sat on the end of the bed.

Harry returned with a glass of amber-colored liquid and held it out to Beatrice, who sniffed it with eyebrows raised.

"Why, Mr. Riley," she teased in whisper. "Bourbon? I'm surprised at you."

"Guaranteed to restore one's moxie," he bantered in return.

Beatrice smirked and took a sip. It burned on the way down but was nonetheless a welcome relaxer. "Moxie restored. So, how'd the hunt go? Suss anything out?"

"It wasn't the library typewriter," Eleanore divulged as Harry leaned casually against the wall. "We went to check the one in Mr. Morrow's office, but . . . it's gone. We never did make it to the last one."

"Gone?" Beatrice repeated, a hand over her throat. She hated losing her voice in any fashion. Colds were her downfall.

"Stolen," Harry jumped in. "The lock was busted."

"Can't have been Mr. Morrow, then," Beatrice reasoned, daring another sip of bourbon.

"Why not?" asked Harry.

"He has a key," Beatrice pointed out. It took more effort to push words out, but she refused to be deterred by the monster she was hunting. "It was definitely his typewriter, though."

"Yeah, only now we can't prove it," Eleanore huffed.

Beatrice understood her cousin's frustration. Things were difficult enough in a courtroom without the addition of dirty cops and corrupt judges. The more evidence they could gather, the more chance there was the guilty party would get put away.

"We're not jimmy-jacked yet," Beatrice assured her. "We can always . . . find more evidence. At least we know which one it was."

"But why steal the typewriter?" Harry wondered. "It only shows their hand."

"Without it, we can't match the typewriter to the killer's note." Eleanore shrugged. "One less piece of credible evidence to give the police."

"Yeah, but . . . wouldn't leaving it in the office just incriminate Mr. Morrow?" Harry thought.

"It could," Beatrice murmured, pondering the idea. In fact, the typewriter was far more incriminating if it had remained sitting on his desk. Why wouldn't the killer want the finger pointed at the hotel manager? What did Mr. Morrow have to hide?

"You don't think Morrow has something to do with this, do you?" said Harry.

"I never rule anything out," Beatrice replied, massaging her throat. "Everyone is guilty of something."

They all fell quiet, each mulling over the possibilities. It gave Beatrice a nice rest from talking, though she certainly wasn't happy about it. She could gab with the best of them on a good day. Her mind lingered the most on Holly's diary entry. If she could figure out who arrived on that day, she might be able to pin down who Holly recognized, and maybe things would start making sense. It felt there was so much to do and so little time to do it in.

"What about you?" Harry asked Beatrice. "Did you find anything before that ape cut in?"

"A little," she croaked.

She went on to tell them about everything she'd found in Holly's room, Mary's haughty interruption, and the missing fuses.

"So the power outage was no accident," Harry uttered.

"No," said Beatrice, "and I bet the storm has nothing to do with the phones either."

"You take me on the best holidays," Eleanore sighed.

Beatrice ignored her cousin's sarcasm. "It doesn't add up."

"What doesn't?" asked Harry.

"Strangling Holly and shoving her body in the nearest closet—that's a crime of passion," Beatrice explained. "Her murder wasn't planned. But the fuses, the typewriter, the phone—those all speak of a careful, intelligent killer."

"What are you saying?"

"I'm not sure yet." She stood decidedly. "We need to check the books."

"Oh, no," Eleanore sang, folding her arms defiantly. "I'm not going back out there. No way, no how! I'm staying right here!"

Beatrice cast her cousin a sympathetic gaze. She supposed she'd put Eleanore through enough, asking her to tread through the dark with a killer on the loose. Eleanore was a secretary, not an investigator, and Beatrice would feel better knowing her cousin was out of harm's way. "Sure, honey," Beatrice conceded. "But you keep the door firmly locked."

"You bet I will," Eleanore replied passionately.

Beatrice set her barely touched bourbon on the desk, exchanging it for her flashlight. Harry pushed off the wall.

"I'm coming with you," he stated. "And no buts about it. Two people are less likely to get jumped than one."

His reasoning was sound, and Beatrice had to admit, she felt relieved at the offer. She smiled, and her eyes sparkled as she said, "Fair enough. Let's ankle, skipper." She pointed a gloved finger at Eleanore. "*Firmly* locked."

Her voice didn't come out as strong as she would have liked, but her meaning remained. Eleanore was not to open the door under any circumstances.

"I'll even move the desk in front of the door," Eleanore joked with a flourish of her hand. "Jet already!"

With a final smile flashed at her cousin, Beatrice took up her handbag and departed out the door with Harry in tow.

The dark hallways felt more dangerous than ever before. Every shadow could be a threat; around every corner, a trap. The long walk to the lobby felt even longer, and Beatrice was keenly aware of her heels on the tile floor. She kept her flashlight close, ambling by the sparse light it offered as if it could burn away any evil that waited in the darkness. She kept exceptionally close to Harry. He smelled strongly of pomade and cologne, which was oddly comforting after nearly being murdered herself. He didn't seem to mind. They moved slowly, inching forward as if it made them invisible. Neither of them said a word until they were halfway to the lobby. It was Harry who broke the silence.

"You know," he whispered, "if we can't find the guy . . . it isn't your fault."

Beatrice was a breath away from replying that it would certainly be her fault when she was struck with a sudden curiosity. "Why do you say that?"

"No reason."

His reply had been quick. Too quick. Beatrice smelled a rat.

"She told you, didn't she?" Beatrice croaked. "Oh, I could just ring her neck!"

Harry didn't joke or smile. His eyes were sincere as he laid a hand on her arm, effectively stopping her in her tracks.

"Someone just tried to kill you, Miss Adams."

"Beatrice."

"Beatrice," he amended fondly. "I'm only saying . . . if he gets away, but you're still alive . . . I like those odds far better."

Beatrice smiled, though it was barely discernible in the dark. His hand was still on her arm, and he was close enough for her to feel the heat from his body, a pleasant reminder that she was still alive. For a moment, she thought he might kiss her, but then the moment passed. He dropped his hand, and the distance between them widened again. It was discombobulating, which was a new sensation for Beatrice. She was usually the one turning heads.

"Well," she whispered, "lucky I have you to watch my back then."

Beatrice could just make out a smile on his face. "Someone has to," he said.

Another breath, another shared smile between them, and Beatrice realized they'd been standing in the same place for too long. She tugged gently on his coat, a silent *Follow me,* then continued on for the lobby.

The hallway grew abysmally dark as they neared, and Beatrice was forced to switch on her light.

"Keep watch," she whispered to Harry, who nodded and took up a post near the lobby entrance.

Beatrice tiptoed behind the front desk and pulled the logbook from the drawer where it was kept overnight. Holly's diary had mentioned a familiar face among the arriving passengers the day before. All Beatrice had to do was find out *who* arrived on that day who was still staying at the hotel. She flipped the logbook to the proper date and scanned the entries with her flashlight. According to the books, Martha and Dennis Vickeridge had come in on that train, as had Donald Flannagan and—Beatrice paused at the last name—Harry Riley.

Beatrice gaped at his name, replaying the day's events in her mind. Harry had *saved* her in the boiler room, hadn't he? It was all so fuzzy now, and the boiler room had been so dark. Was he helping her? Or had he inserted himself into the investigation? She shook her head to throw such a terrible thought away.

Harry noticed. "You okay?" he whispered.

"Everything's jake," she lied and snapped the book shut.

Footsteps echoed down the corridor, and they both froze.

"Someone's coming," Harry hissed, diving urgently behind the desk with Beatrice.

They dropped to the floor in unison, and Beatrice switched off her flashlight. The footsteps neared, maintaining their steady gait. Both Harry and Beatrice held their breath as a dark figure entered the lobby. It was too gloomy to make out a build and height. The stranger's mass blended perfectly with the backdrop, and Beatrice's eyes still had spots from the sudden shift in lighting. The figure crossed the lobby with purpose, and Beatrice dared to peer over the desk, sensing Harry's discontent beside her. As far as Beatrice could see, the dark shape was doing something at the grandfather clock. But what?

Suddenly, the figure turned, and Beatrice dropped in panic. No one spoke. No one moved. Beatrice thought her heart would hammer right out of her chest. Thunder boomed outside like canon fire. Beatrice closed her eyes and kept her ears peeled. The figure was moving again, crossing the lobby toward the desk. Beatrice tightened her hold on her flashlight. Harry tensed beside her. The shadow was almost there. Beatrice coiled like a spring.

And then the footfall turned, heading for the lobby exit. Once sure the figure had gone, Beatrice dared to breathe again.

"Jiminy," she whispered. "I thought we were goners for sure."

Harry smiled in relief. "Yeah. Me too."

It was only when his breath tickled her cheek that Beatrice realized how close they were. She smiled back.

"Come on," she murmured, hopping up with gusto.

The thrill of a new clue filled her with vigor. It was almost as if she hadn't been strangled nearly half an hour previously. Beatrice pussy-footed to the grandfather clock that stood like a sentry against the far lobby wall and switched on her light, Harry skulking along behind her. At first glance, the clock seemed normal, but Beatrice knew there was *something* unique about it; otherwise the figure in the dark wouldn't have been so interested in it. She ran a gloved hand over every inch of the ornate woodwork until one of the wood panels finally gave way.

"A secret compartment," she whispered, pulling the panel aside.

A small slip of paper was tucked inside. She pulled it out and unfurled it to read the following handwritten note:

She's getting too close. If you blow this, you're out.

—M

Beatrice stared at the note in contemplation. Harry read it over her shoulder.

"What does it mean?" he asked.

"It means," she whispered, "that our killer has an accomplice."

Eleanore paced back and forth in Harry's room, beginning to regret her decision to stay behind. The quiet was just as terrifying as the dark, and the rain had yet to let up, pounding against the window panes like a thousand tiny bullets. Rattled, Eleanore threw herself into the desk chair and pulled the case notes she'd started from her handbag. She added new information based on Beatrice's tale and her own excursion with Harry. Things still didn't add up. She drew a circle around Holly's missing two hours. Why drug her roommate? Why not wait until midnight and sneak out? What had Holly found worth killing for?

Eleanore was so wrapped up in what she was doing, she didn't hear a key turning in the lock or the door ease open. A shadow crossed the room with practiced silence, nearing the preoccupied blonde with malicious intent. Just as it was about to reach for her, a floorboard creaked underfoot. Eleanore turned, her eyes wide with fear.

The shadow lunged before she could identify it, forcing a chloroform-soaked rag over her nose and mouth. She didn't struggle for long. The world went dark, and there was no one to stop the shadow from carrying her away

CHAPTER SIX

A THROW OF THE DICE

The realization that the killer might not be working alone only further cast suspicion on Harry in Beatrice's mind. *He wasn't the only name on that list*, she tried to console herself, but she knew well that she had to follow the evidence, not her heart. It was a difficult task. Harry had given her no reason to suspect him. Perhaps that in itself was suspicious.

She was more than aware of his eyes on her, watching and waiting for her to make a decision. They were still standing in the lobby near the clock, the note clutched in her gloved hand, illuminated by the beam of her flashlight. If she paused any longer, he'd know something was wrong. She tucked the note fastidiously into her bag and made for the hall without a word. Harry tagged along in silence, the quiet giving him space to analyze her.

"You're worried," Harry said when she paused in the hall.

"I'm thinking," she replied.

Harry fell silent to let her do so. Beatrice knew her next line of inquiry should be to interrogate him along with the other names on that list. *He could be innocent*, she reminded herself. Sometimes people were simply in the wrong place at the wrong time. For the space of a moment, she hated that he was so gentle and helpful. If he was a complete boob, she wouldn't feel terrible for asking what she knew she must. As Beatrice turned to do just that, the sound of muffled laughter interrupted her thoughts. Both she and Harry turned in its general direction.

"It's coming from down there," whispered Harry, pointing at a cracked Staff Only door down the hall.

The laughter echoed again, and Beatrice nodded in agreement, inching forward on tiptoe. Thunder shook the hotel beneath her feet, signaling the approach of another front. Harry sped up just enough to open the door for Beatrice. She nodded in thanks, holding a finger to her lips to signal quiet. He nodded back. He understood.

The passage beyond the door was pitch black aside from the places stabbed by Beatrice's relentless flashlight. The walls were painted a cheap and lackluster eggshell that had been carelessly dripped over the occasional piping that protruded from the wall and ceiling. The floor was poured concrete, still new enough to be bright gray but used enough to have various wheel marks from things that had been pushed to and fro along the corridor. It was the service hall, Beatrice realized. Passages like these allowed the hotel staff to move about unseen. Could the murderer have used these as well?

Laughter emanated again, not sinister as it had seemed at first, but jovial and layered. More than one person was at it. Beatrice paused to listen at a fork in the passage. The noise came from the corridor to the right, and as Beatrice led the way down it, she became aware of muffled voices talking to one another before another round of laughter ensued. Harry kept close behind, staying silent. Halfway down the hall, sparse light flickered underneath a doorway. Beatrice approached it and set an ear against the wood.

Chattering. Numbers. Something clattered across the floor. More laughter with a groan or two mixed in. Beatrice knew those sounds. A smile crossed her face.

"I do believe we've stumbled upon a midnight gambling spree," she whispered to Harry.

He raised an eyebrow at her. "You don't sound terribly upset about it," he teased.

"On the contrary. I love to place a good bet."

With a wink and a wicked grin, she jerked the door open with a hearty "Hello, boys."

There were three individuals in the room crouched in a small circle near the far wall: two in the maroon of porters and one in bellhop white. All three shrieked like schoolgirls and swore at the ceiling, which drew hoarse laughter from Beatrice's lips. Harry eased into the room behind her, hands in his trouser pockets. The room was small in size, an ugly shade of eggshell like the halls, and housed a few tables and chairs and a small bookshelf with old games and a few books. Candles had been lit and placed about the room, giving the space a moody, warm glow.

"Playing craps, huh?" Harry said, a nod indicating the dice and money in the middle of the break-room floor.

"Winning at craps, more like," the dark-haired porter replied, tapping the stack of money he'd just acquired.

"I still think you're cheating," the bellhop muttered.

"Don't be a sore loser, Fred," patronized the porter.

"Are they his dice?" Beatrice asked.

"No," replied Fred.

"Then how could he be cheating?" she mused.

He gave no answer but instead scooped up the dice to play his turn. Harry grabbed a nearby chair, turned it backward, and sat himself down, arms folded over the back to watch. Beatrice smelled an opportunity.

"Got room for one more?" she wondered aloud, reaching into her bag for her money.

The dark-haired porter laughed. "*You* play craps?"

"No," she said, beaming as she knelt to join their circle. "I win at craps."

This drew chuckles of amusement from all, including Harry. Beatrice, of course, had ulterior motives for wanting to play. The game would provide a much-needed distraction and normal social setting to keep the three hotel employees at ease, which would in turn make them pliable. The best way to get answers, in her opinion, was to make the interview seem less like an interrogation and more like fun.

"You betting in, Mr. Riley?" she dared.

"Who, me?" he replied, chortling. "No way, honey. My vices lay elsewhere."

"Then I shall endeavor to find them out," she teased, smiling at him as she placed five on the floor in front of her. "Don't pass," she bet.

The others placed their own bets, and Fred rolled the dice. They hit the wall and bounced back: snake eyes. Beatrice cheered along with the fair-haired porter, who'd also bet on a don't pass. The dice were passed to Beatrice, and she examined them in her hand, pondering how to proceed.

She placed her bet, then said, "Say, where are the others? I thought there were six of you at tea."

"David and Glenn went for a smoke," the dark-haired porter replied, placing a bet of don't pass.

"And Tommy?" Beatrice pried. "That's the other fella's name, isn't it?"

"Sure is," divulged Fred. He bet pass. "Haven't seen him since before. In the dining room."

Beatrice thought this suspicious. She'd announced her investigation, and suddenly Tommy was missing? Perhaps there was more to Holly's admirer than she initially believed.

"You gonna roll or what, dollface?" the dark-haired porter said curtly.

"Hey, watch it, Mack," Harry warned.

Despite her conjectures, Beatrice suppressed a smile. She had her own ways of putting such an unsavory character in his place, but it was always swell to have backup.

"No, he's quite right," Beatrice said, shaking the dice. She threw them just so, and they bounced off the wall, coming to a three and one. Those who'd bet pass cheered, but the dark-haired porter worked his jaw. The fair-haired one handed the dice back to Beatrice. She shook them again. "Are you sure you still want me to roll?" she patronized.

"You could still crap out," the dark-haired porter replied haughtily.

Fred smirked. "Now who's a sore loser, James?"

With a ruby-lipped grin, Beatrice rolled again and miraculously landed another four. Everyone but James cheered.

"Hot dog!" the fair-haired porter cried. "That's some luck you've got there, Miss Adams."

"One tries," she mused, her eyes sparkling. She passed the dice over, and everyone placed their respective bets.

Thus far, Fred seemed an amiable enough ally. He had a gentility about him that, like Harry, made him instantly likable. James, on the other hand, was clearly a hot-head, and if Beatrice had to guess, he was probably a proper cake-eater too—a real ladies' man. He had that look about him: the sort of man who couldn't take his cheaters off a girl's chassis and expected her to like it. Annoying though it was, Beatrice could work with it. The fair-haired porter was quieter than the other two. As the dice and bets continued around the circle, she soon learned that his name was Theo, short for Theodore, she imagined, and that he seemed to take his cues from Fred.

"Is it the norm . . . for Tommy to disappear?" she asked after another few minutes of gameplay in which she won ten dollars and lost five more.

"Why do you care?" James wondered.

"No," Fred answered as if James hadn't said a word. "But then what about any of this is normal?"

The dice were rolled. Beatrice lost another two dollars.

"Have you got any theories?" she asked. "About what happened to Holly, I mean."

"She was a nice girl," Fred replied. "I can't imagine why anyone would want to off her."

Theo nodded vigorously in agreement, but James scoffed.

"She was a snoop," he spat. "Always sticking her nose where it doesn't belong . . . not unlike *other* people . . ."

"Sounds like she got one over on you," Harry interjected.

It was just the fuel Beatrice needed. With her, James thought himself in charge, but the moment Harry challenged him, James went on the defensive.

"What sort of dame keeps a little black notebook full of secrets?"

James complained. "One that's no good, that's who!"

"What kind of secrets?" wondered Beatrice.

James shrugged. "I never read it."

"But you've *seen* it," pressed Harry.

"Sure. She always kept it in her pocket."

Beatrice frowned. She'd emptied Holly's pockets, and all she'd found was the note from the killer. Had the killer taken it? And if so, why had they left the note?

"I saw it . . . once," Theo began nervously, seeming to second-guess himself.

"Ogle anything interesting?" asked Beatrice.

Theo hesitated.

"You're not on trial, Theo," Beatrice gently reminded him. "I just want to know what happened to Holly."

The craps game was on full pause now, and all eyes fixed on Theo, which only served to make him more nervous.

"Names," he finally said. "And . . . notes. About people."

"Anyone interesting?" pressed Beatrice.

Again, Theo seemed hesitant, but Beatrice's kind eyes eventually did the trick. "The Vickeridges," he uttered. "I dunno why she'd want to take notes on them, but she was. She was all nerves when she caught me lookin'."

James visibly eased, and Beatrice had a sneaking suspicion there was something in that little black book about him.

"They certainly are . . . odd," she commented.

Fred nearly laughed. "You said it. I feel sorry for the poor guy. She's a regular rummy."

"If I had that much dough, I'd spend my days sauced too," James mused.

Beatrice thought subconsciously of her mother, who did exactly that. Money and boredom were often a horrible mix.

"I heard them laying into each other," Fred divulged, lowering his voice as if the walls would snitch on him. "Arguing about her habits while I was unloading the bags. Apparently he tried to file for divorce last year . . . but he couldn't afford it. It's all her money."

Beatrice's eyebrows shot up. "You don't say!"

Fred nodded. "He's tied to the apron string good and tight."

"Good and tight," Theo agreed.

"And anyway, he'd have to prove cheating or negligence on her part to the courts," Fred continued. "You can't be too careful these days."

"No, you certainly can't," Beatrice concurred.

The Depression had turned everything in America upside down. Soup kitchens and bread lines were everywhere, and unemployment was at its highest. If being married to someone like Martha Vickeridge kept Dennis from falling into poverty, Beatrice imagined he would endure anything she dished out. It certainly explained their older but expensive attire. Mrs. Vickeridge was likely keeping a tighter hold of her purse strings. But was it to conserve money or to fund her obvious drinking habit? A yawn presently interrupted Beatrice's thoughts, which she stifled with the back of her hand, prompting Harry to check his pocket watch.

"Gee whiz," he said. "It's already eleven thirty."

"Cup of coffee and I'll be jake," Beatrice said with a dismissive wave of her hand. "Gentlemen . . . you've been swell, but I think this is my stop."

Fred and Theo moaned as she began to put her cash back in her handbag, but James didn't seem to mind.

"Thanks for the extra scratch," he said, giving what he must have thought was a winning smile.

Beatrice wasn't fazed by it in the least. "I tip generously for valuable information," she mused.

She didn't realize Harry had even moved until his hand was before her, offering to help her up. She was reminded of the logbook page and the questions she needed to ask, staring at his hand as if taking it might seal her fate somehow.

"It's just a hand, sweetheart," he reminded her.

Beatrice shook off her internal chatter with a red smile. "Of course," she said, accepting his help.

He tugged her gently to her feet, and she tried not to feel too relieved when he let go. After another farewell to her fellow craps players,

Beatrice and Harry retreated to the gloomy service hall. They walked through the dark in uncomfortable silence until they'd reached the main hallway again. The storm was more audible here, billowing and blowing in a rage outside the hotel. It seemed to have gained in energy while they'd been safely cocooned in the innards of the building.

"So . . . coffee?" Harry suggested with the air of a man asking her on a date.

It was certainly getting late, and Beatrice had to admit, her mind was getting boggled. A cup of coffee might do her some good, and the pause in investigation would allow her to ask Harry the question she couldn't put off any longer.

"Coffee," she agreed with a smile.

They turned for the dining room and continued on, once again falling into awkward silence.

CHAPTER SEVEN
SOMETHING TO KILL FOR

The hotel kitchen was located at the rear of the dining room behind a windowed swinging door. Beatrice's flashlight hardly penetrated the long room when they entered, and she was keenly aware of all the potential weapons hanging from racks overhead and sitting in the knife block near the cutting board. Harry didn't seem the sort to get violent, but it was good to be aware of her options and the potential options of her adversary if adversary he became. They found the coffee brewer on the far counter, and Harry immediately began poking about the nearby cabinets for grounds. Beatrice surveyed his movements with care in case he tried anything funny. The coffee turned up in the third cabinet he tried, and Harry extracted a bag, grinning as if he'd just discovered some ancient treasure lost in an old tomb. Beatrice couldn't help mirroring his smile despite her inner turmoil. It was infectious.

"I'll get some mugs," she offered, daring to leave his side long enough to grab two that sat on a drying rack near the sink. She returned and set them next to the silver coffee brewer.

"Thank you," Harry said. "Could you—" He mimed shining a light at the machine.

"Of course," came Beatrice's reply.

She held her flashlight aloft, allowing the beam to penetrate a larger area, and Harry set to work measuring out coffee grounds. Silence ensued again, and Beatrice took the opportunity to roll her question around in her mind. She tried it several ways, but none seemed to dim the blow she was about to make. She decided it was best to simply get it over with.

"Harry?" she began.

He hummed in reply.

"Did you know Holly?"

The doctor paused midway through dumping grounds into the brewer.

Beatrice tensed, ready to grab the nearest frying pan and crash it over his head if things went sour. She'd already been strangled once that night, and once was enough.

Harry's eyes displayed genuine hurt as he met her brilliant gaze. "What kinda question is that?"

"The kind I have to ask," said Beatrice, visibly easing. "Holly recognized someone on the train yesterday, and your name was on the list."

Harry turned back to making coffee, mulling over the best way to answer. "I've never seen her before," he promised. "But that doesn't mean she hasn't seen me. I've been traveling a lot for job interviews the last few months, and I hate flying. I've stayed at a few Harvey Houses along the way."

Beatrice nodded in understanding. There was no reason to doubt his answer, no evidence to the contrary, so for now, Beatrice accepted his words as the truth. She wondered if Harry had indeed been the man Holly had written about and if the clue in Holly's diary was merely a dead end. After all, Holly hadn't been upset at seeing this stranger, merely curious. What Beatrice really needed was to find that little black book the bell staff had mentioned. If Holly had always kept it on her person, and it wasn't on the body, someone had taken it. Finding that little black book could crack the case wide open, and that was a break Beatrice sorely needed. At present, she felt like she had a slew of information and hardly a single connection that tied it all together. Why was

Holly killed? What was she killed for?

Once the coffee was on, Beatrice and Harry each leaned against a separate counter to wait. Beatrice's question hung, ugly and sharp, between them, and neither seemed to know what to say. A few hours' acquaintance was hardly the basis of a friendship, but Beatrice felt the sting of her accusation as if she'd pointed the finger at her own cousin. A rumble of thunder shook the ground beneath her feet, rattling the pots and pans.

"I'm sorry," she finally broke the silence. "I have to act on the clues, and—"

"Forget it," Harry said graciously.

Beatrice gaped. "What?"

Harry shrugged. "Forget it. There's a killer on the loose. You got a job to do. Don't sweat it."

It was like a weight had been lifted. She averted her gaze to the floor to hide her smile. In all her life, Beatrice had never met someone quite like Harry Riley. He was as amiable as he was handsome, he didn't question her methods, and he seemed to genuinely want to help. Most men simply flung themselves at her, dazzled by her looks and fame, but there was something more in the way he looked at her that she didn't understand. It was something akin to respect, and while she was still seeing Patrick for the time being, she dearly hoped Harry would remain a friend when all this was over. Good friends were hard to come by in a world where people constantly betrayed one another to get ahead. Beatrice didn't even trust Patrick. Not really. It was this line of thought that made her wonder what made Harry tick, and she couldn't help digging into the question once it presented itself.

"So . . . what about you?" she wondered. "You know my story, more or less, and if you don't you can surely read it in the papers. What made Harry Riley take a job in Los Angeles?"

He nearly laughed, surprised at her quick change of subject. "I'll save you the sob story of the poor rich kid from New York," he teased.

"Oh, come on, ace," Beatrice pressed, using her sparkling eyes against him. "The coffee'll be a minute, and my puzzler is tired."

Harry sighed, contemplating. "An answer for an answer?" he

decided. "The tabloids don't cover everything."

Beatrice wasn't sure how much of herself she was ready to give away, but it was only fair. "All right," she agreed. "You first."

Harry shoved his hands in his trouser pockets and shrugged as if his story were nothing special. "Grew up in New York. Pop was into the railroad racket. My mother was distantly related to the Vanderbilts. It made for a charming pair, but it wasn't the life for me."

"So . . ."

He smiled. "So . . . medical school. Harvard University. And here I stand—moved as far away from my family as I can be."

Beatrice got the impression there was far more to the story than Harry's dislike for money and the games of the rich. These days, coming from a wealthy family was the only thing that had saved some from losing it all during the crash.

"Siblings?" she pried.

"An older brother," he returned. "Charlie is more than happy to take up the family business, which leaves me to do as I please. Your turn."

"What do you want to know?"

"Acting is surely more lucrative than sleuthing," he mused. "Why does the murder of one man make such a pretty dame change her whole life?"

Beatrice exhaled. It wasn't difficult to explain, but it was difficult for people to understand. Many still thought she'd been chasing shadows. Mickey Ryan had not died of natural causes, and no one but Eleanore and her fatherly butler, Owens, seemed to believe Beatrice.

"I suppose I was angry," she confessed. "I knew Mickey . . . not well, but he was nice. He always took the time to talk to me if I was wandering around the studio lot. Not all who grace the silver screen are imbued with kindness, I'm afraid."

"So I'm gathering," mused Harry.

"The detective in charge of the case, Mr. Kelley, looked at me like I was nothing but a spoiled little school girl because of who my parents are. The way he talked to me . . . something inside me snapped. I decided to make myself heard from then on. The dead have no voice. It's my job to speak for them."

The smile that lit Harry's face at her words was one of sheer admiration, and Beatrice couldn't help being surprised by it.

"What's that look for?" she asked.

"Nothing," he replied. "I've just never met someone quite like you."

"Of course not," she mused, wearing a smile of her own. "There's only one of me."

She wanted to ask him more, to understand him further, but a sudden pounding on the pantry door made them both jump. They each turned a wary eye to the door. The pounding happened again, this time accompanied by a voice.

"Hey! Lemme out, will ya!"

It was a young man.

Beatrice and Harry exchanged a quiet glance. *Should we open it?* the look said.

Beatrice picked up the nearest cast iron pan and gestured for Harry to open the door.

"I know there's someone there," the voice shouted. "I heard you talkin'! Open up! C'mon!"

Beatrice situated herself to the side of the door frame, out of sight of the pantry's occupant. Harry and Beatrice shared another look.

Ready? his said.

Go! hers replied.

Harry yanked the door open, and a fair-haired man tumbled out and landed in a heap on the kitchen floor.

"Why, it's Tommy!" Beatrice realized, freezing with weapon raised.

Tommy looked up at her and flinched when he saw the frying pan aimed at his head. "Whoa! Easy, lady! Easy! I still got a headache from the last one!"

Beatrice lowered the pan and set it on the nearby counter. "The last one?"

"Yeah," Tommy replied as Harry helped him to his feet. "I was on my way to find ya when some jack-o'-lantern clocked me on the head and stuffed me in there."

He jerked his thumb toward the pantry, gingerly massaging the back of his head with the other hand.

"Can I borrow your light?" Harry asked Beatrice.

She relinquished it, and Harry carefully checked Tommy's eyes.

"He's concussed all right," the doctor concluded, passing the flashlight back to Beatrice. "Nothing serious, though."

"But he's telling the truth," said Beatrice, understanding Harry's purpose. "Do you need to sit?" she asked Tommy.

"Nah," the bellhop negated, instead leaning against the nearest counter.

The three of them settled equidistantly from one another, preparing for a long conversation.

"Did you see who clocked you?" Harry asked.

Tommy barely shook his head.

"You said you were on your way to find me," pried Beatrice. "Why?"

"I was gonna try and talk to ya in the dining room earlier," Tommy explained, "but I never got the chance. And anyway, Mr. Morrow was watchin'. I'd like to keep my job, ya know?"

"Sure," Beatrice replied. "Is he a difficult boss?"

"Just real squirrelly. That guy's a real bluenose. You can't sneeze without him worryin' about the image of the hotel."

Beatrice filed this information away. "What did you want to talk to me about?"

"Holly," he said. "I think she was in some kinda trouble."

"What kind of trouble?" asked Harry.

"Dunno," Tommy continued, "but somethin' bad. She wasn't who she said she was; I know that much."

"What do you mean?" pressed Beatrice.

"Well," Tommy said, "about a week or so ago, I'd finally worked up the nerve to ask her to go to the pictures with me. I found her at the pay phone in the middle of a call. It musta been serious. She was ringing the cord around her fingers like she was anxious or somethin'. I heard her say, 'Yes . . . yes, this is Miss Blake. No. Tell him it's urgent. Yes, I'll wait.' I hid behind the plant in the hall. Didn't want her to think I was snoopin'. Just before I was called away, she said somethin' else—that she'd found it, but all she needed was proof. I think she was some sorta spy or somethin'."

It was like the clouds had parted, allowing Beatrice a brighter view of the puzzle. Excitement bubbled in her chest, and it took all her strength to reign it in.

"Did you hear anything else?" she asked.

Tommy carefully shook his head. "But whatever it was . . . it got her killed."

He'd suddenly turned a sickly shade of green, and Beatrice moved a comforting hand between his shoulders. "Oh, honey, it's not your—"

Her words died mid-sentence. In moving forward, her flashlight had moved in tandem, catching something in its beam.

"Harry," she said urgently, "do you still have that button?"

"Yeah." Harry pulled it from his pocket and passed it to her.

Beatrice held the button from the boiler room up to Tommy's uniform, the latter standing in confusion. It was an exact match.

Harry and Beatrice locked eyes and said in unison, "It was one of the bell staff!"

Tommy's eyes widened, and he opened his mouth to protest, but Beatrice cut him off.

"Do you have keys to the bell stand?" Beatrice demanded of Tommy.

"Sure, but—"

"I need them," she cut him off. "Do you want me to catch the guy or not?"

Her eyes bore into him with the force of a nuclear bomb. Beatrice was half determined to take the keys by force or put her pickpocketing skills into practice, but thankfully neither was necessary. After a short internal struggle, Tommy handed them over without a fuss.

"Just catch the guy, all right? And if anyone asks, ya didn't get 'em from me," he said.

"I'm no snitch," Beatrice promised, kissing his cheek and leaving a red stain behind.

She was out the door before Harry or Tommy could blink, leaving Tommy in a daze. This was precisely the sort of break she'd been looking for. A direction, some sort of trail. If Holly wasn't Holly, if she was someone else entirely, that sort of deception could make someone angry enough to kill. It certainly made the full picture a little clearer. Beatrice was halfway through the empty dining room before she realized she'd left Harry behind. She doubled back and skidded into the dark kitchen, the epitome of a child on Christmas morning. "You comin', Mack?" she asked Harry.

Harry suppressed a smile. "Yeah." He added to Tommy, "Be careful heading back. And come find me if your head feels any worse."

Tommy scooped up Beatrice's discarded frying pan. "Don't worry. I'm not takin' any chances."

They parted ways at that, Beatrice practically dragging Harry by the coat sleeve. He chuckled. "Easy does it. This is my best suit."

But there was no slowing her down. She was like a bloodhound who'd finally caught a scent. Through the dining room and the hall, she dragged him, not relinquishing her grip until they reached the lobby yet again. It was just as gloomy and enigmatic when they returned, but Beatrice looked around as if everything had changed. Excitement replaced the tired slog they'd fallen into, no coffee required.

"It all makes sense!" Beatrice exclaimed, her sore throat forgotten, though she still sounded scratchy. "A bellhop or porter would have access to keys for every room, making it easy to dump the body and come back for it later. I bet my entire coat collection no one was scheduled to stay in our room tonight."

"Must be some collection," Harry mused.

"Oh, it is," she assured him, carrying on. "Our assigned room was having electrical issues, so Morrow set us up in a temporary room, unaware of the body stashed in the closet. A bellhop would have seen it on the books and panicked, thus cutting the power and the phones to leave us in the dark, unable to call the police. The storm will have slowed his getaway. There's no leaving in this weather."

"We still don't know who or why," sighed Harry.

"One puzzle piece at a time," Beatrice replied with a smile.

She approached the bell stand, her excitement keeping the shadows at bay. Tommy's key opened the bell cabinet with ease. The interior was cluttered with lost and found items, crumpled paper, and a logbook similar to the one at the front desk. She pulled the logbook out and flipped through it. Sure enough, there was an order for her and Eleanore's bags. Tommy had signed off on it, so no dice there. She extracted the note from M and held it up against the handwriting in the log. Not one match.

"Well, *foot*," she swore.

"Anything I can do to help?" Harry offered.

"Poke about. If our killer was desperate, he's bound to have left a trace of himself behind somewhere."

It was easier said than done, as Beatrice had the only light, but nonetheless, Harry set to searching the lobby near the bell stand. Beatrice thoughtfully combed the roster of bellhops and porters, hoping something would pop. Not a single one had a name beginning with the letter M. Beatrice pursed her lips in thought.

"So, the killer is one of the bell staff," she puzzled aloud, "but M . . . M is not . . . Unless M isn't in their name at all. It could mean something else."

"Well looky here," Harry sang. "You're never gonna believe what I just found."

Beatrice set the logbook down and turned her glittering eyes to Harry, who was kneeling beside one of the planters. She was at his side in an instant, shining a light over his shoulder and into the bush. Something round and opaque glimmered up at her.

"The missing fuses!" she exclaimed in a whisper.

"Your bell staff theory is holding more and more water," he praised.

"But why dump them here?" wondered Beatrice.

"Morrow sent the staff for candles the moment the lights went out," Harry reasoned. "Maybe he was stopped and had to dispose of them quickly?"

"And no one would think to look in the planters with all the commotion," she agreed.

He would have gone on acting in his line of duty as if everything were normal. Beatrice had looked right at him at some point that night. But which was he? She ruled Tommy out. He couldn't clobber himself on the head and get locked in a pantry. James was definitely hiding something. Theo seemed too quiet for such a coldblooded thing as murder, but then the quiet ones were often the ones to watch. There were only six options, and other than her severe dislike of James, Beatrice had nothing but a single button to go on.

"There has to be *something* here that gives him away," she muttered, feeling her lead slipping through her manicured fingers. She locked eyes with Harry, who still knelt beside the planter. "You were watching closely. In the break room, were any of the staff missing a button?"

"Dunno," Harry replied, rising fluidly to his full height. "I wasn't exactly looking for it. They were all unbuttoned and casual. In fact . . . I don't think James was wearing his uniform jacket at all."

Beatrice pondered this, pursing her ruby lips as she did so. Had comfort been James's motivation for shrugging out of his coat? Or was he missing a button that he knew would point Beatrice right to him? Beatrice put a pin in that idea, then shook it delicately away. It wouldn't do to go accusing a man without all the facts and good solid evidence, something that she could do with more of.

With a sigh, Beatrice turned her light back to the lobby, searching for more clues that might surge them forward. Rain pelted the lobby windows like bullets in the sudden quiet. Her flashlight highlighted the Staff Only door at the other end of the lobby—the bell closet. Beatrice approached it as one might approach a wild animal, her footsteps accompanied by a crash of lightning and thunder. She tried Tommy's key in the lock when she reached the door. It opened without a hitch. Carefully, she eased it open and shined her light around the closet interior.

The bell closet was long and narrow, lined with shelves and cubbies for all sorts of things. Beatrice approached the first row, inspecting the shelves as she passed. Guest packages were piled in neat, organized rows, each with a corresponding label that was, no doubt, in the little mail slots behind the front desk. The next shelf over was stuffed to the brim with supplies—extra towels, soap, shampoo—anything a guest might call down for. Next came the coat rack on which hung a vast assortment: suits that had been pressed, coats that had been checked, and even the odd umbrella. At the very back of the small room was a cart labeled *Laundry*. It was full of white sacks, all of which were labeled according to room number and the date on which the laundry was dropped off. There was something about the way the cart was skewed, as if someone had put it back in a hurry or had been rummaging through it recently. Everything else in the room was placed just so—all except for this.

Beatrice moved instinctively for the cart and started pulling laundry sacks out as if it were some sort of carnival game and she wanted first prize. Harry jumped in with equal vigor.

"What are we looking for?" he asked.

"I don't know yet," she replied. "I just have a . . . feeling."

Harry moved faster than Beatrice, operating with two hands rather than one, her other busy holding the flashlight. When they neared the bottom, Harry hoisted a bag that clinked and was noticeably heavier than the others.

"Is it me, or is that laundry exceptionally loud?" Beatrice quipped as they locked eyes over the cart.

Harry yanked the bag the rest of the way out and set it on the floor, fingers deftly working at the ties. Beatrice waited anxiously, feeling a lead coming on—hoping for it. Time was running out. The bag opened. She shined her light inside, mouth falling open.

"Bottles?" she whispered, reaching inside and pulling out a whiskey.

"Empty bottles," added Harry.

The gears and wheels turned in Beatrice's head. Skulking, payoff, murder, and now empty liquor bottles?

"It's a juice ring," she realized aloud.

"Holly must'a figured it out," said Harry. "But if all the empties are in here, where's the liquor?"

"In whatever they're smuggling it in, I expect. I think it's time for another chat with Mr. Morrow."

"Do you think he's M?"

"I think he's a possible M," said Beatrice. "It's all beginning to look rather fishy."

She carefully slipped the bottle back into the laundry bag, and the pair of them heaped the remaining bags into the cart once more, trying to make it look as if they'd never been there. A juice ring and a missing black notebook in which Holly had been keeping tabs on people. It sounded to Beatrice like Holly was investigating, but who and for what?

"Come on," she said, turning for the door. "The register should tell us where Morrow is staying."

Harry gestured for her to lead the way, following behind her as she made for the lobby. When she reached the bell closet door, it slammed in her face. Beatrice stood in surprise for a moment before she regained her faculties. She closed her hand over the knob and gave it a turn. It wouldn't budge. She jiggled it helplessly. Nothing. They were locked in.

"All right," she huffed. "*Now* we're jimmy-jacked."

Eleanore's first panicked thought when she awoke was that she couldn't see. She fidgeted this way and that, quickly ascertaining that she couldn't move, either. Her hearing, on the other hand, worked just fine. The telltale *click* of a gun hammer made her freeze, and terror struck her like a bucket of ice water.

"You'll stay put if ya know what's good for ya," a deep, scratchy voice warned.

Eleanore's heart thrummed violently in her chest. She nodded vigorously.

"I-I don't want any trouble, mister. Honest," she stammered.

"I know, kid," the deep voice said in mock sympathy. "And that's all that's keepin' you alive. That . . . and your pretty looks. So, sit tight, dollface, and maybe you'll live to see the sunrise."

Fear covered Eleanore in its thick, debilitating clutches. She longed for her desk job at the law office, where criminals were names on a paper and guns the feature of some dime novel. This was more excitement than she'd bargained for. She could feel the adrenaline coursing through her veins, tempting her body to numb and shut down. She knew what would happen if she succumbed to it: She'd faint and be left at the mercy of this horrible man, waiting for someone to find her.

If someone finds me, she thought to herself. There was no telling how long it would be before Beatrice returned to Harry's room to find Eleanore missing. Beatrice had a habit of getting so wrapped up in a case that she completely forgot about things that weren't right in front of her. Eleanore also realized that she was operating under the assumption her cousin was still alive out there. The murderer had already tried to kill Beatrice once, after all. There was nothing to stop him trying again. It was possible that no one was coming, or that it would be too late by the time they did. Waiting for help was a bad idea, Eleanore decided. She had to get out of this herself.

With a slow, intentional breath, Eleanore swallowed back her fear and tried to think about what Beatrice would do in her place. *Probably jabber the guy's ear off,* Eleanore mused to herself. Beatrice could read a person's face and body language as easily as a script and have them tap dancing to her tune. When Eleanore had once asked how she managed it, Beatrice had merely shrugged and said she grew up with an actress. In Eleanore's current position, Beatrice would probably talk her way out. Eleanore knew she had no hope of that. Other than being an excellent gossip and socialite, Eleanore never knew what to say to get people to do what she wanted. What else would Beatrice do?

Her cousin's voice drifted from a distant memory. "*Don't focus on what you can't do,*" it said as a younger Eleanore struggled to get out of an old pair of handcuffs they'd been playing with. "*Focus on what you can do.*"

All right, Ellie, Eleanore schooled herself. *What can you do?*

Her sense of sight and movement were limited, but she could still hear. She tuned her ears more intently on her surroundings, trying to glean any information she could. The storm pelted against the windowpanes, sounding like the Big Bad Wolf attempting to blow the hotel over. Eleanore pulled her focus back from the window, which sounded far from her position, and focused on her captor's footsteps. From the way the man moved, she could tell they were in a closed room, a guest room maybe. He was smoking some horrid cigar while he paced. Eleanore filed this characteristic away for later, along with the gruff sound of his voice. It could help identify him even though she hadn't seen his face.

He didn't say another word to her; he simply smoked and ambulated impatiently as though he were waiting for something. Eleanore wasn't sure she wanted to find out what. Another idea occurred to her, and she cautiously tried to move her feet. They were bound at the ankles but not particularly tight. With some careful fidgeting, she managed to wiggle off one of her heels without making a sound. She paused to ensure she hadn't been spotted. Her captor made no objection, so she continued, feeling her stockinged foot along the floor—it was cold tile. He'd set her in the bathroom. That meant she was likely near the exit. A knock sounded on the door, confirming her suspicion. It was close. She froze as her kidnapper moved to answer it, passing her position to do so. He yanked open the door with an angry "It's about damn time!"

Another voice, a young man's, whispered, "She found it. I dunno how, but the broad found it."

He sounded panicked.

Eleanore's captor swore, then replied in a more hushed tone, "Where is she?"

"I locked her in the bell closet," the young man replied.

"Clearly I'm gonna have to take care of this myself," the kidnapper grumbled. "Find a place. Lay low. I'll find you."

"But—"

"Blow!"

Eleanore heard clamoring. The young man must have run off. The door clipped shut shortly after. Eleanore craned her neck to tune her hearing, certain she hadn't heard her captor walk back. After another few breaths, she murmured hesitantly, "Hello?"

No answer.

He was gone.

Eleanore set to work immediately, yanking and tugging at her bonds. She'd played magician with Beatrice enough times when they were children. Eleanore, of course, had always been the beautiful assistant, which meant *she* was the one getting shoved in boxes and tied up while Beatrice made her "reappear." Beatrice had once forgotten about Eleanore for an entire hour, forcing Eleanore to learn how to get out on her own. This prior experience, coupled with her kidnapper's poorly tied knots owing to underestimation of her, had Eleanore out of her bonds in minutes. She tugged down her blindfold and took a good look at the room beyond the bathroom door while she worked on untying her feet.

The room was a tad bigger than the one she and Beatrice had checked into. There was only one king-size bed. Everything was pristine. Her captor's cigar sat in an ash tray on the nightstand, still smoking. Not far from it sat the phone. An idea sparked. If she could get a hold of the police, they could end this charade and go home. She made short work of the bonds around her ankles, left her uncomfortable chair behind, and slipped back into her abandoned shoe. Walking on tiptoe, she approached the phone hopefully and snatched up the receiver. The nearby candle fluttered.

"Hello," she said into the phone, tapping the switch a few times. "Hello?"

Nothing.

The lines were still dead.

Eleanore hung up, disappointed but not deflated. She was going to get the police if it was the last thing she did . . . and it very well might be.

Determined, Eleanore searched the room for another means of escape. The front door was too risky. Her captor might have someone keeping watch. Her eyes landed on the thick curtains. She raced forward and jerked them open. Yes! He had a room with a balcony! Rain fell in torrents against the glass panes, and Eleanore swallowed hard. It was the rain or a murderer, she told herself. Besides, *someone* had to get the police. With a deep breath to steel herself, Eleanore opened the door and stepped out into the pouring rain. She was soaked in seconds, the rain dousing her perfectly crafted curls and sending mascara down her cheeks. She peered over the side of the balcony, suddenly rethinking her idea. It was a long way down.

"You can do this," she told herself. "Beatrice needs you. You can do this."

Trembling from excitement and nerves, Eleanore removed her shoes and tossed them into the gravel below. A drainpipe ran down the corner of the building, shiny and brand new like the rest of the gorgeous edifice. It would hold her weight all right, but the gap from the balcony to the pipe was severe, at least to Eleanore, whose idea of athletics was usually a trip to the shops. She pulled off her gloves and tossed them below with her shoes, lest the satin make her lose her grip.

Eleanore's conscience kept trying to tell her this was a horrible idea, that her chances of survival were stronger against a psychotic killer, but the rain drowned out all rational thought as Eleanore climbed over the railing and hung from the outside of the balcony. She fixed her eyes on the drainpipe, not daring to look down. Lightning streaked across the sky, momentarily blinding her. She waited for the spots to leave her eyes before fixing them on the drainpipe again. It was now or never, she supposed. After one final deep breath, Eleanore leapt.

Slam! Slip! Eleanore thudded into the drainpipe after a horrifying moment suspended in midair. Her stocking-covered feet clawed at the wall for support, slipping and sliding against the slick surface. She finally managed to get her bearings, her muscles screaming at her to give up and fall.

You can do this, she kept telling herself.

Clumsily, Eleanore made her way down the drainpipe an inch at a time, pausing now and then to reaffirm her grip on the slippery pipe. Lightning flashed again, and the rain seemed to be getting worse. It spurred her on. Help, she reminded herself; they needed help. Finally, her feet touched down on the sodden gravel, and Eleanore couldn't help letting out a surprised and relieved laugh.

"I did it," she said, grinning as her eyes moved back up to the balcony now so far away. Something flowered inside of her as she realized she'd just been taken hostage and held at gunpoint, and she'd escaped all on her own. The thought broadened her pink smile. Perhaps there was something to be said for this moxie business after all.

A rumble of thunder reminded Eleanore that she was still in the open and quite in danger. There would be no outrunning a bullet if she were caught. The wind gusted as she gathered her shoes and gloves, and a shiver passed through her. Even if she had a sweater, she doubted it would keep her very warm in this downpour. Without bothering to put her shoes back on, she took off down the walk at top speed, rain cascading around her. She could have sworn she heard shouting from the room she'd left as she reached the front gate, but it could just as easily have been the wind. Now neck-deep in trouble, Eleanore raced through the darkened parking lot of the hotel and disappeared into the night.

CHAPTER EIGHT

A MIDNIGHT INTERVIEW

The temperature in the bell closet grew stifling the longer Harry and Beatrice remained trapped in such close quarters. Exhaustion began to creep up Beatrice's spine, but she kept it at bay with determination and slight annoyance at the murderer's continual interference. It only made her want to solve the case all the more. With her hands defiantly on her hips, she watched for a good five minutes as Harry bashed his shoulder into the door. Beatrice willed the hinges to give way, but the door didn't budge.

"It's no use," Harry sighed at last, massaging his duly bruised shoulder. "It's too solid."

"Probably blocked from the other side too," added Beatrice. With a groan, she sat atop a box marked Fragile, caring little for the warning under the circumstances. This investigation was admittedly a bit more complicated than the one she'd helped Detective Raglan solve. The killer hadn't been stalking her every move then, and she'd been in disguise, putting her acting talents to far better use than they would have been on a film set. Here, she was only playing herself against an unknown entity who always seemed to be a step ahead of her. It was aggravating.

Harry turned, assessing her defeated posture. "Don't tell me *you're* giving up."

"I'm sitting still," she rebuffed, resting her chin in her hand. "I've yet to find a problem I can't solve by thinking."

Harry shook his head, clearly amused, but he didn't say anything in return. He sat himself atop the nearby toolbox and relaxed against the wall while Beatrice puzzled.

If only the door opened the other way, thought Beatrice. Then they could use the tools Harry sat on to remove the door hinges. If that were the case, she supposed the culprit wouldn't have locked them in so easily in the first place, and they wouldn't be in this predicament. She combed her brain, trying to think of *something* from all the research she'd done on Harry Houdini, but she came up short. There were no locks to pick. A fulcrum wouldn't do. There was no secondary exit. All hope of escape seemed to lay *outside* the door, which didn't bode well. At length, she sighed in defeat.

"I can't think of anything. There's no laundry chute, no air duct—"

"I take it you've used both before?" Harry interrupted.

"Of course," said Beatrice as if this were perfectly normal.

"There's no breaking down the door either," he added. "It's too thick."

"Well, we can't stay in here," Beatrice grumbled. "If he locked us in, he's probably coming back. If only we could reach Eleanore somehow."

"Say!" Harry snapped his fingers. "There's an idea!"

"What do you intend to do? Send her a letter?"

"No. Your cousin is a worrier. I bet you she's wandering the halls looking for us by now. We said we'd be in the lobby, so—"

"That's the first place she'd look," finished Beatrice.

Harry nodded. "Pounding on the door worked for Tommy."

It wasn't the brilliant escape she was hoping for, but Beatrice didn't want to meet the killer face to face on his terms either. "I'm game if you are," she agreed.

The pair of them stood and began beating on the door with their fists, crying for help at the top of their lungs. If Eleanore was anywhere nearby, she'd surely hear them, provided the storm didn't drown them out. Five minutes passed. Ten. The hope of rescue started to diminish, and Beatrice was nearly resolved to give up when movement sounded on the other side of the door as if someone were moving something heavy out of the way. Hope blossomed in Beatrice's chest once more, and she hammered passionately on the door.

"Yes! We're in here! Hurry!" she cried.

The door was pulled open moments later, but it was Martha Vickeridge, not Eleanore, who stood on the other side, dressed in her expensive night robe and slippers. Beatrice was grateful nonetheless.

"Thanks ever so!" she exclaimed, stumbling out of the closet at the first available opportunity, Harry just behind her.

The air was instantly cooler, a welcome relief to both of the closet's former occupants.

"No trouble, sugar," the older woman assured, "but what on earth were you youngsters doing in there?"

"Looking for clues," Beatrice replied.

A knowing look crossed Martha's face, and she smiled. "Ah, I understand. I was young once too, you know."

Both Harry and Beatrice exchanged confused glances before the meaning of Martha's words dawned on them—she thought they'd been necking.

"Mrs. Vickeridge, why would we have someone lock us in?" Harry pointed out, but it did nothing to curb Martha's imagination.

"Young people today. Such wild creatures," she chuckled to herself.

Beatrice could see there was no reasoning with the old woman, so she changed the subject. "What are you doing out of bed at this hour?" she asked instead.

"Me?" Mrs. Vickeridge replied. "Oh, looking for my husband, dear. I'm afraid we've had something of an argument. It won't do to go to bed angry."

"No, I suppose it won't," mused Beatrice, wondering just how loose the old woman's tongue might still be. She decided to take the risk. "Can I ask a . . . personal question?"

Mrs. Vickeridge didn't even pause. "Only if you're sure you really want the answer."

"I heard a rumor . . . that Mr. Vickeridge tried to divorce you last year," said Beatrice, doing her best impression of young and innocent. "Is it true?"

"Oh, you poor rabbit." Mrs. Vickeridge patted Beatrice clumsily on the hand, and Beatrice had a sneaking suspicion she was still ossified. "Having to endure such idle gossip. Well . . . I suppose it is true, though, isn't it? I put a stop to it, though. Told him how it would upset our dear Ned."

"Ned?" Harry repeated. There'd been no mention of a Ned previously, and there certainly wasn't one at the hotel.

"Yes," Mrs. Vickeridge enthused. "Ned, our son. He's a bit older than you," she said, looking Harry over with eyes of appraisal, "but just as handsome. He lives in our old Rhode Island estate with his wife. Lovely girl, though not quite as stunning as you, pet."

Beatrice's smile was an uncomfortable one. There were some people who gave compliments and made her feel fabulous, and others who should never dish out compliments at all. Mrs. Vickeridge fell in the latter category.

"Why would it have upset him?" Beatrice asked. "If you're unhappily married, then—"

"Unhappily married?" Mrs. Vickeridge interrupted. "Whoever said such a thing?"

"He was filing for divorce," Beatrice said sharply.

"Oh, fiddle-faddle. He always threatens divorce after we argue. He'd never go through with it. It would ruin him."

"Because of the money," supplied Harry.

"That and the social scandal," sighed Mrs. Vickeridge, confirming Fred's earlier tale. "These are dark days, but even now, image is everything."

Beatrice couldn't deny that. She lived it every day. The appearance of something was often more valuable than the truth of it. By remaining married, the Vickeridges kept their finances and properties intact—a handy thing when jobs and money were scarce. Another thought piqued Beatrice's curiosity, and she asked, "Mrs. Vickeridge, how often do you and your husband travel on the line?"

"Oh," she thought, "six months out of the year, give or take. Why do you ask, dear?"

Harry must have sensed where Beatrice was headed with this. He stiffened beside her as if bracing for an explosion.

"I thought you might be able to help me with a particular problem. You see, my mother likes her bourbon, and I was hoping to bring some home to her. You wouldn't happen to know anywhere along the line where I could find some, would you?"

The effect was immediate. Mrs. Vickeridge's eye went wide, and her cheeks colored. She puffed up like blowfish sensing danger. "The very idea," she breathed. "Now, see here, young lady. I get my hooch legally. I keep it stockpiled. The very idea!"

Beatrice smiled sweetly. "Of course, honey. I was only asking."

"Well . . . that's that!" Mrs. Vickeridge huffed, and before Beatrice could say another word, Mrs. Vickeridge turned, snatched up her candle from the front desk, and left the lobby in a snit with candle flickering madly.

"Do you think she's telling the truth?" Harry asked.

"Not one bit," replied Beatrice. "A woman with deep pockets and a drinking problem who regularly rides the rails? She's a customer of the juice ring. I'll stake my favorite diamond earrings on it."

"I bet you dazzle at parties," he praised.

This compliment brought a vibrant smile to her red lips. "You have no idea."

She wandered back to the front desk, leaving Harry to stand there and contemplate the image of her dressed to the nines for some Hollywood shindig. She never tired of putting that look on a man's face. When he shortly came back to his senses, he rejoined her at the desk, where she was flipping through the logbook, this time searching for Mr. Morrow's whereabouts. Being ever the studious manager, Mr. Morrow was an avid record keeper, and thusly the books reflected where each of the hotel staff had been put up for the night. Beatrice stared at this page thoughtfully, then ripped it from the logbook, much to Harry's surprise.

"Morrow won't be happy about that," he uttered as Beatrice folded the page and tucked it into her handbag.

"He'll live," Beatrice replied. "I'm tired of the shadows being one step ahead."

She closed the logbook with a snap and stowed it back in its drawer, signaling for Harry to follow her. They returned to the darkened halls on high alert, both walking with determined steps and sealed lips. Beatrice was only half aware of their surroundings, too lost in contemplation to pay them any mind. The juice ring was the epicenter of the whole ordeal, of that Beatrice was certain, but how many people were involved? And why had Holly been killed over it? Perhaps it had something to do with her missing notebook. If she was keeping tabs on people, she might have discovered who was behind all of this. But why had she been keeping such a notebook in the first place?

So tangled were Beatrice's thoughts, she hardly realized they'd reached Mr. Morrow's room until Harry knocked on the door. Sounds of confusion and mumbling came from the other side—Mr. Morrow had been asleep. Harry knocked again.

"Yes, yes. All right," came Mr. Morrow's tired voice.

Noises of shuffling came next, and Mr. Morrow shortly opened the door, wearing a hotel robe and carrying a candle. "Can I help you, Miss Adams?"

"Yes," she replied. "May we come in?"

Mr. Morrow's expression said he'd rather they didn't, but he waved them in regardless. Beatrice smiled in thanks and switched off her light to conserve battery. Together, she and Harry entered the room, which was an exact copy of Beatrice and Eleanore's, only in reverse. Mr. Morrow closed the door behind them. Harry and Beatrice each took up residence on one of the two beds while Mr. Morrow perched himself in the desk chair, setting the candle on the desk beside him.

"What's this all about?" Mr. Morrow demanded, mopping his brow with the back of his hand.

"Are you a nervous sweater, Mr. Morrow?" asked Beatrice, catching him off guard.

"What's that got to do with anything?" he snapped.

Beatrice shrugged innocently. "You could be sweating because this case is stressful—"

"Yes, it damn well is!"

"—or you could be sweating because you lied to us."

It was like watching a bomb go off. The hotel manager was shocked, then defensive. Survival suddenly mattered more than honesty. "Now see here," he stumbled for words, but Beatrice didn't let him get another one in.

"It was your typewriter, Mr. Morrow, that wrote the note leading Holly to the boiler room."

"So what if it was?"

"You don't deny it, then?"

"Someone broke into my office, as I'm sure you well know. It could have been anyone." Again he swiped his forehead with the back of his hand.

"But it wasn't just anyone, was it?" Beatrice pressed. Her eyes were absolutely lethal. "You knew I'd be studying the typewriters the moment I asked if yours was the only one in the hotel. In fact, you were the *only* one who knew of my interest in them at all. What I want to know is why? Why did you do it?"

Mr. Morrow was stunned to silence, and Beatrice had to fight to keep from looking too pleased. She was working entirely on conjecture and a gut feeling, knowing full well that accusation would lead a nervous man to confess *something* even if it wasn't the exact truth she'd been digging for. After a length of silence and her captivating, persuasive stare, Mr. Morrow cracked like an egg.

"First, you must understand that everything I've done is to protect the hotel."

"Oh, sure, and that makes murder all right," Harry jibed.

"What? No!" stammered Mr. Morrow. He couldn't seem to get the words out quick enough. "I admit, I wrote that note asking her to meet me in the boiler room, but I didn't kill her! She never showed!"

Beatrice leaned forward. "What do you mean she never showed?"

"I mean precisely that. I waited for half an hour, and then I returned home to my wife. It's not uncommon for me to leave the hotel late. You can ask her!"

This was a different outcome than Beatrice had originally surmised. She'd assumed the killer had written the note in Holly's pocket, luring Holly to her death. Now Beatrice understood. The notebook had been taken and the note left for this very purpose—to lead Beatrice off the trail and buy the killer time. All roads seemed to lead back to Mr. Morrow. He was either a patsy or he knew more than he'd been letting on.

"Why did you ask Holly to meet?" Beatrice demanded. "What were you paying her for?"

"To lay off the case," Mr. Morrow sighed in defeat. He was sweating in earnest now.

"The case?" repeated Harry.

"Was she an investigator?" asked Beatrice.

"Worse," Mr. Morrow uttered. "She was a reporter."

It was as though the lightning outside had struck within the room.

"*That's* why she kept a notebook with her all the time," Beatrice said urgently to Harry.

Harry nodded. "And why she was undercover."

"She was writing about the juice ring," they said in unison.

Beatrice felt her cheeks warm, and Harry smiled.

"Heavens," grumbled Mr. Morrow. "You know about that too, do you?"

"Of course," replied Beatrice, turning back to the interview. "I'm a detective. How did you know Holly was a reporter?"

"It's my job to know everything that goes on in my hotel," he said, almost affronted. "Mary Todd told me Holly was snooping around, so I looked into it. Rather than risk being sacked, Holly came clean. She told me everything. Who she really was. What she was doing."

"Who was she?" Beatrice pried.

"Tiffany Blake of the Los Angeles Times," he sighed. "She was doing a piece on what it was like to be a Harvey Girl after experiencing it for herself. Naturally, I wanted the hotel written up well, so I kept her secret."

"But she didn't intend to keep yours, did she?" Harry mused.

Mr. Morrow averted his gaze. "No," he muttered, "but I didn't kill her, I swear it! I was trying to protect her!"

"Protect her from what?" asked Beatrice.

"From getting killed!" Mr. Morrow sighed, exasperated. "Look . . . the juice ring isn't mine. I was simply in the wrong place at the wrong time, and I found the empty bottles stashed in the garbage. When I started poking around, I received a warning letter."

"Who from?" Harry questioned.

Mr. Morrow shook his head. "I don't know. They were all signed M."

Beatrice pulled the note she'd found in the lobby from her bag and held it up. "You mean, *you* didn't write this?"

"No. I get letters and payments from M. As long as I'm silent and I mind my own business, I get a nice bonus hidden in the clock once a week."

"How long ago did you get the first letter?" Harry asked.

"Two weeks, give or take."

"So you were being paid hush money," said Beatrice, "and you were trying to bring Holly along?"

"Yes!" Mr. Morrow nodded vigorously. "She'd stumbled on the juice ring and went Nellie Bly on the whole thing. M told me to take care of it, so I offered her money if she'd meet me at midnight. As I said before, she never showed."

Beatrice fell silent, allowing this new information to sink in as she tucked M's note back into her bag. When she finally spoke, it was to Harry.

"If she never went to the boiler room, she couldn't have been killed there."

Harry nodded in agreement. "Our timeline is wrong."

"Tommy said he found Holly on the telephone saying she was Miss Blake," Beatrice thought aloud. "I'll bet you anything she was calling her editor to tell them she'd found a new story. What if she not only found the juice ring, but she also found the person behind it?"

"The mysterious M," Harry intoned.

Beatrice nodded. "She'd cracked the case wide open before we'd even arrived. She was killed to keep the story from reaching the press."

"Or the police," added Harry. "She was probably searching for evidence when she was killed by our bellhop."

"Yes . . . but which one?"

"Bellhop?" Mr. Morrow interjected. "You don't mean—"

"One of the bell staff killed Holly, yes," Beatrice cut him off.

"Tiffany," Harry corrected.

"Tiffany," she amended, waving it off. Her next question was directed at Mr. Morrow. "Can you think of anyone on your staff capable of this?"

"No." He shook his head. "No. They're all vetted extremely before they're hired."

"These are desperate times, Mr. Morrow," Beatrice pointed out.

"I'm sorry, Miss Adams. That's all I know," Mr. Morrow said wearily. "The letters are in my office filing cabinet. I'll get you a key if you need them."

"That'd be aces," she replied with a smile.

After handing over his key, Mr. Morrow showed them out, and Harry and Beatrice returned to the ominous dark halls, navigating by the fading beam of her flashlight.

"What now?" whispered Harry.

Beatrice paused in the middle of the hall, trying to determine that herself by mentally prioritizing what information she had thus far. "First we need to get those letters from Morrow's office," she decided. "Then I might actually need that cup of coffee. Did you ever turn the brewer on?"

Harry chuckled and affirmed that he had. The storm sounded worse than ever as they resumed their trek through the dark, and Beatrice silently hoped her poor cousin wasn't being kept up by it. At least one of them deserved to get a little sleep.

Freezing to the bone and huddled under a store awning for a break from the torrential downpour, Eleanore was beginning to see the flaws in her plan. She had no idea where the police station was, and every single shop was closed owing to the late hour, so she could hardly stop and ask for directions. Worse, she was out in the open. Surely her captor had realized she was missing by now. Would they figure out that she'd left the hotel entirely? Would they come after her?

Eleanore hugged her arms around herself, but it did nothing to stop her shivering. The wind was relentless. It pulled at her dress and her hair, the latter of which now hung lifelessly about her cheeks. Cake mascara ran in rivulets down her face, giving her a sort of gaunt expression. If she could see herself in the mirror now, she would surely have a fit. *Why did I do this?* she asked herself. The answer screamed loudly in her mind: Beatrice needed her. That horrible man was going to kill her cousin if she didn't get help. No one in that hotel was safe.

Lightning struck across the street, sizzling the air and shooting every hair on Eleanore's body skyward. She didn't need telling twice to keep moving. She broke into a run, still in nothing but her stockinged feet, her shoes dangling in her hand. She'd gone another three blocks, fatigue and hopelessness slowing her down, when suddenly, there it stood like a miracle from heaven—the bright lights of a twenty-four-hour diner.

Eleanore nearly cried in relief. Hope burgeoned in her chest, and she put on a burst of speed, racing as if the shadows themselves were trying to stop her. Halfway there. Three quarters. She burst through the door and slammed it shut behind her as if a monster had been at her heels.

The diner was small—no bigger than a train car—and contained only three occupants: two exhausted men dining at one of the booths and the cook behind the counter.

"You okay, sweetheart?" the cook asked, taking in her disheveled appearance.

Eleanore's heart beat furiously in her chest as she tried to catch her breath.

"Police," she stammered, approaching the counter with all due haste. "I need the police. Have you . . . got a telephone?"

"Sure." He pulled a dime from the register and flicked it her way. "On the wall."

Eleanore caught the coin, much to her surprise, and raced to the rotary payphone on the far wall. It took a few tries to get the dime into the slot—she was trembling so badly—but she finally managed, swiftly dialing zero.

"Operator," a cool female voice answered.

"Yes! Operator! I need the police in Winslow, Arizona! It's urgent!"

"One moment, please," the operator replied in as calm a tone as before.

The phone rang. Eleanore held her breath.

"Winslow Police Department," a young male voice answered.

"Hello! I'd like to report a murder!"

CHAPTER NINE
A FIRESIDE CHAT

Mr. Morrow's office door was still wide open when Beatrice and Harry arrived. Judging by how damaged the handle was, Beatrice imagined there would be no closing it until a new knob was installed. They entered the manager's office to find it in shambles. Papers were strewn everywhere, chairs were overturned, and the desk drawers had all been pried open. Beatrice wasn't surprised. In fact, she was glad. If the office had been tossed, that meant she was on the right track.

"Good gravy," Harry breathed. "The killer must be getting desperate."

"Or M," Beatrice added. "Looks like we're shaking the right trees."

The sounds of the wailing storm were muffled inside the interior room, adding to the eerie sensation that they were once again being watched. Beatrice shrugged it off and shined her flashlight on the filing cabinet in the corner. It was dented here and there by sharp blows from a heavy object, but so far as Beatrice could tell, the thief hadn't been successful in getting it open.

"Could you?" She held her light out to Harry, who took it without question, holding it aloft so she could see.

Beatrice used Mr. Morrow's keys to open the topmost drawer of the filing cabinet. Harry adjusted his arm so the flashlight illuminated the metal drawer's contents more fully, and Beatrice set to work rifling through them. Like everything else in his office, Mr. Morrow's filing cabinet was meticulously organized, and Beatrice couldn't help wondering if he applied as much effort to the upkeep of his pencil mustache.

"Anything?" Harry asked.

Beatrice shook her head, combing through each section paper by paper. She found occupancy reports, supply orders, and employee records (James had two demerits already) but no letters. Had Mr. Morrow lied?

Beatrice moved to the next drawer and did the same. Other than more hotel business, she found nothing even remotely related to M. It wasn't until Beatrice opened the bottommost drawer that she uncovered what she was searching for. She pulled a stack of four letters from the very back that was held together with a large rubber band. Beatrice hummed in thought.

"What is it?" Harry wondered.

"These envelopes," she said. "The handwriting on them is different from the note we found."

"Maybe it's Morrow's?" Harry suggested.

"Maybe."

Beatrice moved to the desk and rifled through the papers strewn over it until she found one that contained the manager's scrawl. She held the bound envelopes up to it. The handwriting was indeed Henry Morrow's. Beatrice fleetly unwrapped the band around the letters and spread them out on the desk, Harry leaning over her shoulder with the light. Each envelope was marked with a different date.

"Clever man," Beatrice praised. "He's kept a record of the date each note was left."

"Which means?"

"Which means we may be able to use them to figure out who M is," Beatrice explained. "Morrow must have expected things to turn sour."

"They always do," Harry mused.

Beatrice heartily agreed. In her experience, if anything could go wrong, it would. It was best to plan for every eventuality. Mr. Morrow's obsessive need to do just that currently worked in her favor.

Beatrice rearranged the letters on the table so they were organized in ascending order from the first letter Mr. Morrow had received to the last. She pulled the note she'd found in the clock from her handbag and placed it on the desk beneath these. Once everything was mapped just so, she opened the first letter to read:

Look any further into this business, and things could get messy. If you keep your trap shut, I'll leave you a little surprise in the lobby clock at midnight. I created a secret compartment in the molding. I'll know if you open your mouth. I have eyes everywhere.

—M

Beatrice compared this note with the one she'd found earlier and confirmed that the handwriting was the same. The M who had written to Mr. Morrow before and the M now stalking the hotel were the same person. Satisfied, Beatrice stuffed the first letter back into its envelope and opened the next one. It congratulated Mr. Morrow on his wise decision and informed him that continued silence would equal more hush money. The third note read almost the same. The fourth, however, was another set of instructions.

Holly Albright is asking too many questions. Take care of it, or I will.

—M

Beatrice stared at this note a moment longer than the others. The letters certainly corroborated Mr. Morrow's account of events, which let him off the hook for murder. It didn't, however, leave him entirely blameless. He'd known Holly was really a reporter doing an undercover story, and he'd known about the juice ring. If he'd done his job from the start, Holly—Tiffany—might still be alive. Mr. Morrow may not have hurt her, but in Beatrice's eyes he was as good as an accomplice, and she would see the police knew of his involvement.

She decidedly stuck the final note back into its envelope and banded the letters back together.

"Why do I get the feeling we have to go back to the lobby?" Harry mused as she slipped the envelopes into her brimming handbag.

"Because you have razor-sharp intellect," Beatrice replied,

beaming as she took her flashlight from him. "Ever think of changing professions?"

Harry chuckled. "I think I'll stick to the medical side of things."

"Pity. You make a crackerjack sidekick," Beatrice teased.

They shared a smile.

"Come on, skipper," said Beatrice. "We can check these letters against the ledgers."

She led the way back into the dreary hall, Harry just behind her. Thunder shook the hotel, and lightning flashed outside the windows. Beatrice was about to turn for the lobby when another glow down the hall caught her eye. It was too bright to be a candle, but it was definitely flickering. Curious, Beatrice turned toward it instead, walking on careful tiptoe in case an unsavory character waited ahead. About halfway down the hall, she came across a short set of tiled stairs that led up into a long and vast room. If all the furniture was moved, Beatrice wagered a party could be held in there for at least a hundred people. The floor was polished wood, decorated here and there by a colorful handwoven rug. Pillars separated the space into thirds, and the overhead beams were painted bright colors of turquoise and yellow, almost a tapestry in their own right if viewed from a certain angle. At the very end of the long space was a fireplace that was currently alight and surrounded by comfortable armchairs. Sitting in one of these smoking a putrid cigar was Mr. Vickeridge. Beatrice and Harry headed toward him, the former no longer quieting her steps. The click-clack of her heels alerted Mr. Vickeridge to their presence.

"Ah, Miss Adams," he greeted as he turned to face her and Harry. He shook some ash from the end of his cigar into the ashtray on the side table. "And . . . Mr. Riley, is it?"

"That's right," Harry replied.

"Mind if we join you for a spell?" asked Beatrice. "That fire sure is nice."

"Not at all. Please." He indicated the two chairs opposite him.

Beatrice switched off her light and took a seat. Harry sat in the other chair. The three of them enjoyed a comfortable silence for a few minutes, listening to the lulling crackle of the fire and the pelting of the rain against the hotel exterior. Beatrice feared she might drift off to sleep if she stayed silent any longer.

"Where's Mrs. Vickeridge?" she asked conversationally. She knew full well where Martha Vickeridge was, or at the very least, where she had been.

"Oh, I left her in the room," he said. "We had a disagreement, and I wanted some peace and quiet."

He took a puff from his cigar, tired eyes lingering on the fire. It matched with Mrs. Vickeridge's tale, which likely meant it was the truth.

"Must have been some argument," Beatrice mused.

"It doesn't take much with that woman," Mr. Vickeridge muttered. "She's a regular volcano. You never know when she might erupt."

"I can imagine," Beatrice sympathized. "It must be difficult . . . being married to a rummy."

Mr. Vickeridge opened his mouth as if he were about to protest, then decided against it. "Noticed that, did you?" he grumbled instead.

"It's hard to miss," mused Harry.

Mr. Vickeridge shook his head in distaste at the situation and perhaps with a bit of pity toward himself. "She's always been heavy-handed. Do you know, that woman made me change *my* name when we married? Can you imagine?"

"You don't say," Beatrice uttered thoughtfully. "Did she give a reason?"

"She likes to be in charge, my wife."

"What was your name before?" asked Harry.

"Hmm? Oh, Martin. Dennis Martin," he answered, gazing into the fire. "I suppose it wasn't fancy enough for Martha. She lives for extravagance, that woman."

Beatrice and Harry shared a glance, and Beatrice felt a chill that had nothing to do with the dreary weather.

Martin, Harry mouthed.

M? she mouthed back.

Mr. Vickeridge hadn't noticed their exchange, far too lost in his own thoughts. He puffed on his cigar and tilted more ash into the designated tray.

"Is that . . . why you tried to divorce her?" Beatrice asked carefully.

Mr. Vickeridge jerked as if she'd slapped him. "Where did you hear that?"

"Never mind where," she replied.

There was a moment when Beatrice thought he might close up and end the interview immediately, but the moment passed. Mr. Vickeridge merely puffed his cigar and appraised her with old, wise eyes. "You're a very clever young woman. I'll give you that," he said. "Yes, it is *one* of the reasons I wanted to divorce her. When you're tied to Martha Vickeridge, you're tied to trouble."

"What kind of trouble?" wondered Harry.

"Martha likes her games," replied Mr. Vickeridge, and Beatrice didn't care for his tone. "Especially if they benefit her in any way. She'd throw money at the wall if you told her she can keep what sticks."

Beatrice filed this information away, intelligent eyes studying him, looking for chinks in his armor. "A juice ring wouldn't happen to be her latest game, would it?"

Harry stiffened beside her, prepared to pounce if things got out of hand. It was certainly a comfort having someone at her side who could throw a decent punch if needed.

Mr. Vickeridge took his time to answer, watching the smoke curl from the end of his cigar. "I try to remain ignorant of my wife's affairs," he said. "But . . . if there is a juice ring nearby, I imagine my wife will find it if she hasn't already."

Thunder crashed so loudly that Beatrice jumped in her seat. The resulting adrenaline was a good reminder of time running out. She still needed to check the logbook against M's letters, and then she would look in on Eleanore. Hopefully her cousin had managed a few winks of sleep.

"Thanks for chatting," Beatrice said as she stood.

Harry took his cue and rose to his feet as well.

Mr. Vickeridge shrugged indifferently. "Sorry I can't be of more help," he said, sounding the exact opposite of sorry.

Beatrice had a feeling he knew more than he was letting on, but why keep such secrets? To protect Martha? Or to hide something else?

CHAPTER NINE

After bidding Mr. Vickeridge goodnight one last time, Beatrice and Harry returned to the dark hallway. Beatrice switched on her light, and they headed once more in the direction of the lobby.

"You don't think *he* could be M, do you?" whispered Harry.

Beatrice shrugged and shook her head. "I don't know," she answered earnestly. "There are so many Ms surrounding this case. Mary, Martha, Martin, Morrow . . . he's definitely hiding something, though."

"Who isn't?" Harry quipped, and Beatrice nearly laughed.

"You might be on to something, detective," she teased.

The storm continued its barrage against the hotel, and Beatrice was starting to wonder if it would ever let up. They entered the lobby with all due caution, treating the shadows with even more care now than they had before. Beatrice did a careful circle with her light to ensure they were quite alone, then made her way toward the front desk. Harry followed. They stopped short of reaching it. Like the manager's office, the front desk had been tossed. Papers were scattered all over the floor, drawers were yanked open, and it looked as though the till had been broken in to. Beatrice made straight for the drawer where the ledgers were kept, her heart sinking.

"They're gone," she uttered in disbelief. "All of them . . . gone."

Beatrice didn't know whether to be angry or feel despair. Aggravation also reared its ugly head, and if she'd felt any more of it, she could have punched the wall. She took a long, measured breath to calm herself.

"You okay?" asked Harry earnestly.

"Aces," Beatrice lied with another sigh. "Absolutely aces."

Eleanore had taken refuge in the corner booth after calling the police. Though the officer on the other end of the line had said someone was on the way, she had heard disbelief in his voice. Eleanore supposed it was utterly unbelievable. No one wanted to think murder could happen in their sleepy little town, and from what Eleanore had seen of it, that's exactly what Winslow was—a little refuge on the side of the highway where nothing ever happened.

The storm howled outside the diner windows, and Eleanore felt a pang of guilt for making anyone drive in this weather. She'd barely survived it herself. The thought made her glance down to examine the damage, and she sighed in incredulity. Her beautiful green dress was tattered and mud-stained from her excursion, and her shoes, which sat sopping wet beside her, would likely never be the same after such a soaking. Eleanore would have to dispose of the whole lot, a realization that sent a prickle of irritation through her. Why couldn't Beatrice *plan* to get into trouble? At least that way Eleanore could be prepared if she got dragged into it. Trousers and flat shoes would be a start.

"You okay, sweetheart?" a voice interrupted her thoughts.

Eleanore jumped, a shocked squeal escaping her. She placed a hand over her heart and looked up to see the kindly cook standing over her holding a pot of coffee in one hand and a fresh mug in the other.

"Yes," she said with a nervous smile. "I mean . . . no. Oh, I don't know. It's been a very long night."

"Coffee?" he offered, holding up the pot.

"Oh . . . no. I don't have any money with me," Eleanore uttered, her eyes expressing her thanks.

"On the house, honey," he said, and he placed the mug on the table, filling it with steaming hot caffeine.

A tired, genuine smile crossed Eleanore's lips. "Thank you."

"Sure thing. Say, you must be in some real trouble to be out in this weather."

Eleanore cupped her mug in her hands, the warm ceramic providing relief to her chilled hands. "You could say that," she murmured, aware that the two motorists across the way were staring. There was only one booth between her and them. Anything she said would be overheard, and until the police showed, Eleanore trusted no one.

"Well," he said, "if you need an ear. . . ."

He let his words trail off, the invitation left open to cash in whenever she chose. Eleanore smiled again in thanks, and the cook returned to his place behind the counter.

Eleanore averted her eyes to the coffee in front of her, watching the steam curl in ringlets, reminding her of the difference between hot and cold. She shivered, suddenly craving the comfort of a blanket and a warm fire. Neither were on offer. She tried to put it from her mind, but the longer she sat there, the more exhaustion crept up her spine and tempted her muscles to collapse. She rested her forehead in her hand, ignoring the stares and whispers. Like herself, the two motorists were trapped by the storm. Eleanore wondered where they'd come from and where they were headed. Why were they traveling so late at night? Perhaps they'd stopped for a bite and been trapped. It hadn't been that late when the first of the rain had fallen. The thought that other people would have a different story to tell about that night seemed foreign to Eleanore. It would always make her think of murder. The image of Holly's body falling from the closet presented itself, and Eleanore shuddered, pulling her coffee closer.

She hoped the police would be there soon.

CHAPTER TEN
A WARNING FROM M

It felt to Beatrice as if she'd been playing a child's game of detective up to present, and now the real game had begun. Tony Baker's murder had been a cakewalk in comparison. She'd been assisting the police then. This time she was on her own, and it seemed M was no longer underestimating her. No more games, she decided. If M wanted to tango with her, Beatrice would show she knew all five steps.

Back in the kitchen once again, Beatrice paced up and down, a cup of steaming coffee on the counter behind her.

Harry was leaning against the opposite counter, one hand around his own coffee and the other in his trouser pocket. His eyes followed her progress back and forth as she stewed in silence. After about five minutes of this, he said, "Geez. Would you just drink your joe and hold still a minute?"

Beatrice started as if she'd forgotten he was there and leaned contritely against the counter near her mug, arms crossed and lips pursed.

"Coffee too," Harry said, an amused look on his face. "Doctor's orders."

Beatrice huffed and picked up her mug. "Oh, all right," she grumbled.

At the first sip, it was as if all the oxygen had returned to her brain. She took another, and the fog in her mind cleared a little more.

"Better?" asked Harry.

"Much," she replied.

With a smile and a nod, Harry sipped his own coffee, seemingly satisfied.

"The good news is, we know M was looking for the letters," Beatrice began.

"And the bad?" Harry wondered.

"I have them, which means M will be coming at me even harder."

She took another careful sip of coffee, pleased at the opening it seemed to be creating in her head. She was still tired, but it no longer affected her thoughts.

"We'll just have to unmask M, then," Harry said.

Beatrice nearly laughed. "You say that as if we haven't been trying to do that already."

"And we're nearly there."

Harry was right, of course. They were only hitting brick walls now because they were getting close to the truth.

"Maybe we're looking at the puzzle the wrong way," Beatrice thought aloud.

"How do you mean?"

"Ever since we found that note in the clock, I've been so worried about M, I haven't much thought to the original murderer."

"You're sure they aren't the same?"

"Absolutely and how!" Beatrice enthused. "None of the bell staff's handwriting matches M's letters. The murderer must be taking orders from M too, same as Morrow. Something must have gone wrong."

"You can say that again," Harry mused.

"What do we know?" said Beatrice, taking to pacing again. "We know Holly wasn't Holly, but Tiffany Blake. We know she was a reporter doing a story on the Harvey Girls. We know she kept a little black book, likely with all her notes on the story. The bellhops would mistake it for a tally book, naturally, not knowing what she was *really* up to."

"Don't forget, our original timeline was wrong," Harry observed.

Beatrice paused. "Time," she repeated. "Holly's missing time."

"What about it?"

"Miss Acre and Miss Bishop both confirmed that Holly was missing for exactly half an hour the day she was killed. The bell staff was all out smoking."

"I'll just bet one of them knows where she went," Harry said, smiling.

Beatrice smiled too. "We need to talk to Tommy again."

Suddenly, a gut-wrenching, horrified scream ripped through the hallways of the hotel, jerking both Harry and Beatrice from their relaxed stances.

"Either I'm hearing things," Beatrice uttered.

"Or something else has happened," finished Harry.

They shared a glance and then, as if released from a spring, abandoned their coffees and sped toward the swinging kitchen door. The dining room was empty and glum as they crossed it, almost hauntingly so. Beatrice shined her light in every corner, looking both for the source of the scream and for the culprit who'd caused it.

"Do you hear anything else?" whispered Beatrice.

Harry shook his head.

They both paused under the archway at the dining room's entrance and trained their ears. Nothing. Lightning flashed outside the windows, and Beatrice felt for a moment as if she were trapped in a haunted house and the murderer was a spirit. Though it went against her very nature, Beatrice called out, "Hello?"

"Help!" came a cry from down the main hall. "Oh, somebody, please help!"

"It's coming from the library!" cried Harry.

The pair of them took off at a run, no longer checking the shadows as they should or bothering to quiet their steps.

When they arrived at the scene, they found Essie Hartman—Beatrice knew by the E on her silk pocketed night-robe—standing in the entryway, trembling in a fit of sobs. Her candle had fallen out of her hand and diminished on its way to the floor. Harry was immediately at Essie's side, trying to calm her. Beatrice followed Essie's frightened gaze to one of the armchairs, her flashlight beam illuminating the figure of a staring corpse.

It was Mrs. Vickeridge, her eyes open and glassy, holding her last emotion of terror. Her throat had been cut from ear to ear, and a small slip of paper was clutched in her hand.

The first emotion to hit Beatrice was shock. She'd seen Mrs. Vickeridge alive a mere hour ago, soused up and bright-eyed without a care in the world. Guilt reared its ugly head next, condemning Beatrice for leaving the old woman alone in such circumstances as this. Would she still be alive if Beatrice had seen her off to bed? Beatrice cast such thoughts aside. She couldn't allow them to affect her. She shouldn't. This knowledge did nothing to squash the pain in her chest, and those thoughts resurfaced. This *was* her fault. She hadn't completed the puzzle quickly enough.

Beatrice moved forward and respectfully closed Mrs. Vickeridge's staring eyes with a heavy heart.

"What's in her hand?" asked Harry, hardly aware of Essie, who was sobbing into his chest for comfort.

Beatrice carefully pulled the note from the dead woman's hand and unfurled it, reading by the light of her flashlight:

If you don't lay off the case, I'll kill another.

—M

Beatrice barely suppressed a gasp. She crumpled the letter as if it were M's throat.

"What'd it say?" Harry wondered.

Beatrice met his eye and gave an infinitesimal shake of her head. She couldn't tell him now, not with Essie listening. The last thing she wanted to do was start a panic.

"Miss Hartman," Beatrice began in the tone of a concerned older sister, "what on earth are you doing out of bed? It's well after midnight."

Clearly disappointed that the older and handsome Dr. Riley wouldn't put his arms around her, Essie ceased her sniveling and turned her attention to Beatrice.

"I couldn't sleep," Essie answered with an innocent shrug. "I came to find a book."

"All on your own? With a killer on the loose?"

"Sure. What would he want with me?"

Beatrice didn't buy it. "You can be straight with me, honey," she said. "What were you really doing out of bed?"

Essie rolled her dazzling eyes. "I said already. I was looking for a book."

Beatrice tilted her head just so and placed a hand in the curve of her hip. "Look, I'm no dumb Dora. That robe—real silk, embroidered with a fine thread? Must have cost a pretty penny. And those duds you and your sister were sporting at dinner were just as fine. You come from money, but you're traveling alone. No chaperones. You're looking for trouble, you and Tunie. More specifically, I'd wager you're looking for the best speakeasies money can get you into. And now I've found you standing over the dead body of a woman who might be attached to a juice ring. Somehow I get the impression it wasn't a *book* you were after, so spill."

Essie gaped at her, mouthing like a suffocating fish as she stumbled for another excuse.

"I'd sing, honey," Harry recommended. "She'll find out the hard way if you don't."

Beatrice's heart soared at his support, and she tried to push it back down. Now wasn't the time to go getting excited.

"Boy," Essie puffed out. "You really are a detective, huh?"

"Did you think I was playing a part?" Beatrice replied.

"Kinda."

"Well, I'm not. Two women are now dead, and some very dangerous characters are lurking in the dark. I suggest you help me before anyone else gets hurt."

Essie sighed. "Oh, all right." She hugged her arms around herself as if it created armor against the coming storm. "I wasn't looking for a book. I was meeting Mrs. Vickeridge."

"Why?" asked Beatrice.

"She said she could get me and Tunie some hooch real cheap. I thought, why not? You know? It'd make the next stretch of track more interesting."

Harry and Beatrice shared a look.

"I'll bet that's why she was in the lobby," he said.

Beatrice agreed with a nod. "And why she was so bent out of shape by our questions. Did she say anything else to you?" she asked Essie. "Anything at all?"

Essie shook her head. "She was going to explain everything when I got here, but . . . well . . ."

"You found her like this," Beatrice supplied.

Essie nodded.

Beatrice considered for a moment, once more casting a somber gaze over the silenced Mrs. Vickeridge. If the old woman was about to get him another client, why would M kill *her*?

"When exactly did she talk to you about meeting here?" asked Beatrice. "I don't recall you talking at tea."

"Sometime after dinner. That slimy salesman was making a pass at me, and she swooped in to bat him off."

"Flanagan?" Harry asked.

"Yeah. He seems to have a thing for younger women. He's a little too far outside the pasture for my liking, if you get my drift."

"I do indeed," Beatrice murmured in thought.

"Anyway," Essie continued. "She took me to the ladies, and we had a chat. It's a real bummer . . . her ending up like this."

"Does your sister know where you are?" asked Beatrice.

"Of course," replied Essie. "We tell each other everything."

Thunder crashed so loudly that all three of them jumped and subconsciously inched toward one another.

"Well, then, why don't we get you back to bed?" Beatrice suggested. "I'm sure she's waiting up and worried sick."

Essie nodded. "Yeah . . . that's Tunie, all right. Say," she added, perking up. "Can I have your autograph to take back? That'd cheer her up."

Beatrice cast Essie a look crossed between supreme annoyance and incredulity. It wasn't that she minded being famous or anything—it was all she'd ever known—but she wanted to be famous for her mind rather than her looks. A few starring roles as a child and copious red carpets with her mother had certainly shot that horse in the face.

Essie felt the heat of Beatrice's stare and backtracked, sounding dejected. "Sorry I asked. . . ."

Harry looked at Beatrice as if to say, *What harm could it do?*

Beatrice sighed. "It's just that . . . I have nothing to sign at the moment," she amended. "Maybe when this business is all cleared up."

Essie lit up like a dozen New Year's fireworks exploding at once. "That'd be the cat's meow!"

Beatrice smiled, but it didn't touch her eyes. "Go on, then. Off to bed. Harry can escort you."

"No way. I'm not leavin' you on your own," he countered passionately.

"Don't be such a worrying Waldo," huffed Beatrice. "I'll be fine for five minutes, you boob."

"That's what we thought last time, and look how that turned out," he mused.

"And what about Miss Hartman?" Beatrice said. "What if something happens to *her* on her way back? I can look after myself."

For a moment, they shared a heated stare, Beatrice settling her hand defiantly on her hip. There was no matching her gaze or her stubbornness. In no time at all, Harry melted completely and bent down to scoop up the diminished candle from the floor.

"It's your funeral, sweetheart," he muttered, signaling for Essie to follow him.

Essie practically glued herself to Harry's side as he led her, lightless, back into the darkened corridors. Beatrice felt the sudden absence of their presence profoundly. The storm seemed louder and more menacing when she was on her own, and every nerve in her body became hyperaware as if the shadows would jump her at any moment. She allowed a few seconds to tick by, testing this theory. Nothing happened.

Satisfied that she was quite alone aside from a cadaver, Beatrice turned her attention to the murder scene. The use of a blade suggested intimacy. This was a different killer altogether than the first. M had done this themself, and it was far from a crime of passion. It was premeditated, deliberate. The angle of the cut suggested that she was attacked from behind, and by the direction of the laceration, Beatrice deduced that the killer was right-handed. Had he crept up behind Mrs. Vickeridge and taken her by surprise? Beatrice shook her head at that conjecture. The angle of the armchair made it impossible to enter the room without being seen. M could have been waiting in the shadows, she thought next. The library did have curtains. Following this line of inquiry, she moved to the window to examine the hangings. One tug of the fabric nixed that idea. They were faux curtains, barely large enough to hide a small child. How, then, had M managed to successfully off Mrs. Vickeridge? There were no signs of a struggle. Mrs. Vickeridge looked like she'd been caught unaware. *Perhaps*, Beatrice thought on, *perhaps she knew the killer.*

If Mrs. Vickeridge knew M's identity, she would think nothing of his waltzing into the library while she waited for Essie Hartman. They could have been talking, Mrs. Vickeridge sitting and the killer pacing. Beatrice returned to the body, leaned closer, and sniffed. The smell of alcohol lingered, unsurprisingly, accompanied by a strong scent of cigar ash. Of course, Mr. Vickeridge smoked cigars, so Beatrice was hardly surprised at the smell. This remembrance sent another chill down Beatrice's spine. Mr. Vickeridge, formerly Mr. Martin. M?

Mrs. Vickeridge would have recognized her husband if he'd entered the library. She wouldn't have felt endangered by his presence. They could, logically, have rowed, leading Dennis to kill her. Perhaps their fortune was ill gotten, and with Mrs. Vickeridge out of the way, Mr. Vickeridge would have it all.

Thunder rolled, drawing Beatrice back to the present. She shook her head to clear it. It was a good story, but so far, it was all speculation. She needed more proof.

Resolved, she shined her light on the floor around Mrs. Vickeridge's chair in search of more clues. The bulb began to flicker.

"Oh, fiddlesticks," Beatrice grumbled. She tapped the metal cylinder in her hand a few times, and the light came back on. Beatrice cursed herself for not packing a spare battery, but then she supposed she hadn't expected to get caught in a powerless hotel all night with two killers. *Always expect the unexpected,* she chastised herself.

Beatrice searched the library further, combing the floor, the shelves, and the desk for anything that might identify M before they struck again. Her efforts were fruitless. Not one thing seemed out of place. Nothing but the note still crumpled up in her fist. She sat with a sigh across from Mrs. Vickeridge as if the latter were simply taking a nap. Though her heart was torn at the death of the poor woman, the husk left behind didn't frighten her. It was up to Beatrice now to be the dead woman's voice, to bring her justice.

"Why were you really killed?" she whispered to the corpse. "What did you know? Why was M so afraid of you?"

Tommy had been knocked out and stuffed in a closet when he'd gone to tell Beatrice something of importance, so why had Mrs. Vickeridge been so unlucky? Had she been about to tell Beatrice something too?

If killer number one was indeed a bellhop, it made sense for him to knock Tommy out. They were likely friends. The killer only had to make it to morning or the end of the storm at the very least. He hadn't imagined Beatrice and Harry would find Tommy and let him out. Mrs. Vickeridge, on the other hand, was killed by a far more calculated and well-practiced killer. Tiffany's murder had been sloppy. This one was well executed and clearly positioned to send Beatrice a message. Even so, she didn't think sending a message was M's original intention. It didn't fit with the original pattern. When Mr. Morrow had gotten too close, M paid him off. When Tiffany Blake figured things out, M didn't off her either. No, something must have changed to make him kill Mrs. Vickeridge. Studying the body now, Beatrice believed with absolute certainty that Mrs. Vickeridge had known her killer. Perhaps that made all the difference in staying dead or alive. Tiffany had presumably known M's identity too. If only Beatrice could find that little black book, or at the very least, the missing ledgers.

On and on, Beatrice puzzled in silence, sitting still as her mind whirled. She could feel the helpful effects of coffee beginning to wane. Solving a murder over the span of a week was cake. Solving a murder in one night was a feat Beatrice had never tackled before, and she was starting to wonder if she could actually do it. Had she been too presumptuous in declaring her plans to a room full of suspects? Would it have made a difference if she'd kept things quiet for longer? Beatrice knew the answer was no. It would have been impossible to get interviews if everyone hadn't been told of the situation. She only wished she could have prevented a second murder. No matter how anyone consoled her, Beatrice would always feel this was somehow her fault.

Harry returned to the library then, pausing in the doorway. Beatrice sat so still she looked as much a corpse as Mrs. Vickeridge in the dark.

"Not you too," he breathed, rushing forward.

Beatrice turned toward him, and Harry nearly jumped out of his skin.

"'Not me too,' what?" she asked.

Harry placed a hand over his heart as if it would slow his ticker down. "Nothin'," he muttered. He took a breath and loosened his tie.

It only took Beatrice half a second to understand, and a smile crossed her cherry lips. "Harry Riley, you were worried about me," she teased.

A breathy laugh escaped him. "All these cadavers can make a fella nervous."

"You're a doctor."

"No kidding. My job is to keep people from ending up like this."

Beatrice's smile widened. Harry was a rare breed, always looking out for others at a detriment to himself. The shiner forming on his eye said as much. Her beau, Patrick, was more likely to tell her "*I told you so*" if she were ever to get hurt.

"So," he continued, shoving his hands in his trouser pockets, "you gonna fill me in, or do I have to guess?"

The lighter atmosphere diminished instantly, and Beatrice's countenance shifted to a somber expression. She held the note from M, still crumpled in her hand, out to Harry. He took it from her and tilted it toward her flashlight to read it. His face, too, grew somber.

"You don't *really* think that's why he killed her, do you?" Harry asked.

Beatrice stared at Mrs. Vickeridge, again feeling a sense of guilt. "No, I don't. I think her corpse just happened to be convenient. He killed her for some other reason. I just don't know what."

Harry handed the note back, and Beatrice tucked it into her handbag, which was now brimming with items. She'd run out of room soon if she wasn't careful.

"What should we do about her?" Harry asked.

"Leave her," sighed Beatrice. "As much as I hate to, this is a crime scene."

Besides that, there was a lot of blood, and while Beatrice wasn't particularly squeamish, the thought of getting blood all over the place wasn't particularly appealing. It was best to leave Mrs. Vickeridge for a coroner.

The appearance of another body had placed a far greater worry on Beatrice's mind: Eleanore. It had been nearly two hours since they'd left her alone in Harry's room, and while Beatrice knew the door was locked, she suddenly had a bad feeling that wouldn't be enough. When she expressed her concerns to Harry, he readily agreed it was time to go back, and they returned to the hall, walking with renewed determination. Beatrice's flashlight faded with every step, the beam hardly bright enough to light their path. Neither of them said a word the whole way. When they finally reached the door to Harry's room, it was wide open. Beatrice's heart plummeted. They rushed inside. The candles still burned where Eleanore had placed them, but their igniter was nowhere to be seen. Beatrice searched the room diligently, combing the bathrooms and closets, looking frantically for any trace of Eleanore and trying not to panic. There were no signs of a struggle. No telltale markings or overturned furniture. Beatrice approached the desk, spotting the papers spread over it.

"She was looking over the case notes," she commented as she perused them with a curious eye. Beatrice could see where her cousin had added things in, and from the looks of it, Eleanore had been on the verge of making a connection when her pen strokes suddenly jerked and spattered. Beatrice took the notes in her hand and brought them closer to her face to observe the marks.

"Oh, Ellie," she murmured. It was exactly the sort of thing she'd been looking for—evidence that her cousin had been abducted.

"Beatrice," Harry said near the door.

She didn't care for his tone, turning tentatively toward him. When she followed his gaze, she spied another note on the back of the door, held in place with a letter opener. It read:

I have your cousin. Leave well enough alone, and I'll return her at dawn.

—M

It was as if the sharp point of the letter opener had pierced Beatrice's heart rather than the door. All the air left the room, and Beatrice collapsed in the desk chair, clutching her heart as emotions spilled over the walls of her carefully constructed boxes. Tears welled in her eyes. Angry, worried, and exhausted tears. Harry was at her side in an instant, kneeling in front of her.

"Hey . . . it's gonna be jake," he encouraged her. "Just take a deep breath."

"I can't do this," she uttered. "I can't do this."

"Yes, you can," Harry said sharply. "You're just over exhausted."

"Is that all I am?" she demanded. "Or am I just a sap? Thinking I could go around playing detective and save the day? Now Mrs. Vickeridge is dead, and M has Ellie. . . ."

Harry took her hand in his. "Breathe," he reminded her.

Beatrice could feel the heat of his hand through her glove. It distracted her enough for her panic to melt away, and the kindness in his eyes did the rest.

"I'll never forgive myself if anything happens to her," Beatrice whispered.

"I know. And it won't. In the few short hours I've known you, I've yet to see you give up. Don't start now."

Beatrice took a long, deep breath. Harry was right. She couldn't fall apart now, not when the stakes were so high. And they had certainly never been this high before. A little voice in the back of her mind kept telling her she wasn't good enough, that this would be Mickey Ryan all over again, only it'd be Eleanore she lost.

Harry seemed to guess at her most likely train of thought, saying,

"Hey . . . kidnapped isn't dead. M can't take her far."

Beatrice's countenance shifted. "That's true," she murmured thoughtfully. An even louder, more determined voice screamed in her head. She'd more than proved herself capable. Eleanore needed her, and M had crossed a line. M underestimated her. M thought she'd behave like a good little girl if he took what she loved. *Well*, Beatrice thought, *M is about to be disappointed.*

Beatrice's frustration bubbled into new determination within her, and she was suddenly more resolved than ever to solve the case. All she needed was an edge of her own. Anonymity was M's strength, as were the shadows the power outage had caused. Both M and Tiffany's killer were using the dark to create fear. If Beatrice took that away, she might be able to regain the high ground.

"We need to even the playing field," she said.

"I take it you've got something in mind," mused Harry.

"I do," Beatrice replied, her ruby smile returning. "And it comes with revenge for that forming shiner of yours."

She hopped up with gusto and tucked Eleanore's case notes into her handbag. When she turned back, she nearly ran straight into Harry, who'd stood in the meantime.

"Easy, tiger," he teased. "I'm on your side."

Her smile widened. "You really are, aren't you?" she uttered sincerely, searching his eyes.

"I am," he murmured. "God help me . . . It's those damn blue eyes. I can't say no to them."

Beatrice felt her cheeks color, and not for the first time that evening, she thought he might kiss her. The realization that she might let him filled her with guilt, and she took a step back to remove the temptation.

"Thank you," she said, suddenly finding the floor more interesting than his deep hazel eyes. "For not letting me panic, I mean. You're absolutely right. Over exhausted."

Harry smiled. "Even Sherlock Holmes had a doctor around to make sure he didn't work himself to death."

Beatrice nearly laughed. "You would compare yourself to Dr. Watson."

Her flashlight flickered and died, drawing a sigh from her lips. "Well . . . that's that, I suppose. Grab a candle, would you? And a spare sheet from the closet?"

Harry did as she asked, and Beatrice led the way back into the hall, feeling like a complete nincompoop for nearly letting her exhaustion get the best of her. Beatrice had been in dangerous spots before, and she'd certainly gotten Eleanore into trouble, but until now, Beatrice had never put Eleanore in real danger. She could already hear her Uncle Theo's lecture if Eleanore got hurt . . . or worse.

Don't think about that, Bea, she chastised herself.

Solving things was a particular skill of hers. She'd figure this out. She always did. And if she was earnest with herself, Eleanore wasn't entirely helpless. In all their reckless adventures as children, Beatrice had taught her cousin a few things, and like Beatrice, Eleanore was highly intelligent, simply in a different fashion. Beatrice hoped—she had to hope—that her cousin would know what to do. The howling storm outside seemed to jeer at Beatrice, trying with all its might to discourage her, but Harry's encouragement had done its job. There was only one way M would leave that hotel—in handcuffs.

CHAPTER ELEVEN

The Return of a Soldier

Detective Joe Mason was a middle-aged man with a boxer's build and salt and pepper hair. He'd been fitter in his prime, but copious night shifts with little action and eating to pass the time had added a pot belly to his already-large frame. He'd taken a bullet during the war, but thanks to a skilled medic, Mason had not only survived the ordeal, but he'd also been able to keep his leg; he now walked with a limp. The injury flared up every time it rained in Winslow, putting Mason in a sour mood. Presently, he sat at his desk at the police station rubbing his knee in annoyance as he perused the day's newspaper, which laid flat on his desk. It was full of more depressing news. Unemployment still skyrocketed, and wages were cut. The paper criticized Hoover's inability to fix the problem, to which Detective Mason merely grunted. He didn't see how the president *could* fix such a problem, even if it was in his power.

Just as he was turning the page, the telephone at the front desk rang. He paused and glanced toward the front of the station, fully expecting a prank or another drunken brawl. Collins, the officer on duty, answered the phone. Mason watched curiously as Collins reached anxiously for a pen and began jotting down information.

"O-Okay. Slow down, miss," Collins said. "Uh-huh. Yep. And where are you now? Are you safe? Good. Stay there. I'll send a detective straight away."

Detective Mason raised an eyebrow at this. Though he was usually on call during night shifts, he rarely saw any action. The younger officer hung up the receiver and turned excitedly for Mason's desk. "You better get out there, Mason. There's been a murder."

He handed the slip of paper with his notes over to the detective, who took it with a mildly amused grunt.

"Murder, my ass," he said. "It's probably another prank by those damn kids across the tracks."

"I dunno, Mack," replied Collins. "She sounded pretty upset. Said she's at the diner on 2nd Street."

Detective Mason held up the slip of paper. "I see that." With another rub of his sore leg and a sigh, he said, "I'll get on it, Collins. You can go back to your crossword."

Collins nodded, seeming to take no offense to Mason's jab. Everyone knew Mason could be a grump, especially with the weather like this.

After a brief moment to collect himself and switch gears, Detective Mason reached into his desk drawer and extracted his gun and badge. He slid the gun into his shoulder holster, then pulled his suit jacket from the back of his chair, slipped it on, and tucked his badge into the interior pocket. Lastly, he plucked his fedora from the top of his rolltop desk and placed it on his head. Any other night, he'd be glad of the call just to get him out of the station, but tonight it wasn't ideal. If it was those pesky kids again, Mason wasn't going to go easy on them this time.

He walked with a slight limp for the coat stand near the door and pulled his trench coat on over the rest of his ensemble, Collins watching with interest. Mason turned toward him and grumbled, "Keys."

Collins reached for the keys to the squad car, which were stowed behind the desk, and tossed them to Mason, who caught them with ease. With one final pause to look out the glass door in distaste at the rain, he turned up the collar of his trench coat and headed out into the unforgiving storm. The walk from the station door to the police department's beaten-up Model A drenched Mason from top to bottom, which didn't leave him in good spirits. Worse still, the rain made driving difficult. It was thirty minutes before he pulled up to the diner the woman had mentioned on the phone, which was coincidentally a favorite haunt of Mason's.

Mason exited the car, once more ensnared in the rain's icy clutches, and made his way to the door. The diner bell rang when he entered, and the cool air immediately disagreed with his wet clothes. He caught sight of the cook behind the counter, who jabbed a thumb toward the girl sitting alone in the corner booth nursing a cup of coffee.

Whatever Detective Mason had been expecting, it hadn't been the blonde bombshell seated there. Even with her makeup running down her face and her blonde curls deflated, she was the epitome of glamour and beauty. Not for the first time that year, he suddenly wished he had his youth back.

Mason hung his trench coat and fedora on the stand by the door and made his way toward Eleanore's shivering form. All his predisposed anger melted away in the presence of this delicate angel, and sympathy took its place.

"Hey, kid," the cop said gently as he neared her booth. "I'm Detective Mason. You the one that called?"

Her brilliant eyes traveled up to his face, seemingly frightened at first by the sheer size of him, but she shortly registered who and what he was. She nodded feebly, every line of her posture indicating the strains of exhaustion.

Mason sat across from Eleanore and pulled a pen and a notebook from the inside of his suit jacket. "You wanna tell me what happened?" he asked.

She shifted her coffee mug closer to disguise a shiver. From the lack of steam that usually issued from a hot cup of coffee, Mason wagered the coffee inside had long since grown cold. He glanced the cook's way and signaled for two new coffees, his grumpy mood dissipating with each passing second. A moment later, the cook appeared at their table with two new mugs and poured fresh coffee into each.

CHAPTER ELEVEN

"Thanks, Earl," said Mason, taking a much-needed sip of the miracle brew.

"Sure thing, Joe," Earl replied.

The graveyard shift had brought Mason through the diner many times over the years, and if he hadn't presently been there for a case, Earl, knowing Mason's usual order by heart, would have whipped up a double cheeseburger, hold the onions, the moment Mason walked through the door. Tonight, however, the young woman across from Mason changed the routine.

He watched her for a moment, cupping the warmer cup of coffee the same as she had the other, not daring to take a sip. Again, she shivered, and Mason felt a twinge of fatherly instinct despite never having been one himself. He stood, slipped off his suit jacket, and draped it around her shoulders, exposing his suspenders and the holstered gun he wore.

"Thank you," she said.

She sounded frail. Tired. Mason knew at once this was no prank. He would never forget the first time he'd seen a dead body taken from this world by the cruel hands of another human being. One minute, the guy had been standing next to Mason on the front lines, and the next, a flurry of bullets had dropped him. Nineteen-year-old Mason had never been the same. He saw that look now in her eyes.

"What's your name, sweetheart?" he asked gently, sitting across from her once more.

"Eleanore Hughes," she answered.

Mason wrote it down in his notebook. "Address?"

She spouted off her Pasadena address almost mechanically.

As Mason wrote this down, he was glad to see her attempt a sip of coffee. He imagined her adrenaline had waned in the half hour it'd taken him to get there. "You told Collins there's been a murder," he pried carefully.

She nodded.

"Who?"

"I left the case notes . . . back in the room," she uttered. "Wrote it all down. One of the Harvey Girls up at the La Posada."

Mason paused. Case notes? A Harvey Girl? Who'd bump off one of them? The Fred Harvey Company had been well respected for almost fifty-five years. They only hired the most clean-cut, educated women they could find. Mason couldn't imagine a Harvey Girl being murdered, and yet he couldn't deny the look in Eleanore's eyes.

"You remember her name?" he asked.

"Holly Albright," Eleanore replied, steadily regaining herself.

Mason jotted that down. "And how did you find her?"

"She fell out of our hotel room closet. My cousin said she'd been strangled."

"Your cousin?" He said, writing in illegible scrawl.

"Mm," Eleanore hummed. "She's a private detective."

Mason's pen stilled, and he met her gaze unsure if he'd heard her correctly. "*She's* a PI?"

His disbelief seemed to have sparked some of Eleanore's waning adrenaline. "That's what I just said," she fired back.

Detective Mason had a hard time believing a dame could be a detective, especially if she were in the same looks category as the bombshell sitting across from him, but he wrote it down nonetheless. "What's her name?"

"Beatrice Adams," Eleanore said proudly.

The name struck a chord. "The actress?"

"Honestly," Eleanore huffed. "A girl does a few pictures, and everyone thinks she's capable of nothing else."

Mason didn't comment further. He wrote Beatrice's name down and took a sip of java. "So, the body fell out of your closet, and you came here . . . why?"

"The telephone lines are down at the hotel," Eleanore supplied. "The power too. The murderer cut them."

Mason briefly wondered if he'd fallen asleep reading a dime novel at his desk, but he decided to keep his doubts to himself. "Did that happen before or after you found the body?"

"After. Bea was sure the killer was still about, and we couldn't call the police, so she started investigating."

Now that he had her talking, Eleanore seemed to be more vibrant and less shell-shocked. Mason readjusted himself and poised his pen over the notebook. "What time was this?"

"Gee, I don't know," Eleanore admitted sheepishly. "Maybe around nine? We popped into the dining room before we went upstairs."

Mason wrote the time in his notebook with a question mark beside it, deliberately taking his time so he could form his next inquiry. He had a feeling the answer would be just as flabbergasting to him as the others. "When you say investigating . . ."

"I mean just that," replied Eleanore. She took a sip of coffee, suddenly more animated now that they were in the flow of conversation. "Bea called a conference downstairs in the lobby. You could cut the tension in that room with a knife, and how!"

"Lemme get this straight," said Detective Mason. "You find a dead body in the closet, you're trapped in a hotel by a storm, the power goes out, and your cousin announces to the murderer that she's looking into it?"

"Well . . . yes," Eleanore answered tentatively. "But that's my cousin for you. She never thinks of the danger before she does things."

"She sounds like quite the live wire," Mason mused.

A tired laugh escaped Eleanore. "You have no idea."

Mason enjoyed the sound of her laughter, even if it was strained by fatigue. He couldn't remember the last time he'd really heard anyone laugh. It reminded him of his late wife. He quickly shoved the thought to the rear of his mind, wondering why it'd surfaced.

"You said you kept case notes?" he asked.

"Oh, yes," Eleanore replied enthusiastically. "That's my job, see. Bea is a terrible typist, and her handwriting is atrocious. I do a lot of work for my father at his law firm, so organizing case notes is nothing new to me. This is the first case I've really helped her on. I usually stay out of it all . . . until she drags me into it."

"She's been at this for a while, then?"

"Mm-hmm," Eleanore confirmed. "But this is really only her second case as a proper detective . . . and I'm not even sure you could call the first official. She helped the police on a murder investigation back home. Went undercover and everything. Of course, she's been getting into trouble and studying up on investigation since we were kids."

"I'm guessing she found a body," Mason mused. That was usually how these obsessions got started.

"Saw the murder," Eleanore corrected. "They never caught the guy."

Detective Mason couldn't believe what he was hearing. It was all too fantastic to be true, and yet, he knew it must be. Fabricated stories weren't usually so detailed, and there was always a thread that unraveled them. "Did she find anything in her investigation?"

"Oh, yes," Eleanore replied with a vigorous nod. "Oodles. You just wouldn't believe the scandal going on up there."

"Care to fill an old man in?"

"Oh, hush," she waved a hand. "You're not that old."

Mason smiled. It was impossible not to like Eleanore Hughes.

"And anyway," Eleanore continued. "I don't know much. I got kidnapped, see . . . not long after the guy tried to kill my cousin. It was horrible."

"Kidnapped?" Mason repeated incredulously. This case got better all the time.

"Uh-huh," Eleanore sang. "Tied to a chair and everything. But I got away when he left the room. Climbed down the drainpipe and ran for the nearest phone to get help."

"In this weather?" Mason said, impressed. "You're a brave young lady."

"Gosh, I don't know about that. I just don't want him to hurt anyone else."

"Did you see his face?"

Eleanore shook her head. "No. The ape knocked me out. I was blindfolded when I woke up."

Mason wrote furiously across his notepad, now on a second page just to fit everything in. Judging by what he had so far, he knew he'd have to throw procedure out the window. He had a gut feeling that not only was Eleanore telling the truth, but everyone inside that hotel was in danger. She was lucky not to get struck by lightning trying to find him. The hotel was a good distance away.

CHAPTER ELEVEN

Detective Mason tapped his pen against the notepad in thought. As far as the case went, he needed details from Beatrice Adams to fill in his report. He knew where the killer was, an unusual occurrence at the start of an investigation. It was numbers that were needed here, he decided. He needed to send in the troops.

"Finish your coffee," he instructed Eleanore as he slid out of the booth.

"Where are you going?" she wondered, obediently lifting her mug off the table.

"To call for backup."

Eleanore sipped her coffee as he lumbered toward the payphone and pulled a dime from his pocket. He called the station, gave his badge number, and shortly had Officer Collins on the phone.

"This is no prank," he informed. "Call everyone you can. I want every available squad car to meet me in the parking lot of the La Posada Hotel immediately."

"Sure thing," Collins replied through the speaker. "It might take a while, though. This storm is a rager."

"Trust me, I know," grumbled Mason. "Just do it."

"Yes, sir."

After hanging up, Detective Mason ambled back to the table, his leg protesting. "Come on, honey. No, you hang on to that," he said when she tried to hand him back his suit jacket. He tossed some cash on the table for the coffees and a tip. Times were too hard not to.

Eleanore slid gracefully out of the booth and slipped her arms through the sleeves of his jacket, which nearly swallowed her. Mason returned his sopping fedora to his head and pulled on his trench coat.

Earl paused in his task of wiping down the counter to say, "You be careful out there, Joe. This storm is a doozy."

"No kidding," Mason replied, tipping his hat to signal farewell.

He held the door open for Eleanore, and together they stepped into the rain, the La Posada their destination.

CHAPTER TWELVE

WHODUNIT

With Eleanore missing, another murder, and the threat of more bodies being dropped, Beatrice had to throw the old process of elimination out the window. If she had more time, she could easily chat with Tommy and get the dirt on the rest of the bell staff, then weed out the lies from the truth. Beatrice was particularly skilled at spotting a liar. Time, however, was not on her side, so Beatrice had to do something a little more drastic. After explaining her plan to Harry, he heartily objected, claiming it as foolhardy and unpredictable. There was too much room for error. Even so, he had been unable to suggest a better plan, and thus they found themselves once more in the lobby, this time taking extra care to check the shadows and corners for any onlookers. Beatrice couldn't afford to have either M or Tiffany's killer know what she was up to. When they were sure they were quite alone, Beatrice retrieved the fuses, which were mercifully untouched, from the lobby planter. The little glass bulbs glittered in the light from Harry's candle.

"It's amazing how so small a thing can have such an impact," whispered Beatrice.

Harry agreed, then said, "Let's not hang about. It feels like the walls have eyes."

Having no more room in her handbag after stuffing her dead flash-light inside it, Beatrice clutched the little glass bulbs to her chest to keep from dropping them and led the way back to the boiler room. *If only we could fix the phone lines*, she thought to herself. While Beatrice was quite capable of solving a mystery, there always came a time when she need-ed to involve the police. Even when they caught the killers, for Beatrice had every confidence that they would, an arrest still had to be made. That part of the job Beatrice had no authority in. She could only hope Harry's knot-tying skills were exemplary. Once they ripped up the sheet she'd asked Harry to grab, the strips could be used in lieu of ropes until the culprits could be delivered to the police. It was a good plan as long as nothing went wrong, and so much could go wrong.

When they reached the boiler room, Beatrice instructed Harry to start ripping up the sheet. He set the candle down and did so. Beatrice approached the toolbox she'd tripped over when the killer had been strangling her and rifled through it with her free hand until she found a large wrench. It was perfect for knocking someone over the head.

"Here," she said, passing it to Harry.

He paused in his ripping to take it from her. "Are you absolutely sure about this?" he whispered for the third time that evening.

"No," she replied, also for the third time. "But it's the only plan we have, and I'm not about to leave Eleanore in M's hands."

Harry nodded, and Beatrice hoped he understood. A half-baked plan was better than no plan at all.

Once Harry finished preparing the sheets, he took up the candle and approached the fuse box with Beatrice, holding the light up so she could see.

"Now remember, he can't see you," Beatrice reminded Harry.

She examined the fuses in her hand and peered carefully at the empty spaces, trying to determine where each went.

"I know," Harry sighed. "Are your vacations always this exciting?"

Beatrice smirked. "Only when bodies find their way into my lug-gage," she teased.

She set to work replacing each fuse with care. They were like round jewels, each as easy to screw in as a lightbulb. All Beatrice had to do was ensure she didn't mix up the wattage. Owens had taught her well. One by one, the lights came back on throughout the hotel. Beatrice smiled as she twisted in the last one, illuminating the boiler room.

"Well . . . that should put a bee in his bonnet," she mused.

Harry deftly blew out the candle, and the pair of them took refuge behind one of the massive boilers, Harry keeping watch. Time slid by glacially, which was a detriment to Beatrice's adrenaline. She reminded herself to breathe, taking careful, measured breaths. Oxygen was her friend. It cleared her thoughts and slowed her heart, allowing her to keep her wits about her despite how much she wished she could sleep. When all this was over, she promised herself a lie-in.

The heat from the boilers offered another problem. It wasn't until they remained still in such close quarters that Beatrice realized how hot it was in that room. She could feel sweat starting to bead on her forehead and her chest, forcing her to fan herself. Other than loosening his tie, Harry seemed not to notice. His eyes were fixed on the fuse box as if nothing else mattered. A good five minutes passed, though it felt a great deal longer. Beatrice was beginning to wonder if her plan was a bust when, suddenly, Harry tensed. Someone was coming. Footsteps hurried across the long room, accompanied by panicked muttering.

"No, no, no," it stammered.

Once the figure had ripped open the fuse box, Harry skulked forward and bashed it over the head with the wrench. The figure crumpled in a heap on the floor. Beatrice left her hiding place, finally laying eyes on the man who'd ended Tiffany Blake's life. Her heart clenched. He wasn't a man at all. He was only a boy, no more than nineteen if Beatrice had to guess. He was six feet tall with broad shoulders and hands that had clearly seen their fair share of work. Dark wavy hair covered his forehead. There was a cut on his hand that looked to be caused by clawing fingernails. Beatrice checked his coat. It was missing a button.

"This . . . can't be right," she murmured.

And yet, she knew the moment she saw him that he was the one. He perfectly fit the profile she'd constructed in her mind. The desperation and sloppiness of his work made sense. He'd probably never killed anyone before now. Something had made him panic. There was a deeper story here, and Beatrice intended to get to the bottom of it.

"Let's tie him up," said Harry, his conscience seemingly clear.

Together, Beatrice and Harry bound the bellhop in the strips of sheet, Harry ensuring the knots were good and tight before they both stood back to observe their prey. The boy didn't look at all like a cold-blooded killer when he was unconscious. M must have put him up to it, Beatrice reasoned, but she wouldn't know for sure until he awoke. His demeanor on being caught would tell her exactly what sort they were dealing with.

Beatrice stood with folded arms, staring at their captive as she tried to draw her own conclusions. *Why* had he done it? Was this still about the juice ring? Or was something bigger going on?

"He was sitting next to Tommy at tea," Beatrice thought aloud. "Must be how he knew Tommy was going to look for me."

Harry nodded, observing her with an analytical gaze. "What's wrong?"

"Nothing," Beatrice muttered, unfolding her arms with a heavy sigh. "I just thought he'd be . . . older."

"He's old enough to know right from wrong," noted Harry.

"Maybe."

Beatrice had fully expected to find James at the other end of Harry's wrench, and if she had, she wouldn't have felt a shred of sympathy for the figure crumpled up like a wounded spider on the boiler room floor. The young man before her, however, had the full force of her sympathy. It must have shown on her face because Harry felt the need to say, "He tried to kill you."

"I know," Beatrice replied, a hand subconsciously touching her neck where dark bruises had begun to form. She could still feel his hands around her neck, the heat of his body against her back, and the rising panic as her vision had begun to fade. Young and baby-faced or not, the boy at her feet was guilty of murder. She couldn't afford to forget that, but it didn't make her heart any lighter. More than anything, she wanted to know why he'd done it. Strangulation was no accident. He had deliberately intended to end Tiffany's life. Why? What made someone so young and full of possibility commit the worst crime known to man?

Soon, the boy began to stir, and Beatrice steeled herself for the conversation ahead. The path forward was entirely dependent on the boy's reaction to being caught. His eyes slipped open, and a groan issued from his lips. He moved as if to press a hand to his throbbing head, only to realize he couldn't. Panic ensued, and his eyes shot wide open. Beatrice stood over him, watching carefully as he took her in and then shifted his gaze to Harry. Everything Beatrice needed to know was etched right there on his face: panic, fear, and desperation. All at once, the boy began to cry. The jig was up, and he knew it. Having a clear idea of his personality, Beatrice knelt beside him as if they were equals, her sparkling eyes reflecting sympathy.

"What's your name?" she asked, her tone calm and kind despite what he'd done to her.

"Please . . . please don't kill me," begged the bellhop.

"I'm not going to kill you," Beatrice replied patiently. "I just want to know your name."

Confusion painted the boy's face, the emotion strong enough to quell his terrified tears.

"P-Phillips," he stuttered. "David Phillips."

"David," Beatrice repeated, taking the intimate approach. "That's a lovely name."

David merely stared at her. Harry stood just behind her, hands in his pockets and a look of stone on his face.

"Listen," Beatrice went on, folding her hands in her lap. "I know it was you who killed Holly. I know you were working with someone called M. What I want to know is why? What does a young man like you have to gain?"

David's incredulous expression grew. "Are you for real, lady?"

"She's for real," Harry answered, his tone a little harsher than Beatrice's. "Answer her question."

David shook his head. "I can't."

"How about I give you a matching shiner, huh?" threatened Harry.

Beatrice cast him a scathing look, and Harry backed off. She didn't need violence to get what she wanted. She simply needed to get David talking. She turned back to the bellhop.

"Did you know Holly was a reporter?"

"What? N-no," stumbled David. "No."

"Then why did you kill her, David? I want to understand."

Beatrice kept her blue eyes locked on David's gray until he had to avert his gaze to avoid the heat of them. She could see the answers she needed lurking just behind his irises, begging to be set free. He had a guilty conscience.

"I didn't . . . *want* to," he muttered. "I had no choice."

"There's always a choice," said Harry.

"What do you mean, no choice?" asked Beatrice. "What nixed your options?"

"M told me to," he replied in defeat. "And when M tells you to do somethin' . . . you do it. No questions asked."

"Why did he want you to bump her off?" wondered Beatrice. "What *happened*, David?"

"I went out for a smoke with the guys that day," he explained. "She came by and said she needed to talk. I thought maybe she was sweet on me or somethin', but when we got to the end of the station . . . she changed."

"Changed how?" asked Harry.

David's gaze shifted to the doctor as he continued. "She became more . . . bossy, I guess. In-charge like. That was when she laid it all out in front of me. The juice ring, the payments. She knew about all of it. She wanted to know who was running it, but I wouldn't tell her. I knew if I did, he'd kill me."

"M?" asked Beatrice.

David nodded. "She was insistent. Said she could help me. When I told M, he said to keep an eye on her . . . take care of it if she got too close. He said there was too much at stake."

"But she figured out who M was on her own, didn't she?" said Beatrice.

"Yeah," David uttered. "She confronted me about it . . . in the bell closet. I just wanted to get home. My ma . . . she's real sick. She doesn't like bein' home alone. And then Holly started going on about exposing the operation, but she needed my help. She needed proof. I . . . I couldn't let her do it. I was so . . . *angry*. She wouldn't shut up. She just wouldn't shut up."

"So you strangled her," Beatrice realized, "because you needed the money for your mother, and you couldn't let her mess that up."

David nodded shamefully.

The weight in Beatrice's heart grew heavier. She wondered if these circumstances would still have played out were they not in the middle of an economic crisis. Could David have supported his mother on his wages alone? Would juice rings still exist if prohibition hadn't provided a means to profit from them? Desperation has a way of turning the most innocent people into terrifying monsters.

"Your mother . . . how sick is she?" wondered Beatrice after a pause.

The subject was clearly a painful one, but David answered nonetheless. "She needs surgery," he answered quietly. "We didn't have the money."

"And when M came along, you thought your prayers had been answered."

He nodded.

"You know who M is . . . don't you?" said Beatrice, now treading as if tiptoeing on thin ice.

Terror colored David's face, but there was no denying the truth in his eyes.

"He took my cousin, David," Beatrice went on. "I just want to know if she's alive."

The bellhop visibly eased. "Yeah . . . yeah. She's alive. I think she got away. Dunno where. M was pretty bent about it. Broke a lamp."

It felt like some of the weight had been lifted from Beatrice's shoulders. If Eleanore was safe, M no longer had an ace up his sleeve. She could feel the tide turning in her favor.

"I need you to think, David," Beatrice spoke. "There was a little black book that Holly kept with her. It would have been in her pocket when you killed her. Did you take it?"

David nodded that he had.

"I need to find it. Do you know where it is?"

"I gave it to M," he muttered. "He said it was dangerous. She had all these facts and figures in it. All the specifics, even who he worked for. That broad was scary good."

"Who does M work for?" Harry interjected.

"I'm not sure. Honest," David replied. "But I'm pretty sure it's one of the mobs."

It was the puzzle piece Beatrice had been waiting for all night, the one that made all the other pieces clear. Bootlegging was common those days, and Beatrice could hardly walk out her front door without stumbling on some form of illegal hooch or another. But murder? Payoff? This was all part of a much bigger operation, one that had, no doubt, been going on for some time.

"I need to know who M is," Beatrice said.

David immediately clammed up, shaking his head fervently. "No way. I can't. I just can't."

"I know you're worried for your mother," Beatrice tried again. "I can't keep you out of prison for what you did, but I *can* help her. Tell me what I need to know, and I'll put up the money for her operation. How's that sound, hmm?"

Her words seemed to strike a distant chord. David's eyes watered. "You'd do that?"

Beatrice smiled. "I would."

And she meant it. As horrible as his actions had been, David's initial motivation had been a good one. There was no sense in letting a poor woman die over her son's bad decisions. Beatrice wouldn't have it.

David contemplated for a long while, and Beatrice watched his face hopefully, trying to keep her anticipation at bay. She was so close to solving the case. All she needed was M's identity and evidence against him to put the case to bed, and bed was exactly where Beatrice longed to be.

The decision came suddenly to David's eyes, and Beatrice held her breath. He opened his mouth to speak.

"M is M—"

BANG!

A shot rang out, and David slumped sideways, a gaping hole in his chest. Harry was immediately at the injured man's side, ripping off his own tie and using it to stem the bleeding. Another shot pinged off one of the boilers, narrowly missing Beatrice. She gasped and ducked for cover behind the nearest boiler, heart hammering as her gaze sought Harry. He was still out in the open, hands keeping pressure on a quivering David's wound. Instead of seeking cover, he'd shielded the bleeding bellhop with his own body, turning his eyes toward the door to spot the gunman.

"He's gone," he uttered after a tense moment of silence.

Beatrice peered around the edge of the boiler, adrenaline fueling every cell in her body. M had been there. M had tried to kill her. And now M was getting away.

Beatrice's adrenaline turned to anger, which morphed into determination. "Can you save him?" she asked Harry.

Harry looked the sputtering David over, still keeping pressure on the wound. "Maybe . . . but I'll need my medical bag, and M is out there with a gun. He could be waiting for you."

Beatrice scooped up the wrench Harry had used to clock David. "To *hell* with M," she spat. "I'm getting the bag! Keep him alive, Harry."

Before Harry could protest, Beatrice took off toward the staircase and raced down the hall toward his room. There was no sign of M as she went. The coward was likely hiding. But who was it? Who of her suspects would carry a gun? Who would know how to use it? Beatrice shoved the inquiries from her mind, willing her legs to go faster. Saving David was all that mattered. His testimony could close the whole case. She needed him alive.

Harry's room was, mercifully, still unlocked from the last time they'd dashed out. Beatrice skidded inside, took up Harry's bag, and raced back down the hallway. The corridor seemed to stretch the faster Beatrice ran. Finally, she turned down the narrow hall that led to the boiler room and practically fell down the steps in her haste. She didn't stop until she reached Harry. Huffing and puffing, she held out his medical bag. It was only then that she noticed the grave look on Harry's face. Her heart sank, eyes traveling to David's limp form. His eyes were glassy, his chest still. Beatrice dropped the medical bag with a noise of extreme aggravation and threw the wrench violently at the wall, eyes stinging with livid tears.

Harry jumped, but he didn't reprimand her. He simply reached into his medical bag with a somber expression and pulled out a cloth to wipe the blood from his hands. Once through, he respectfully closed David's staring eyes.

Beatrice couldn't remember the last time she'd been so angry. For every step she took forward, M seemed to shove her two steps back. There were now three bodies lying in various places around the hotel, and even though David was responsible for dropping one of them, Beatrice could entirely trace the blame for all three murders back to M. She paced angrily back and forth, racking her brain, trying to sort the facts. Could it have been Mr. Vickeridge who had every reason to want his wife gone? Or could it be Mary, whom Beatrice had written off as incapable of committing the crime so early in the investigation? Perhaps it was Mr. Morrow, who was so meticulous at planning? Was he intelligent enough to fake the letters? Beatrice needed evidence. She needed data. She paused in her pacing and turned her gaze to Harry.

"Did he say . . . anything?" she asked desperately.

Harry looked up at her gravely. "Not much," he uttered. "There was a lot of fluid in his lungs. He said something about a bottle and the word 'Follett.' Mean anything to you?"

Beatrice's face twisted in concentration. "Follett?" she repeated. "Are you sure?"

Harry nodded. "That's what he said."

Beatrice let this information roll around in her head a little longer, then put a pin in it, eyes returning from their glazed state to meet Harry's. "Are you all right?"

"Me?" he replied, surprised. "Sure. I'm dandy."

"I mean, really," Beatrice pried. He was a doctor who'd had a chance to save the third victim. Even if David was guilty of murder, Beatrice didn't imagine it was easy to have a patient die on his watch, no less beneath his very hands.

Harry's shoulders slumped, and he let out a measured sigh. "Disappointed . . . but I'll live. I'm more worried about that jack-o'-lantern hurting someone else."

Beatrice nodded in understanding. That was also on her list of concerns. Gratefully, Eleanore was out of the line of fire for the moment, at least, if David's words could be trusted. The same couldn't be said for the rest of the hotel guests, whom Beatrice could hear talking out in the hall. The gunshot must have woken some of them. An idea suddenly occurred to Beatrice, and she pulled the page she'd ripped from the ledger out of her handbag, careful not to spill anything else from her bag on the floor.

"Do you think you can get everyone back in the lobby and keep them distracted for half an hour?" she wondered.

Harry thought on it. "I'm sure I can come up with something," he reasoned.

"Swell," said Beatrice, a smile curling on her red lips. "You work on that. I'll need a full half hour."

"What are you going to do?" he asked.

Beatrice extracted Tommy's keys from her handbag as well. "A bit of old-fashioned snooping."

Eleanore had never ridden in a squad car before, but as she sat in the front seat with Detective Mason at the wheel, she decided it was an experience best had once. Rain collided with the windshield as if it were trying to break the glass, the sound so loud, it nearly drowned out Eleanore's thoughts. Flashes of lightning blinded them at odd intervals, and the resounding thunder shook the car. Mason let up on the gas each time, further slowing their progress toward the La Posada Hotel. Still drowning in Mason's large suit coat, Eleanore hugged her arms around herself for warmth and protection. Though the fabric would do little to stop a speeding bullet, it felt to her as if it kept the night's darkest horrors at bay. She couldn't seem to get the resounding *click* of her kidnapper's gun from her mind or the idea that if he found Beatrice, her cousin was armed with nothing but a flashlight and a little moxie. She remembered the younger voice at the door saying he'd locked *her* in a bell closet. Beatrice was the only "her" Eleanore could think he'd meant, and if her captor had gone to take care of it himself, Eleanore imagined he'd taken the gun too. What if Beatrice was still trapped in the closet? What if Eleanore was too late and her cousin was already dead on the closet floor?

Detective Mason must have sensed her distress. "You did the right thing," he assured her. "We'll take care of the rest. Nothing will happen to your cousin. I promise."

Eleanore nearly laughed. "You don't know my cousin, Mr. Mason. If something *can* happen to her, it usually does."

The weather had them driving more slowly than even a snail dared go, and Eleanore was starting to doubt her plan. Perhaps she should have focused more on figuring out who her captor was. She should have followed him out the door and crept through the shadows. That's what Beatrice would have done. Eleanore's daring escape was suddenly starting to seem like the coward's way out.

"Your cousin sounds like quite the character," mused Detective Mason conversationally.

Eleanore knew he was trying to keep her talking to distract her—she'd spent enough time around lawyers and the like—but she found she didn't mind. Talking kept her from envisioning Beatrice's corpse mangled in a million different ways.

"Oh, she's a hoot, all right," Eleanore assured him. "She got kidnapped for ransom when we were teenagers, and would you believe she jabbered the goons into turning themselves in?"

"You're pulling my leg," he replied.

"Not even a little!" Eleanore enthused. "It was the soberest I've ever seen Aunt Ginny."

"Rummy?" asked Mason.

"Mm," confirmed Eleanore. "I wish it weren't so, but she's all washed up now that talkies are all the rage."

"Why would that make a difference?" wondered Mason.

Eleanore realized she was gossiping again, and a small voice in the back of her head told her to stop being such a chatty Cathy about business that wasn't really hers, but she knew the moment she stopped talking, the worry and anxiety would return to replace the high of a good tale. "Well," she explained, "before sound, all you really had to be was good-looking. As much as I love Aunt Ginny, she has a terrible voice for cinema. Too many cigarettes, I think."

"Huh," Mason grunted as the information sank in. "Well, if that don't beat all."

"Maybe there will be a part for her one day," Eleanore said hopefully. "I mean, she's only in her forties."

Though Eleanore had to admit forty seemed a long way off to her at merely twenty-three, it wasn't as if Virginia Adams were hideous. She still had her good looks plus a few laugh lines. Eleanore thought it was silly that a little thing like one's voice could keep them out of work, but that was the world they now lived in. No one wanted to hire her aunt, and everyone wished Beatrice would take a crack at it.

Silence fell, and the rain once again took center stage. Eleanore wished they could go faster. She would never forgive herself if anything happened to Beatrice. She stuck her thumbnail in her teeth and chewed anxiously, a nervous habit she'd had since she was a child. Somewhere in all this mess she'd completely lost her gloves, and, surprisingly, Eleanore didn't care. All her thoughts were wrapped up in the dark corridors of the hotel and the monster now stalking them in search of her cousin.

CHAPTER THIRTEEN

THE LAST PUZZLE

When Beatrice had first asked Harry to distract everyone for a half hour, he'd readily agreed. Now, standing at the end of the boiler room hall, he was beginning to second-guess himself. He wasn't an actor or a detective, merely a doctor. What could he possibly do to distract so many people? The idea came at once, and Harry dashed into the hall, running up and down it, screaming at the top of his lungs.

"MURDER!" he shouted. "THERE'S BEEN ANOTHER MURDER!"

The few people already mingling in the hall turned his way with shocked gasps and murmurs. Those who hadn't yet ventured into the corridor poked their heads out of their doors as he ran down the hall screaming about murder. It did the trick, probably aided by the bit of blood on his shirt and suit coat that had spattered when David had been shot. Within minutes, people were milling down the hallway, hugging robes around themselves and clearly trying not to panic. Harry trailed along behind them, pleased with his progress. Maybe he wasn't so bad at this detective thing.

Once everyone was gathered in the lobby, Harry took center stage, and all eyes turned expectantly on him. Stage fright threatened to overtake him, but it shortly dawned on him that this wasn't unlike talking to a waiting room full of people. The thought gave him courage, and he stood a little taller, prepared for the barrage of questions he knew were coming.

"Well? Who was it? Who's died now?" demanded Mr. Morrow before Harry could open his mouth.

The room was silent other than the rain, which was now pattering against the window rather than pelting. Everyone seemed to be holding their breath. Harry knew if he mentioned two more murders had happened, there would be a panic. Moreover, there were certain details of the case he wasn't sure Beatrice wanted known yet. This was about catching M, after all, and Harry had a feeling M was standing in that room watching him curiously. He decided to go with the murder that would cause the most shock.

"I'm sorry," he murmured, looking at Mr. Vickeridge. "It was your wife. There was nothing I could do."

The effect was immediate. Gasps and whispers abounded, some sorry, others sounding unsurprised. Mr. Vickeridge turned a sickly shade of white and swayed on the spot.

"Oh, someone help him!" Miss Bishop cried.

James and Tommy, who were nearest, caught Mr. Vickeridge as he swooned, and they helped him into a nearby chair that Sarah Acre had fleetly vacated.

"Fetch him some water, Sarah dear," Miss Bishop instructed.

Sarah nodded and set off to do so, hugging her night-robe around her small frame.

It took Mr. Vickeridge a few minutes to regain himself, stuttering when he did, "W-who? How?"

Harry knew it went against his Hippocratic oath to lie to a patient or the family of one, but this was a murder investigation, not a hospital, and everyone present had heard the gunshot. He consoled himself that Mrs. Vickeridge hadn't been his patient, which made his following fib easier. "She was shot . . . point blank. There was nothing I could do. I'm sorry."

Mr. Vickeridge immediately broke into sobs and buried his face in his hands, his entire body heaving. Sarah returned and held out the glass of water to him, but he was too lost in grief to notice, so she set it on the end table beside him. Essie Hartman, who had witnessed Mrs. Vickeridge's body earlier in the evening, locked eyes with Harry from across the room, her gaze questioning him. He gave an infinitesimal shake of his head, a warning to say nothing. She gave an equally small nod accompanied by a look that said she'd do anything he asked. Harry couldn't tear his eyes away fast enough.

"James was talking to her at dinner," the salesman pointed out.

James fired a glower in the man's direction. "You got some mouth, Flanagan," he spat.

Mr. Vickeridge recovered himself, Flanagan's words having sparked a thought. "Yes . . . you were making eyes at her earlier in the evening. I saw you!"

"That's a lie!" barked James.

"It is not!" chimed Tunie. "I saw her slip something in your pocket when Mr. Vickeridge was out for a smoke after dinner!"

Harry's eyebrows rose. Things had taken a much bigger turn than he'd anticipated. Once the ball was rolling, there didn't seem to be any stopping it. A raucous argument broke out. Everyone shouted across the room to each other as if the yelling would get their points across, and soon it was impossible to hear anything over the cannonade. Harry rubbed a hand over his face, debating if he should stop it. Beatrice wanted them distracted, after all, and they were certainly distracted.

Unfortunately, so was he.

Beatrice hid out in the boiler room while Harry gathered everyone in the lobby. The gunshot had drawn people into the hall already, and with a bit of exaggeration on Harry's part, it wasn't difficult to get the onlookers to comply. Beatrice beamed with pride and made a mental note of Harry's exceeding usefulness in dangerous situations. It took several minutes to herd everyone into one room, and Beatrice took that time to observe the logbook page in her hand. Rifling through every single room would be too time consuming, so she mentally highlighted the ones that would be of most use, deciding on the Vickeridges' first. Once sure there was nobody left in the hallways to see her, Beatrice tiptoed out of the boiler room and slipped swiftly down the hall in the direction of the guest rooms.

If Beatrice had been tired before, it was all but erased now. A fresh batch of adrenaline coupled with infuriation and the thrill of sneaking around recharged every sinew and synapse in the redhead's body. This wasn't just a case anymore; it was a hunt for the shadow that haunted those corridors, and she was determined to catch it this time. The Vickeridges' room was located on the first floor not far from Harry's room. *Close enough to nab Eleanore without being seen,* thought Beatrice.

She tried the handle on approach, unsurprised to find it locked. It always amused Beatrice how people thought a locked door was enough to keep their things safe. She rifled through Tommy's key ring until she found the appropriate skeleton key, then inserted it in the keyhole, smiling as it unlocked. Her heart pounded with excitement as she edged into the room and flipped on the lights. It was amazing how much difference a few volts of electricity could make.

The room was decent in size, with a king-size bed rather than the two-bed setup Beatrice and Eleanore had been assigned. At first glance, nothing seemed out of place other than the perfectly made bed. Beatrice already knew both Mr. and Mrs. Vickeridge had been wandering the halls, so she was hardly surprised it hadn't been slept in. It still raised a flag in her mind. Surely one of them had at least sat on the bed that night. Judging by the lack of creases, it seemed neither of them had done that either.

Beatrice edged around the bed toward the trunks set in the corner of the room. The more ornate of the two was clearly Mrs. Vickeridge's. Various scuffs and dents in the aged brown exterior told Beatrice of

Martha Vickeridge's frequent travels. Beatrice moved to open the trunk, but it was locked tight. Scowling, she set her things on the nearby desk. Searching for the trunk key would waste valuable time, and she doubted Harry could keep the others occupied for longer than the half hour she'd requested. The human attention span was only so long. So, Beatrice knelt beside the trunk and pulled two pins from her short, red bob. Her hair was deflating anyway, she told herself.

Teaching herself to pick locks and crack safes had all been fun and games to Beatrice when she was young. Harry Houdini had made it seem so easy, and after what she'd witnessed at age twelve followed by countless bouts of falling into trouble, Beatrice reasoned it would be good to always be prepared. Thankfully the locks on a steamer trunk were much simpler than those on a large door, and with the pins twisted just right, Beatrice shortly managed to open Mrs. Vickeridge's trunk. Contents spilled out at once, causing Beatrice to gasp as she tried fruitlessly to save them from gravity's clutches. They fell to the floor anyway, most of them silks and scarves to Beatrice's relief. She'd hate to break any of Mrs. Vickeridge's things, even if the woman would never use them again.

A quick rifling through the drawers and hangers inside the steamer trunk turned up very little other than a curiosity. Why had the trunk been such a mess? It was almost as if something had been hidden carefully inside it and someone had rifled through it in a hurry and then locked it tight to hide their mess. But who had it been? Dennis or Martha Vickeridge?

Beatrice rolled this thought around in her mind as she searched the rest of the room. She turned up a case of Montecristo cigars in the side table along with an engraved gold lighter. An empty glass sat on the other nightstand. Beatrice approached and held it under her nose. There was a faint smell of whiskey, and the bottom of the glass had trace amounts of the liquor still trapped in its hexagonal edges—no doubt the night cap Mrs. Vickeridge had before she'd gone to meet Essie, rescuing Harry and Beatrice along the way.

Beatrice returned the glass to its perch, thinking. Both of the Vickeridges claimed to have had an argument, but what had it been about? And who had won? A further search of the closet and bathroom turned up nothing of interest other than to tell Beatrice the argument had escalated in the bathroom. A perfume bottle was smashed on the floor, likely swatted out of Mrs. Vickeridge's hand, judging by the spread of the glass. No one had bothered to clean it up, which struck Beatrice as odd. Perhaps that was when they'd both parted ways.

Deciding that she'd found all she needed, Beatrice took up her things and returned to the brightly lit corridors, heading in the direction of Essie and Tunie Hartman's room on the second floor. The storm still swirled outside, but with the power back on, it seemed to have lost its chilling power. Up the curved steps and down a narrow hall, Beatrice walked with a spring in her step. She didn't bother trying the knob on the Hartmans' door when she reached it, opting instead to use Tommy's keys on the first go.

"Oh, my," Beatrice uttered when she entered the room.

The lights had been left on when the girls departed, and the mess inside the room was unbelievable. Clothes were strewn about, trunks had been left open, and the bathroom was a nightmare. If Beatrice didn't know any better, she might have thought someone had given the place a good toss. The mess, however, was clearly a deliberate disregard for decorum, and Beatrice was hardly surprised. The Hartmans clung to the free spirit of the Jazz Age with everything they had left in them as if throwing a fit that it'd ended before they could have their turn. Beatrice wagered this trip of theirs was a last hurrah before the money dried up and the penny-pinching began.

She ran her eyes over the mess, unsure where to begin. The storm flashed behind the drawn curtains, and Beatrice could almost feel her time running out. The other guests and staff might be patient, but M was not. If she took too long, M would know she was up to something. With a sigh, she started with the mess around the beds, turning up discarded girdles, stockings, and knickers. The dresser was much the same. Beatrice paused in the middle of the room to think. Her suspicions were solely with Essie Hartman, as she was the one who'd been out of bed. Essie had been forthcoming about the reason for her meeting with Mrs. Vickeridge, but Beatrice had a sneaking suspicion there was still more to the story.

It was then that something caught her eye on the dresser. Something barely peeking out from underneath a carelessly tossed stocking. Beatrice neared and threw the stocking aside to find a half-empty bottle of perfume. This in itself was nothing extraordinary, but the name across the bottle struck Beatrice with delight: Follett.

She snatched it up, yanked off the lid, and took a sniff. It was definitely whiskey. A grin of absolute glee crossed her lips. It was the perfect disguise. Many of the day's popular perfumes were amber in color, and no one would think to check the bottle sitting on a lady's dressing table with the rest of her things. Even Beatrice might not have guessed it without David's hint. With another thrill, she recalled the smashed perfume bottle on the floor of the Vickeridge's bathroom. Mr. Vickeridge must have caught his wife taking a swig and realized the truth, thus leading to their argument. Comprehension lit Beatrice's eyes like the setting sun catching the ocean on fire.

"I know who M is," she thought aloud.

CHAPTER FOURTEEN
UNMASKED

Detective Mason and Eleanore gabbed on and off as their drive toward the La Posada Hotel continued. The more he talked to Eleanore, the more Mason remembered why he'd taken a job with the police force, and the more he felt protective of Miss Hughes and the cousin she talked so much about. They'd made it halfway to their destination when the rain began to let up, and Mason stepped on the gas as much as he dared. From what little Eleanore had been able to tell him, it sounded like they were dealing with a desperate killer, and he wouldn't put it past a cornered murderer to kill again. They covered the last half of the drive twice as fast as the first, and it wasn't until they pulled to a stop in the parking lot outside the hotel that Mason realized Eleanore had been holding on for dear life.

She released the handle on the side of the door and leaned forward, squinting through the window. "The power is back on," she remarked.

Mason had noticed that too. It didn't bode well. A fully illuminated hotel would make it harder for the murderer to hide, which could make the killer more violent. There was no telling what lay in wait for them inside that building, and it was for that reason he turned to Eleanore and said, "You should wait in the car."

Eleanore looked flabbergasted. "What? No! I'm coming with you!"

"Look, kid, it's brave what you did, but you need to let me take it from here."

Stubborn indignation colored Eleanore's face. "I'm coming with you," she said sternly. "I won't get in the way. I'll stay in the back. Besides, you'll need me to point him out . . . if Bea doesn't have him already."

They had a brief staring contest, but Mason could see he'd already lost. He sighed. "All right, but stay in the back."

Eleanore beamed with triumph as she hopped out of the car in unison with Mason.

The rain, though lighter, still fell in a steady stream, gathering in the brim of Detective Mason's hat and running off the edges like miniature waterfalls. Four other squad cars were parked outside the hotel awaiting the arrival of Mason and Eleanore. Ten officers climbed out of them, all eyes fixed on the detective. Mason observed the hotel for a moment. He'd been there only once before to have a late dinner at the restaurant. The food was much better than the burger and fries he usually consumed, the latter of which contributed to his growing physique, and the famed Harvey Girls had all been friendly and welcoming. For such a nasty thing as murder to occur within those walls was almost unbelievable.

"Orders, sir?" the nearest officer asked.

Mason was called back to the present. He turned his attention to the waiting policemen. "I want five of you on me," Mason said. "The rest of you spread out and cover all the exits. This bastard isn't escaping on my watch."

Nods and movement accompanied his words, and half of the officers split off to cover the rear of the hotel. The remaining five followed Mason as he moved up the front walk for the door, Eleanore trailing behind them. When Detective Mason entered the hotel lobby, the scene he found was incredible. James and Tommy were duking it out in the middle of the room while Harry attempted to pull them off of each other. The onlookers gave cries mixed between encouragement and disdain.

"All right, that's enough!" shouted Mason, but no one seemed to notice the police. He pulled his gun from its holster and fired at the ceiling. Everyone paused in fright, looking even more contrite when they realized the police were standing in the entryway. Tommy and James immediately separated, and Harry straightened.

"Miss Hughes?" Harry said, catching sight of Eleanore standing at the back.

Eleanore beamed and waved at Harry.

"You know this man?" Mason asked Eleanore.

She nodded. "Harry Riley. He's been helping my cousin."

Mason stepped forward and offered Harry a hand. "I'm Detective Mason. Your friend here filled me in on most of the details."

They shook hands briefly, Harry seemingly in shock. He looked back and forth between Eleanore and Detective Mason as if he couldn't believe his eyes.

Mason continued, "We can get to the formalities later. Right now, we need to apprehend this joker. Where is Miss Adams?"

Harry pointed toward the hallway. "She went to search the guest rooms. She should be on her way back by now."

This brought cries of outrage from those gathered in the lobby, and Mr. Morrow stepped forward.

"Henry Morrow," he said, "hotel manager. I would like it on record that I did not give permission for this obvious invasion of privacy."

Detective Mason wasn't impressed. One look at Mr. Morrow, and he had all he needed to build a profile. Oily hair, a perspiring forehead, and a perfect pencil mustache told the detective this was a man who liked everything just so, and the manager's speech sealed the deal—he was slimy.

"We'll deal with that later," Mason assured him, turning back to Harry. "Anything else I should know?"

"Yeah," replied Harry. "The killer has a gun."

Detective Mason nodded in understanding. It would complicate matters, but it wasn't the first time Mason had dealt with an armed culprit. "You two," he pointed at the nearest officers. "Stay here and start gathering witness statements. You," he pointed at Eleanore, "stay with the doctor. And no buts."

Eleanore had opened her mouth to protest, but at his final statement, she closed her mouth and gave a feeble nod, moving to stand beside Harry.

"Hang on," Harry said in a tone that Mason didn't favor. Harry's eyes roamed over the room. "Someone's missing."

The words sent a chill through the air.

"He'll go straight for Beatrice," Eleanore uttered to Mason.

"She'll be fine," the detective replied earnestly. "I promise."

With three of Winslow's finest, Detective Mason moved for the corridor, keeping his gun aloft in case there was trouble.

It had taken Beatrice the full half hour to conduct her search, but as she stood in the final room on her list, she knew her hypothesis was correct. A chair stood in the bathroom surrounded by discarded ropes as if someone had been tied up and had escaped. *Eleanore*, Beatrice thought. She still had yet to find her cousin, and she hoped with all her might that Eleanore would be in the lobby when she went back downstairs. An ashtray held an extinguished cigar, and a sniff told Beatrice it was the same that she'd smelled earlier on Mrs. Vickeridge's body. She turned out the bed covers and opened all the drawers. It wasn't until she looked under the bed that she found what she was looking for: a giant case.

Beatrice had to shimmy a little way under the bed to grab the case's thick handle, but she managed to tug it out after a bit of careful maneuvering. The clasps opened with a satisfying *click* as she unlatched them. She held her breath and pushed the lid open. Inside the case, perfectly protected in their own individual pouches, were at least twenty bottles of Follett perfume.

"Hello, gorgeous," she murmured, running her gloved fingers over one of the bottles. She pulled it out, twisted off the lid, and gave it a sniff. It was whiskey.

Beatrice returned the lid and tucked the bottle of smuggled liquor back into its place, her eyes catching the pocket fixed in the case's lid. She doubted M was the sort to keep all his eggs in one basket, but nevertheless, she dug a hand into the pocket, fully expecting it to be empty. Surprise colored her face when her fingers found a small rectangular object. She pulled it out with a victorious grin—it was the missing notebook.

Beatrice hastily opened it and began thumbing through the pages. The notes were in a kind of shorthand, but Beatrice had no trouble in making it out. At the start, Tiffany was only taking notes that pertained to her Harvey Girl story. There were passages about the long hours, the comfortable lodging, and the decent pay. She had several pages of first-hand stories likely from conversations she'd had with the other girls. She spoke often of their kindness and noted more than once that there was a camaraderie among the girls she'd never experienced anywhere before. Halfway through the notebook, the tone changed. Tiffany seemed to be studying people who acted in a strange way. Beatrice reasoned this must have been after she found some inkling of the juice ring.

Mary was the first person under the microscope. Tiffany noted that Mary had a sour disposition when not in the presence of Mr. Morrow or Miss Bishop. She was a very controlling and bossy girl who'd announced her desire to be a house mother one day, to which Tiffany made a side note: *not suitable.*

Beatrice reasoned that Mary disliked Tiffany for more than "sweeheart stealing." She recalled Miss Bishop's emotional words at the tea party earlier in the evening. It was clearly Miss Bishop's view that Tiffany, as Holly, would have made an excellent house mother one day. Beatrice had to wonder if this was the first time Miss Bishop had ever expressed such views aloud and if the information had ever reached Mary's ears.

Next, Tiffany had taken an interest in James. He often disappeared at odd times, claiming to go off for a smoke or that he wasn't feeling well. Sometimes he'd disappear without warning altogether. It was evident from her notes that Tiffany had thought she'd found a lead at last. After searching for him one evening after the dinner rush, Tiffany had found him departing a guest room. Beatrice raised her eyebrows at the next part. He had been tangled up in the arms of one of the female guests who slipped an extra tip into his chest pocket after a steamy farewell kiss. Beatrice could see why he was so apprehensive of this black book. One word of his entertaining female guests for extra money would have him sacked and on the streets looking for work he'd probably never find.

Beatrice flipped even further ahead, knowing Harry was still stalling downstairs. She found the pages pertaining to David Phillips and the discovery of his involvement in the juice ring. The writing here was rushed, excited. Beatrice could relate to Tiffany's enthusiasm. Nothing was quite so invigorating as a mass of puzzle pieces finally coming together to form a clear picture. It seemed Tiffany had stumbled on David transferring whiskey from its original container into empty perfume bottles. He'd denied everything at first, but Tiffany was persistent. She soon discovered the secret compartment in the clock, which impressed Beatrice. From there, it didn't take her long to coincide David's staying late with the arrival of a particular guest who came at least once a week since opening. Tiffany had seen M at another Harvey House along the same line before she'd transferred to La Posada. It was this connection that had led her, per her notes, to believe the juice ring was a much bigger operation. As a journalist, Tiffany had access to all sorts of connections, one of which she'd used to trace M back to . . .

"Leaping lizards," Beatrice murmured aloud.

If Tiffany's notes were true, then M worked for Nikki Donavan, the most dangerous mobster on the West Coast. Donavan controlled most of the criminal activity in Los Angeles. No one had been able to pin anything on him in years. Had Beatrice just stumbled on the one bit of proof that could bring finally him down?

"Drop it, sister," a gruff voice demanded from the doorway.

Beatrice gasped and whirled toward the voice to find Donald Flanagan, the traveling salesman, standing there with a gun trained on her.

"How did you get past Harry?" she asked.

"Creating a distraction was easy with James and Mr. Vickeridge in the same room. I instigated a little shouting match. Your pet doctor doesn't even know I'm gone. Now . . . drop the notebook and stand up."

Beatrice complied, dropping the notebook atop the perfume bottles, eyes fixed on the Colt pistol with apprehension. She rose slowly to her feet with her hands up in surrender.

"I was going to give you a chance to unmask yourself in front of everyone," Beatrice mused. "Now you've gone and spoiled the fun."

"Sorry, sweetheart," Flanagan said, "but nothin' doin'. You and I are gonna take a little trip to get you fitted for concrete shoes."

"Concrete isn't really my color," she quipped.

"It is now," he said firmly. "Keep your hands where I can see 'em, and walk toward me . . . slowly."

Beatrice had no doubt that he would shoot her if she played this the wrong way. She'd have to play it safe until she found an edge.

"So . . . you work for Donavan, huh?" she said conversationally. "Out of curiosity, does he pay well?"

"Only if you're willing to get your hands dirty, little girl," he retorted, yanking her by the arm once she was close enough. He threw her into the hall with so much force, she collided with the opposite wall. "One misstep and I'll give you a lead-lined goodbye."

He cocked the hammer back on his gun for emphasis, and Beatrice swore internally. This wasn't going at all how she'd hoped.

"Which way, skipper?" she asked.

He waggled the gun. "Toward the stairs."

Beatrice moved in the designated direction at a deliberately glacial pace. She needed to buy herself time. It was like playing casual chess against a known champion. Beatrice was good, but Flanagan had been at the game for longer.

"Donald Flanagan," she said, testing the waters. "Where does the M come from?"

He didn't say anything.

Beatrice gave an exaggerated sigh. "If you're going to kill me anyway, there's no harm in a little jabber."

Flanagan grunted. "Chitchat with you is more dangerous than Russian roulette with a full gun."

"Really?" Beatrice beamed over her shoulder, stopping in her tracks. "I'm flattered, Mack. I truly am."

"Keep walkin'," Flanagan barked, poking her with the cold tip of his gun.

Beatrice turned front again, walking slower still. She had to get him talking. Though she was sure she had all the pieces of the puzzle, she needed to be certain she hadn't left anything out. Moreover, the longer she kept him busy, the less he'd be focused on making her and the evidence disappear. Admittedly, Beatrice had never thought about what she would do when she caught the culprit. Unmasking him in front of an audience would have left too many witnesses, and he would have been forced to surrender or do something drastic to escape, in which case he'd likely make a mistake. Presently, he was in complete control, and Beatrice didn't like it.

As they turned the corner, she said, "You can at least tell me what you've done with my cousin."

"She musta jumped out the window. Phillips was watchin' the door. No one went in or out. But she'll turn up . . . and I'll take her down too."

Beatrice suppressed the smile that came to her lips. If Eleanore was out there somewhere, the first thing she'd do is go straight for the police. It was something Beatrice could always count on her cousin for. Even when they were children, Eleanore had never hesitated to call on the boys in blue when she thought Beatrice might be up to her neck in trouble. As things looked now, Beatrice was positively drowning. With Harry added to the mix, hope blossomed in her chest all the more. They weren't out of the woods yet, and neither was Flanagan.

"It really is an impressive operation you've had going," Beatrice praised. The stairs were now in sight. Her time was running out. "I'm guessing you have a supplier? You buy perfume in bulk, dump the bottles, David refills them, and then you resell them at a higher price, all while the world thinks you're peddling perfume."

"You know, for a broad, you're not as dumb as I thought you'd be," mused Flanagan.

"Oh, you're too kind," Beatrice replied. "I honestly couldn't have done it without Tiffany's help."

"Who?"

Beatrice rolled her eyes. "Holly. The girl you had killed . . . The reason we're all in this mess."

She took the stairs one at a time, hoping there wasn't a nearby back door he'd prefer. The rumble of thunder outside was farther away than it'd been all night. It didn't even shake the hotel. The storm was retreating, which was bad news for Beatrice if they made it outside. Flanagan could make his getaway with her and the evidence still tucked in her purse. The thought didn't terrify her as it should. Instead, she felt a growing motivation to survive.

Flanagan didn't seem to notice her tactic of slow movement, or if he did, he didn't mind it. Now that she had him on a subject, it was as if he couldn't help contradicting her. "I never told that rat to kill her. I said *'Take care of it.'* He decided to kill her all on his own." He scoffed. "And *you* . . . making puppy eyes at him, promising him you'll look out for his mother. What kinda dumb sap are you, huh? The kid has murder in his veins. His own pop got put away for it. Your doctor friend had the right idea."

For some reason, this information hurt Beatrice, which was likely its intended effect. Someone so young and so seemingly innocent shouldn't be capable of murder. She refused to believe David was predestined to kill. He had a choice. This notion made her heart clench all the more. David did have a choice, and he had chosen wrong. Why was that so hard for Beatrice to grasp? She wanted so desperately to believe this was all Flanagan's fault, that M was responsible for everything.

"Violence should never take the place of kindness or mercy," she said quietly.

Flanagan held back a disbelieving laugh. "Mercy? Where has that gotten you, sweetheart?"

Beatrice wanted to answer that it'd gotten her pretty far, but she knew a man like Flanagan would never understand. Kindness would work on someone like David who had made a mistake in anger and still retained some semblance of humanity. Flanagan, on the other hand, clearly held no value for human life. The manner in which he'd dispatched Mrs. Vickeridge said as much.

"Why did you kill Mrs. Vickeridge?" she asked while the topic was on her mind. They'd reached the bottom of the stairs and were now ambling down the long hall toward the station and the lobby. "You already had Eleanore, so it wasn't *really* to send me a message, was it?"

"That dumb broad was gonna squeal on the whole operation. Tell you everything. I couldn't have that, now could I? Bodies were already cropping up. What was one more?"

"But why would she turn stool pigeon? I thought she was a loyal customer?"

"She was more than a customer," Flanagan said. "She was a mule too. She'd smuggle in the perfume bottles whenever she traveled. It's less conspicuous when a high-class lady buys perfume in bulk. The second a body turned up, she started getting fidgety."

"You can only carry twenty bottles at once," mused Beatrice. "I take it there's more than one way station along the line."

"You bet there is, but I ain't sayin' where."

"So . . . what? She wanted out?" Beatrice pressed.

"Nah, the broad wanted more money," Flanagan answered. "As if she doesn't have enough dough already. She was four sheets in the wind and completely off her rocker, talkin' about the 'right thing.'" He scoffed. "The world ain't been right for a long time. That dumb Dora wouldn't know *right* if it bit her on the nose. Kept goin' on and on about you like you're some sort of hero. *You*. An actress!"

Beatrice quirked a brow. "You know, if you keep judging women so harshly, they'll be your downfall one day."

Flanagan had a laugh at that. "Even with all your snooping, you've never been where I don't want you to be. I'll always be two steps ahead."

"Or three steps behind," a gruff male voice interrupted.

Detective Mason stepped out of the lobby and into the hall, gun raised. Three armed officers flanked him. Eleanore, drowning in Mason's coat, stood like a wet kitten in the lobby behind them, Harry at her side.

"Ellie!" Beatrice enthused, beyond relieved to see her cousin alive.

Flanagan yanked Beatrice back and held her tightly against his body, the cold tip of his gun pressing into her temple. He smelled strongly of cigars and too much cologne.

"One wrong move and I redecorate the wall with her brains!" he barked.

CHAPTER FIFTEEN

The Chase

It was incredible the effect a hostage could have in a dire situation. Though they could see very little through the lobby arch owing to the police blocking the way, it wasn't difficult for the gaggle of onlookers gathered there to grasp what was happening. Many of them huddled nearer to one another for safety, while others, like James, behaved indifferently. Eleanore tried to rush forward, but Harry yanked her back, and not for the first time that evening, Beatrice was grateful for his presence in this unraveling catastrophe.

"Did you hear what I said?" barked Flanagan, pressing the gun more firmly into Beatrice's temple. She winced.

"I heard it, pal," Mason replied. "I'm not sure I believe it."

"He's already killed two people tonight," said Beatrice. "I wouldn't rile him if I were you."

"SHUT UP!" Flanagan yelled.

"It's over!" cried Mason. "You're all washed up. Miss Hughes told us everything."

Beatrice mused to herself that there was loads Eleanore didn't know, so her cousin could hardly have told Mason *everything.* The fact that she'd known something, however, seemed to be enough to rattle Flanagan's cage. He tightened his grip painfully on Beatrice, and Eleanore again tried to surge forward. Harry held her back with ease.

"I'll deal with Miss Hughes later," Flanagan growled, moving inch by inch toward the door that led to the tracks. Beatrice knew she was a goner the moment they made it outside. "For now, this bird is coming with me."

Beatrice racked her brain for a way out of her predicament that didn't end in her corpse on the floor. Unfortunately, with Flanagan's gun cocked and ready to fire, one wrong move on Beatrice's part could end badly. Despite this, Detective Mason maintained the cool air of one holding all the aces. Beatrice wondered what he knew that she didn't, but as mind reading was merely a cheap carnival trick, she'd just have to wait and see what he had up his sleeve.

"Drop your weapons!" Flanagan demanded.

He now sounded desperate and—dare Beatrice think it—afraid. M was cornered.

The three cops around Mason all looked to their superior, asking silently for orders. Mason held his ground.

"DROP THEM!" screamed Flanagan.

Beatrice winced. "Geez, not so loud, honey," she murmured.

He yanked her hair. "Quiet, you—"

BANG!

Several screams accompanied the gunshot, and Eleanore broke free from Harry's grip, racing forward. Beatrice stood in shock, expecting to fall to the floor at any moment. But something else fell to the floor with an almighty clatter instead. It was Flanagan's gun. Flanagan clutched a bleeding hand, and all eyes turned in wonder to Detective Mason, whose gun was still poised. Beatrice could have sworn she saw a wisp of smoke curl away from the barrel.

"That was a damn good shot," she praised the detective.

"Did a stint in the army. It's done wonders for my aim," he mused, turning to the swearing mobster. "Hands where I can see 'em, slimeball!"

Glowering, Flanagan slowly raised his hands in surrender, the right one bleeding profusely and trembling slightly. Beatrice nimbly slipped behind the police only to be nearly choked to death in Eleanore's tight embrace.

"Darling, I can't breathe," Beatrice teased, though she was hugging her cousin just as tightly.

"On your knees," Mason growled at Flanagan. One of the other officers had already produced handcuffs.

The cousins pulled apart to watch what they thought would be a victorious arrest. Flanagan had barely lowered an inch when the door to the tracks opened behind him. He bolted, flattening the unsuspecting officer on the other side.

"After him!" shouted Mason.

All three policemen charged after the fleeing mobster, Mason hobbling at a run behind them. It was evident from his limp that he had a bad knee, and Beatrice doubted the other cops were as good a shot. Three seconds were all it took for Beatrice to come to a decision and scoop up Flanagan's dropped gun. As she turned toward the lobby's front door, Eleanore cried in exasperation, "Where are you going?"

"To catch a killer," Beatrice answered. "Keep an eye on her for me," she said to Harry.

Neither Harry nor Eleanore had a chance to protest before Beatrice took off at a run and burst through the door.

Outside the rain still fell, but it was no longer the torrential downpour it had been. Beatrice edged along the side of the building without a care for her hair and makeup, which were by now diminished anyway. She heard shouting and gunshots from the other side of the hotel. Though the few lamps outside were freshly glowing, the rain still made visibility poor, and Beatrice doubted even Detective Mason could land a good shot on Flanagan. Not good news for Beatrice's lack of experience. She squinted through the rain and fixed her eyes inquisitively on the parking lot in front of the hotel. If escape was truly Flanagan's aim, Beatrice wagered he'd double back for the parking lot once he'd lost the police. Hiding in the rail yard was too risky and far too obvious. Flanagan was bolder than that. When she reached the side of the hotel, Beatrice paused to listen, gun aimed skyward. More shouts came from the other side of the building, but no further shots rang out. From the sound of things, they'd already lost their quarry in the rail yards, which meant, if her theory held any merit, Flanagan would soon be heading her way.

After a quick survey of her options, Beatrice crouched behind the low garden wall that separated the front courtyard from the small parking lot. It didn't take long for her ankles to protest the position, but she knew giving in to gravity would mean sacrificing necessary spring, should Flanagan show. Rain slid down Beatrice's face and neck, bringing goosebumps to the surface of her skin. Seconds ticked by as hours. What if Flanagan didn't come this way? What if the police had already caught him? She would never live down the shame of letting M get away. She could see the headlines now: *"Actress Plays Detective and Gets the Hook."* She had to make this work. She needed her name to mean something more.

Beatrice's ankles were absolutely screaming, and she was on the verge of giving up when the sound of crunching gravel met her ears. She froze, holding her breath, and tightened her grip on the gun. The footsteps were harried yet careful, like someone trying to run without creating too much noise. As they neared, it dawned on Beatrice that, short of shooting Flanagan, she had no idea how she was going to stop him. The steps were nearly on top of her, heading fastidiously toward the parking lot, a smorgasbord of getaway vehicles.

Beatrice shot up, her gun poised. "Hold it right there, mister!"

Flanagan took flight at full speed, which was the opposite of what Beatrice had intended. She couldn't very well shoot him in the back. She wanted to stop him, not kill him.

"I really need to work on this part of the job," Beatrice muttered to herself, bolting after him.

Distant voices shouted, presumably the duped policemen.

"I heard something over there!"

"Head for the front!"

"Don't let him get away!"

Flanagan and Beatrice raced clumsily through the parking lot, the latter keeping up well, considering she was running in heels.

"Stop!" Beatrice shouted, as if it'd do any good against an admitted mobster.

Flanagan dove into the nearest car—a blue Packard Speedster—and turned the engine over. The owner of the car had unfortunately left the top down in this weather, exposing the interior to the elements. Beatrice jumped out of the way as Flanagan reversed, nearly flattening her. Angry, Beatrice took aim and fired as he sped forward. She missed him, the bullet pinging off the car's metal side with an angry spark.

Beatrice seized the opportunity to jump into the nearby Cadillac roadster. The engine roared to life when she turned the key. She reversed the car and sped after Flanagan as best she could, the police clambering into their squad cars behind her. It was an immense relief to be out of the rain, but the weather still made visibility poor. Beatrice didn't dare slow despite this lest she lose sight of the blue car ahead of her. If she could just run him off the road, the police might have time to catch up. She hoped they hadn't gotten too far behind.

Resolutely, Beatrice slammed her foot down on the accelerator with no thought for the danger or the slick, flooding roads. Thunder rumbled distantly. The storm was finally moving on, but it still had a little kick left in it before it left them behind. Beatrice steadily overtook the blue Speedster. Flanagan and Beatrice were now neck and neck. She had the advantage of a roof overhead to keep the rain out of her eyes Flanagan didn't notice her until it was too late.

Beatrice jerked the wheel and slammed the Cadillac into the side of his car. Flanagan veered toward the side of the road but miraculously course corrected. It wasn't his first car chase. Skillfully, he rammed her back. Beatrice gasped, trying to correct herself and nearly hydroplaning in the process. She crashed through the scaffolding surrounding the front of Saint Joseph's Catholic Church before wrenching the wheel back the other way.

The impact had cracked her windshield, but she could still see Flanagan's swerving car ahead of her. He'd gained the lead again, turning the corner a good three seconds before Beatrice followed suit. The moment she was on a straight stretch, Beatrice slammed her foot down on the gas pedal, gaining on Flanagan's teetering Packard like a lioness after a jackrabbit.

As soon as she was level with Flanagan, she yanked the wheel violently and smashed into the side of his car. The wet roads impeded the mobster this time. He skidded off the street, taking out a mailbox before he returned to the pavement, muttering swearwords that were lost to the wind. The force of the crash had slowed him down, and Beatrice was now in the lead. She glanced behind her and let off the gas, veering down a side street as Flanagan changed course. She could make him out at every cross street. He'd gained momentum again, and Beatrice swore, risking lost time by snaking an S down one street and up the one he'd chosen. The gap between them was noticeably wider, and Beatrice could feel the car slipping and sliding along the road beneath her. Though it went against her better judgment, she mashed the gas pedal again, gaining on Flanagan with ease. Sirens blared distantly behind them, the police a good two blocks away. Flanagan barreled past a sign for Route 66, and Beatrice suddenly understood his plan. The highway went back to Los Angeles. He was retreating to his boss, and once he had mob protection, there was no way the police would get their hands on him. At this revelation, Beatrice jammed the gas pedal as far down as it would go, effectively closing the gap between the two cars.

They raced across the town line, exchanging the streetlamps and charming buildings for the vast painted desert. The occasional telephone pole whizzed by, nothing but a blurred shadow. With a cracked windshield and low lighting, visibility was almost impossible to Beatrice, but she could see well enough to notice the blue Packard slowing. Flanagan's run-in with the mailbox had smashed in the Speedster's fender and grill, and something must have sprung a leak. Beatrice eased up on the gas to match his speed. There was no way he'd make it all the way back to Los Angeles now. She just needed to run him off the road for good.

They must have driven into the path of the retreating storm, because the rain abruptly doubled and Beatrice heard a low rumble of thunder overhead. This was suicide, and Beatrice knew it, but she wasn't giving up now, not when she was so close. She took a deep breath, steeling herself for another attempt at ramming Flanagan off the road when, suddenly, lightning streaked across the sky and struck a telephone pole ahead of them. Beatrice screamed as it fell across the road, barely swerving out of its path and skidding off the road in a dangerous one-eighty. Flanagan hadn't seen the obstruction fall. There was a deafening *crunch* as the Speedster slammed into the thick pole and stopped dead in its tracks.

Panting, Beatrice threw open her door and stumbled out of the car, mud staining her gloves and dress as she fell to her knees. Two beaten-up squad cars pulled up to the wreck, their headlamps illuminating the scene. Officer Mason hopped urgently from his vehicle, shouting orders to his men that Beatrice couldn't hear over the ringing in her ears. Three of them raced for the crashed blue car. Mason, still lacking a coat and now drenched for the second time, approached Beatrice where she knelt in the dirt on the side of the road.

"You all right, miss?" Mason asked, holding out a hand to help her up.

Beatrice hadn't even realized she was on the ground. Exhaustion, adrenaline, and shock weren't the best company mixed together.

"I think so," she uttered, accepting his hand.

Mason pulled her to her feet.

"Flanagan! Is he—"

"The boys'll take care of it," Mason assured her, glancing over to the wreck.

She followed his gaze. From the look of things, Flanagan had been thrown from the vehicle on impact.

"You've done enough, Miss Adams," Mason continued. "Let's get you back to the hotel, and you can tell me all about it."

Tired and suddenly hungry, Beatrice gave a feeble nod and allowed Mason to steer her toward the front seat of his squad car. He only took one other officer with him, leaving the rest to clear the scene. Beatrice was too dazed to ask the burning questions on her mind, choosing instead to lean her head against the window and stare at the water droplets running in rivulets down the glass. It seemed so surreal to think that she'd been speeding down the road in a car chase mere minutes ago, or that she'd nearly wrecked. Now that she was sitting still, her hands shook noticeably, a sign that she was over exhausted in the extreme.

She laced her fingers together to disguise it and let her mind wander as Detective Mason guided the squad car back toward the La Posada.

For her first *real* case, a case in which she'd done more than merely assist the police, Beatrice had to admit, it hadn't been quite so terrible. Both murderers had been caught, one way or another, and justice would be served for those who'd lost their lives. Even so, Beatrice couldn't help feeling a little disappointed in the outcome. More lives had been lost than she would have liked, and there was still the concerning connection of Flanagan to Nikki Donavan. Was Flanagan the only courier? How many way stations did the juice ring have? Who was the supplier?

Beatrice's head positively spun with questions, but it was nearly impossible to connect any more dots now. She'd have to think it over in the morning after some sleep and a strong cup of coffee. Yes, she decided. No more sleuthing tonight. Once everything was safely in the hands of the Winslow Police Department, Beatrice Adams was signing off.

CHAPTER SIXTEEN

A CASE CLOSED

The drive to the La Posada was mostly held in silence. Even the officer sitting in the back seat didn't dare ask questions, leaving Detective Mason and Beatrice the luxury of quiet to mull things over. The rain slowed to barely a drizzle the nearer they came to their destination, and Beatrice was relieved. Now the air was clear and cool. Hope seemed to be on the wind, and Beatrice relished in it. The worst was over. As this realization dawned, a tired smile graced her lips and a sparkle came to her brilliant eyes. The worst was over, and everything would be jake.

When they finally pulled up to the hotel, Eleanore practically yanked her cousin from the car, embracing Beatrice as if she'd come back from the dead. Beatrice didn't even have time to be startled.

"Are you loony!" Eleanore exclaimed. "You could have been killed!"

"Nonsense," Beatrice retorted, her voice a little shaky. "I know how to drive."

Eleanore pulled back, her hands still on Beatrice's shoulders. "Then why is your Lincoln in the shop?" she said pointedly.

Beatrice laughed and hugged her cousin again. "Oh, Ellie. You really are such an anxious Annie," she teased.

For once, Eleanore didn't get offended but rather seemed glad at her cousin's ribbing. Beatrice too was glad. Eleanore's nerves, while often incomprehensible to Beatrice, had served them all well that night. They were more than family, Beatrice often thought. They were partners—Beatrice there to get them into trouble and Eleanore to get them out.

"Let's take this inside, ladies," said Detective Mason, who'd been standing quietly nearby.

The girls readily agreed, and the three of them made their way up the walk and into the hotel. Miss Bishop immediately threw a towel around Beatrice's shoulders when they walked through the door. More officers were gathered here. One of them was interviewing Harry, who looked over with a heart-stopping smile at the sight of Beatrice alive. Beatrice smiled back, relieved it was all over, at least for the night. The crowd had mostly thinned, many spreading to the dining room for tea and hot chocolate. A second officer interviewed Mr. Vickeridge, who sat solemn and puffy-eyed in the same armchair he'd fallen into earlier. For someone who supposedly tried to divorce his wife, he seemed awfully torn up by her murder, and Beatrice couldn't help feeling sorry for him.

Mason led Beatrice and Eleanore into the dining room, and they settled at a table in the back where they could talk undisturbed. Sarah brought over a piping-hot pot of tea, and Alice set a plate of cucumber sandwiches beside it. Beatrice wasted no time digging in. Eleanore too finally bothered to eat, though far more gracefully than her ravenous cousin. Mason requested a coffee, which Alice promptly brought over with a smile. For a moment, the table's three occupants sat in silence, reveling in the relief and ease that came in the wake of chaos's end. Beatrice had never enjoyed cucumber sandwiches so much in her life. They were the best thing in all the world, she thought as she polished her plate.

Once they were all satisfied and relaxed in their seats with a second cup of tea and another coffee for Mason, the police detective pulled his notebook from his pocket and flipped to the appropriate page. "As much as I'd love to sit here all night," he began, "I'm sure you ladies would like to get to bed, so let's get to it, huh?"

"Fire away," Beatrice said, looking more content than she had all night.

Detective Mason looked down at his notes. "Miss Hughes said this all started with a body falling out of your closet?"

"That's right," Beatrice confirmed. "It fell out when Ellie opened the closet to hang her dresses. She was all nerves."

Mason scribbled on his notepad. "What happened after that?"

"Well, that's about when Mr. Morrow showed up with Tommy, the bellhop. I sent Ellie downstairs straight away and asked for Dr. Riley."

Beatrice went on to explain how she'd examined the body and employed Harry's expertise to help her form a theory. She pulled the note she'd found in the dead girl's pocket from the depths of her overflowing handbag. Detective Mason stared, clearly impressed.

"What else have you got in there?" he asked curiously, a half-joking lilt to his tone.

"Enough to put Flanagan away, I hope," Beatrice replied with a ruby smile. "Anyway, there was nothing for it but to announce the murder. Mr. Morrow is a bit of a blabbermouth, and my cousin had let slip about my being a detective. I set up some interviews in the manager's office to get my bearings and started investigating from there. You'd be surprised the things people say when they learn there's been a murder."

"And the things they do," added Eleanore who was contently sipping her tea.

"Oh, yes," Beatrice agreed. "Murder has a way of dragging out the dirty laundry, if you know what I mean."

"All too well," Mason mused, suppressing a smile. "Please continue."

Beatrice explained how she'd sent Harry and Eleanore to test the typewriters so they could find the one that had written the note to the victim. She detailed the clues she'd found in Tiffany's room and the encounter she'd had with Mary.

"She's quite the peach," Beatrice said with heavy sarcasm. "How someone like *her* ever got a job with the Fred Harvey Company, I'll never know."

"So, the diary pointed you . . . where?" asked Mason, writing furiously.

Beatrice grinned. "Hang on, skipper. I'm getting to it," she teased. "I went to check the boiler room next. That's where I learned that the storm hadn't blown a fuse as we'd originally thought. The fuses had been stolen altogether."

Detective Mason looked up, his expression one of disbelief. "You're kidding," he said.

Beatrice shook her head. "Not even a little. That was when I got jumped from behind." She pointed to her neck, where David's fingerprints were still forming in shades of black and blue.

"Flanagan did that to you?" Mason wondered.

"Oh, no!" Beatrice exclaimed. "There were two killers. Did I not say?"

Detective Mason set down his pen and rubbed a hand over his face.

"Wait, two?" Eleanore interjected.

Beatrice had quite forgotten how much her cousin had missed since they'd left her. She nodded in excitement. "Oh, yes. David Phillips and Donald Flanagan. I still haven't worked out why he called himself M."

"You've lost me," sighed Mason.

Beatrice realized she'd gotten ahead of herself, so she backtracked, explaining that they'd all regrouped and left Eleanore in Harry's room, thinking she'd be safer there. It was in the lobby where Beatrice had checked the ledger for the day mentioned in Holly's diary.

"Of course, I was *so* focused on Harry's name that I completely ignored Flanagan's name on the list. I didn't even realize who he was until later when I was searching the rooms. And then, after discovering a note from M hidden in the lobby clock, it was all a game of conjecture. I was so sure it was Mr. Vickeridge."

"Why?" asked Mason.

Beatrice described the craps game she and Harry had stumbled on, giving the names and description of each person present in turn.

"You play craps?" Mason interrupted before Beatrice could finish.

"Would you like to hear the story or not?"

Mason signaled for her to continue, and Beatrice went on to tell him about the Vickeridges' near divorce and their clear unhappiness.

"I don't see how that made him this M person," said Mason.

"Well, we found Mrs. Vickeridge dead later, so that sort of had me suspicious."

Detective Mason gaped, and Eleanore ejected, "Heavens, no!"

"Another body?" said Mason incredulously.

"There are three bodies, Mack. Would you prefer I tell the story in reverse?"

Mason let out a long, stressed sigh, and Beatrice sympathized with him. It was a lot to take in, and Beatrice couldn't seem to get it out fast enough. The sooner she left this mess in the hands of the police, the better. When Mason signaled for her to go on, Beatrice skipped to the kitchen where they'd found Tommy. The police detective wrote energetically as she recounted Tommy's tale of Holly's mysterious phone call. She pulled David's button from her handbag and set it on the table.

"It matched Tommy's uniform, so we knew it had to be one of the bell staff. I took his keys and went to check the bell stand. That's when Harry found the missing fuses in the lobby planter. We figured the killer must have dropped them in there amid all the confusion."

"I take it that's how you got the lights back on," Mason mused.

Beatrice hummed in agreement and barreled on. "Up to then, nothing made any sense. What sort of trouble could a waitress in a respectable establishment possibly get into? Well, I found my answer in the bell closet."

Mason and Eleanore both leaned in, and Beatrice tried not to laugh.

"There were empty liquor bottles hidden in with the laundry bags," she supplied.

"But," Eleanore said, "That means . . ."

"A juice ring?" Detective Mason guessed.

"You bet. All up and down the railroad. And I'm pretty sure I know who owns it."

"Who?" asked Mason.

Beatrice realized she was getting all mixed up, telling the story out of order, but she was so excited it couldn't be helped. "I found proof that links the juice ring back to Nikki Donavan."

"The mobster?" Mason replied.

Beatrice could tell he thought it too fantastic, but she grinned like a Cheshire. "Oh, yes," she said. "I purposefully left Holly's notebook upstairs in Flanagan's room atop the smuggled liquor just in case something happened to me. He was so focused on the evidence I'd already gathered, he didn't realize I'd left the most important evidence behind. You see, Holly was actually Tiffany Blake, a reporter. Mr. Morrow can corroborate that."

There was silence as Detective Mason tried to remember every detail she'd just given, writing in cramped shorthand.

"What on earth was she doing here?" Eleanore asked.

"Originally she was doing a piece on the Harvey Girls after being one," explained Beatrice. "But she stumbled on the juice ring and thought she'd caught a break. I'm almost certain the call Tommy overheard was to her editor."

Mason made note of this. "I can check that with the paper. Which did she work for?"

"Los Angeles Times," answered Beatrice.

Mason wrote it down.

"Anyway," Beatrice continued. "After getting locked in the bell closet by David and being let out by a sauced Mrs. Vickeridge, we went to have a chat with Mr. Morrow. That's when we discovered that he wasn't M but that M was paying him to keep things quiet."

"Morrow was accepting hush money?" Eleanore exclaimed, wide-eyed.

Beatrice nodded as if it were the best gossip in all the world, knowing how well her cousin loved to partake in it. "You bet he was. I don't think he should be allowed to stay on after that."

Her statement was directed at Detective Mason, who nodded in agreement and said, "I'll see what I can do. No one likes a mouse."

Satisfied, Beatrice plunged forward, detailing her fireside chat with Mr. Vickeridge and the missing logbooks. "It was shortly after that we heard Essie Hartman scream, and we went running. That's when we found Mrs. Vickeridge in the library . . . with her throat cut."

Eleanore shivered and closed her eyes as if the body were sitting right in front of her, and Beatrice patted her cousin's hand. Cadavers were not Eleanore's strong suit.

"Flanagan did that one?" asked Mason.

Beatrice confirmed that he had. "It turned out that Mrs. Vickeridge was going to blow the whistle on the whole operation, and Flanagan couldn't have that. He'd lose more than his life if he upset Donavan."

Detective Mason readily agreed. "Did you get a statement from Miss Hartman?"

"Not a statement, exactly," Beatrice replied. "But I did interview her and discover that she was supposed to meet Mrs. Vickeridge to get some hooch. Mrs. Vickeridge was a regular to M and a mule for their bottles."

Again, Detective Mason wrote like the wind. Beatrice stifled a yawn and then continued.

"They were smuggling the liquor in perfume bottles, see," she explained. "Mrs. Vickeridge would buy them in bulk and smuggle them when she traveled to each of Donavan's way stations. An appointed helper would then dump the perfume and refill the bottles with liquor for Flanagan to pick up. It really is rather clever."

"I'll say," agreed Eleanore. She rested her chin in her hand, like Beatrice, seeming to fade.

"Not clever enough to stump you," Mason praised. "I must say, I haven't seen anything quite like it."

Beatrice felt her cheeks warm, and she smiled modestly. "I'm just good at figuring things out, that's all."

"What happened to this David fellow?" asked Mason, eyes going back over his notes. "You said he's the one who killed Holly—er, Tiffany—and then tried to kill you?"

"That's right," Beatrice said. "But he's dead now too."

"Good heavens," sighed Eleanore, resting her head on the table.

"Harry and I managed to set a trap for Phillips using the fuses to restore the power," Beatrice explained. "We were questioning him when . . . Flanagan shot him from the shadows."

It was still awful to remember. The way David's face had contorted in pain before his body slackened. The gaping hole in his chest. Harry's panicked voice. Beatrice shook her head to clear it all away.

"He was trying to help his sick mother. When Tiffany got too close, he was afraid of losing everything, so . . . he killed her."

Mason wrote it all down, then sighed as if he'd just run a marathon and set his pen down. "Is that everything?"

"The highlights, at least," Beatrice said. "I can have Eleanore type up a case report in the morning . . . if she doesn't object, that is."

She looked to her cousin, who sat up once more as the conversation turned her way.

"I don't mind," Eleanore said, much to Beatrice's delight. "After a good night's sleep, that is. I'm absolutely beat and no good to anybody just now."

Beatrice laughed. "I'm arriving there myself, darling."

"Where did you say you left the evidence?" asked Detective Mason.

At this, Beatrice pulled everything else out of her purse, keeping Eleanore's case notes so Eleanore could use them in the morning to type them up properly. She pointed out Flanagan's room number on the logbook page she'd torn out.

"It should still be sitting on the floor where I left it. I'd search the room further too, if I were you. I didn't get the chance to dig any deeper."

Mason nodded and took the evidence off her hands, much to Beatrice's relief. This part of the case, at least, was over.

"Say, any chance you can mail me that notebook when you've finished with it?" she asked.

Mason looked at her questioningly. "We'll see," he answered. "It depends on how long it takes Flanagan to sing. What do you need it for, anyhow?"

Beatrice was just about to say, when Eleanore interrupted her. "Oh, no. No, no, no. You're not done with this whole thing, are you?"

"No," Beatrice answered simply. "Flanagan is caught, but the case isn't closed, is it? I mean, there's still a supplier out there somewhere, and so long as the juice ring is operational, Donavan could have another courier by tomorrow. It's not over until we shut it down."

Respect and admiration glittered in Detective Mason's eyes. "I'll see what I can do, kid," he promised.

"Aces!" Beatrice beamed, reaching into her handbag for a business card. She passed it over to him. "Just mail it to this address as soon as you can."

Mason whistled when he looked at the address on the card. "Bel Air, huh?"

"Yep," Beatrice answered, resting her chin in her hand. "Mother wanted to move away from the hustle and bustle and the prying eyes. It's a bit of a drive in either direction, but the seclusion is nice."

Detective Mason tucked her business card safely in his pocket. "Anything else I can do for you?"

Beatrice pondered, then said with a smile, "The address and number for David Phillips's mother would be lovely too. I have a feeling she's going to need some financial assistance in the near future."

"You got it," Mason said.

At that moment, a young officer approached the table to give Mason a report. They spoke in hushed tones a moment while Beatrice and Eleanore sipped their tea, which by now had grown cold. Beatrice set hers distastefully on the table. Mason shortly dismissed the officer and turned back to the ladies.

"Well, the good news is Flanagan will go away for a long time," he mused.

"And the bad?" wondered Eleanore.

"He'll spend a few weeks in the hospital first, cursing both of your names."

"Serves him right," said Eleanore.

Beatrice hid a relieved smile behind a mechanical sip of her discarded tea, followed shortly by a grimace at its glacial temperature. This time when she set it down, she made sure to shove it away. She was glad to hear that Flanagan had survived the crash. Beatrice had only wanted to stop him. If his death had been on her conscience, the guilt might never have left her, even if it had been an accident.

Detective Mason stood, pulling Beatrice from her reverie.

"I think I'll let you kids get some sleep," he said. "I've got a lot of work to do to wrap this up."

Eleanore shrugged out of Mason's massive suit coat and held it out to him. Mason draped it over his arm, tilting the brim of his fedora her way in thanks.

Beatrice beamed up at him. "Thanks ever so."

"What for?" Mason curbed a laugh. "You did all the work, sweetheart."

"For not laughing at me," she replied. "For taking me seriously."

Detective Mason's following smile made his eyes glitter with the personality of a kind soul. It was a lovely contrast to his grumpy exterior. "If there's one thing the war taught me, it's to never judge a thing by appearances."

Beatrice smiled wider.

"You kids take care now," Detective Mason said.

With final farewells and promises to keep in touch, Mason left their table to take control of the mess left in Flanagan's wake. Harry approached moments later, still flecked in David's blood and entirely disheveled, but no less attractive for it.

"That was a risky move," he said, "jumping in the car like that."

He sounded more impressed than exasperated, which caught Beatrice off guard. Patrick despised her risk taking and often treated her like a china doll that might break. Harry had known her all of one day, and there was more respect in his eyes than she'd seen out of Patrick in four months. That was just the way of things, she supposed. People in serious relationships never got along. Arguing was part of it. Even her father, who'd been married to her stepmother since Beatrice was five, never stopped arguing with his spouse. Whatever the case, Beatrice knew in that moment that she didn't want to lose Harry after this business.

"It was an impulse," Beatrice said, a gentle smile on her lips.

"I'm just glad you're all right," he said.

"Me too."

Eleanore yawned more animatedly than was necessary and pushed herself to her feet. "Well, I'm going to go find Mr. Morrow and see about a new room for the night. Surely there's still an honest bellhop around here somewhere. . . ."

She let her voice trail off and ambled through the dining room, leaving Harry and Beatrice alone.

"I never did say thank you," Beatrice said as Harry took a seat.

"What for?" he wondered.

"For your help. You didn't have to."

"What can I say? I enjoyed the company," he mused.

Beatrice chortled musically, drawing a charming smile from Harry. No more was said aloud. Their eyes did the rest of the talking, conveying their relief, their thanks, and their burgeoning kinship. A few moments passed as such before Beatrice withdrew her gaze.

"Well," she said decidedly, rising to her feet. "I'm beat. See you in the morning?"

Harry gave a short nod. "See you in the morning."

Beatrice felt her heart skip at the prospect, which was a foreign but not altogether unwelcome sensation. They shared a final smile before Beatrice turned toward the dining room's exit. Eleanore was at the front desk getting a new key from Mr. Morrow. Tommy went ahead of them, accompanied by an officer to move their bags. Morrow said nothing to Beatrice, but his parting smile was forced, and Beatrice couldn't help thinking that she'd just made her first enemy. He would lose his job for this, but in comparison to all the lives lost that night, Beatrice thought it a fair trade.

Arm in arm, Beatrice and Eleanore made their way upstairs, neither saying a word. They could think only of the two empty beds calling their names.

CHAPTER SEVENTEEN
The Telegram

Time seemed to speed up again with the murderers caught, and Beatrice was glad for it. It was as though they'd been trapped in some strange time bubble from an H. G. Wells novel that had burst the moment her head hit her pillow. Morning came much too quickly, but what a glorious morning it was. Sunshine streamed through the crack in the curtains, victorious over the long dark night, and the air was crisp and clear as it often was after a storm. Beatrice roused slowly, blinking back sleep, and stretched with a satisfied yawn. She could easily have slept for another few hours, having only managed three, but after such a treacherous evening, she and Eleanore had agreed to cut their vacation short, and they now had an eight o'clock train to catch. With this in mind, Beatrice managed to peel herself out of bed.

"Come on, darling. It's time to get up," she chirped at Eleanore, who had a pillow covering her face to block out the flecks of early morning light the curtains missed.

Eleanore groaned in response, her following words unintelligible.

Beatrice grinned wickedly and swiped a pillow from her bed, fleetly smacking her cousin with it. Eleanore popped up in a shock, letting loose a swear of frustration.

"Now, that is hardly ladylike," Beatrice teased. "Up you get. You have a case report to type up before we leave, remember?"

Eleanore groaned and fell back against her pillow, seeming to regret her offer from the night before.

Satisfied that she'd at least woken her cousin up, Beatrice turned for the bathroom and set about getting ready for the day. It felt like heaven to get cleaned up and put on a new face. The bruises from David's fingers had fully manifested by now, and no amount of makeup could truly hide them, so Beatrice accessorized with a lovely blue silk scarf to complement her bright-green dress. Eleanore was out of bed and moving by the time Beatrice left the bathroom.

"I'm going to get us a seat on the train," she said as Eleanore pulled on her robe.

"See if there's a compartment, would you?" asked Eleanore.

"Oh, don't worry. I will," Beatrice replied passionately. There was no way she'd face the day without a little more sleep, and a twelve-hour train ride was the perfect time to catch up. "Should I send someone up with coffee?"

"Please," answered Eleanore. "But to the library. I'm sure I'll be at the typewriter for a while."

With a nod of assent, Beatrice departed the room, surprisingly chipper for someone who'd had the night she'd had. The hotel seemed washed anew with sunlight streaming through it. Gone were the shadows that had seemed so daunting and the empty halls that had felt so long and eerie. Erased was the fear of failure. Walking through the hotel now, Beatrice never would have guessed that three murders had taken place the night before. She made her way to the station master's office to see about procuring a compartment on the train, then took fifteen minutes to call her mother and let her know what had happened before the papers could. Afterword, she headed to the dining room for breakfast, asking the nearest Harvey Girl to send a pot of coffee and plate of biscuits to the library for Eleanore. Once sure everything was in order, she sat at a table alone and ordered a coffee for herself. Harry soon joined her, looking every bit as tired as she was and sporting a wicked shiner.

"Heading out this morning?" she asked.

"Yep," he answered, setting his fedora on the table as he sat. "I start work next week. How's your throat?"

Beatrice touched her neck subconsciously. "Well, I don't sound like a frog anymore," she mused. "And your eye?"

"Looks worse than it feels," he assured her.

Sarah delivered Beatrice's coffee and asked what Harry would like. He ordered a coffee and a full breakfast, eying Beatrice with a look of concern. "Aren't you going to eat something?"

"I'm not really one for breakfast," she mused.

"She'll have the same," he told Alice, to which the Harvey Girl smiled and walked away. Beatrice was about to protest, but Harry interrupted her with, "Doctor's orders. You need to eat something. I'll even get the check."

Stubborn indignation tempted Beatrice to be annoyed, but another quieter voice murmured that it was almost sweet. "Thank you," she said quietly.

Alice came back with a coffee for Harry, and the two sat in silence for a moment, enjoying the stimulant. Beatrice used this moment to think, which must have shown in her eyes because Harry asked not a moment later, "What's on your mind?"

"Hmm?" she replied. "Oh . . . nothing. I'm just . . . pondering."

"I've known you for one night," Harry said, "and I know better than to think Beatrice Adams is ever just pondering."

Beatrice couldn't help smiling. "It's . . . well, there are just so many unanswered questions I still have."

"Such as?"

"We know Mrs. Vickeridge was supplying perfume bottles," said Beatrice, "but who was supplying the hooch? If we could figure that out, we'd shut down the whole operation."

"I like the way you say 'we,'" mused Harry.

Beatrice's cheeks colored. "Only if you want to, that is. I can't deny you've been extremely useful. Eleanore has no choice in the matter," she joked.

"I suppose someone has to watch your back while you watch your front," he said.

"Yes, you do take a punch rather well," she teased.

Harry subconsciously touched the shiner on his eye. "Don't remind me," he murmured.

Their food arrived then, piping hot, and Beatrice's stomach growled at the smell of it: bacon, eggs, toast, sausage, and jam. She had to give Harry credit for ordering her food. Apparently she was hungrier than she realized. She'd never say this aloud, of course. Her pride wouldn't allow it.

"Do you have any leads?" Harry asked as Beatrice peppered her eggs.

"Tiffany's notebook," she answered. "I didn't get very far—Flanagan interrupted me—but if the answers aren't there, a clue surely is. Detective Mason has agreed to mail it to me when he's through with it."

"Can he do that?" asked Harry.

"It probably isn't protocol," she admitted. "But he's agreed to do it anyhow."

"I have a feeling you get an awful lot of people to agree with you," Harry mused.

Beatrice nearly laughed. "Oh, please. You've caught me on a good day. Sparkling eyes can only get you so far."

Harry looked as though he wanted to comment on the latter subject, but Alice came by to refill both of their coffees before he could.

"Thanks," Beatrice said, beaming. She grazed over her eggs a little more, returning to her thoughts as the Harvey Girl walked away.

Harry sipped his coffee before shifting the conversation. "You girls staying after all this?"

Beatrice gingerly shook her head. "Heavens, no. I booked us a compartment on the first train home."

"We're taking the same train, then," he said.

Beatrice smiled. "Looks that way. Perhaps we can meet in the dining car later this afternoon. I'm sure I'll sleep most of the day away."

"You earned it."

They shared a smile.

"So did you," Beatrice replied. "I wouldn't have managed without you."

"I'm sure you would have," Harry said modestly.

"Darling, if it weren't for you, I'd be on a slab in some morgue and the murderer would have gotten away," she pointed out, using her butter knife for emphasis. "I highly doubt Eleanore would have taken Phillips on in the dark."

"I think you underestimate your cousin," said Harry.

"What makes you say that?" Beatrice wondered curiously.

"Sounds to me like you've been getting her into trouble for a long time," he mused.

"So?"

"She's still following you around, isn't she?"

Beatrice had to admit he had point, but she didn't voice it aloud. That would be to admit he was right, and Beatrice was too stubborn for that.

They finished their meal shortly after and said their farewells. Beatrice made her way back upstairs to see that everything was packed. Thankfully one night and a murder hadn't given them much time to unpack, so there wasn't much to do. Eleanore returned moments later with the completed case files. Beatrice looked them over, in awe of Eleanore's organization. The police couldn't have compiled a better report themselves. Beatrice carefully folded these and tucked them into an envelope from the desk, writing "*Joe Mason*" in her flowery but barely legible handwriting across the front. A knock on the door announced the bellhop, whom Eleanore let in with a smile. It was one of the boys who hadn't been on duty the day before, which was just as well, because neither of the girls felt much like talking about the murders after only half a night's sleep.

Once all their things had been loaded and carted off, the girls retreated arm in arm to the lobby, carry-ons and handbags in tow. Beatrice checked out with the front-desk clerk, also a fresh face, and left the envelope with him. Mason was set to pick it up later in the afternoon. Beatrice very much doubted Henry Morrow would still be the manager by the end of the week. Even if, by some miracle, he wasn't charged for accepting hush money from a mobster, the Fred Harvey Company was far too prestigious to keep such a man on staff, and Beatrice couldn't say she blamed them.

Eight o'clock soon arrived, and with it, the train. The station was a buzz of activity as porters rushed back and forth from the hotel to the baggage car. Passengers boarded and took their seats, the lucky few to snag compartments heading for the sleeper car. Once the train was rolling and the tickets had been collected, Beatrice and Eleanore happily climbed into their bunks and went back to sleep, lulled into dreamland by the steady rhythm of the train clacking along the tracks.

It was past two in the afternoon before Beatrice stirred, rising with a much-needed stretch in the top bunk. Eleanore was already awake, perched in the small armchair with a book.

"Morning, sunshine," Eleanore greeted.

"Morning indeed," Beatrice mused, climbing carefully down from her roost.

She disappeared into the tiny bathroom to freshen up. A bit of lipstick, some powder to her nose, some adjustments to her curls, and Beatrice looked as if she'd never spent the last six hours asleep. She leaned out of the bathroom.

"Hungry?" she asked Eleanore.

"Starving," came Eleanore's enthusiastic reply.

Together, they left their compartment behind and headed for the dining car. Harry was already at a table, perusing a newspaper, when they entered.

"Mind if we join you?" asked Beatrice as they approached.

Harry glanced up, smiling when he saw who'd spoken. "Not at all," he replied, gesturing to the two adjacent chairs.

"Anything interesting in the paper?" Beatrice intoned as she and Eleanore took their seats, Beatrice directly across from Harry.

"Oh, just something about a murder and a gorgeous redhead who saved the day," he joked, a sparkle in his eyes.

Beatrice gave a ruby-lipped smile. "I had a little help."

She nudged her fair-haired cousin, who smiled modestly.

"I didn't do that much," Eleanore murmured.

"You got the police!" Beatrice exclaimed. "Our goose would have been cooked without you!"

A faint blush tinted Eleanore's cheeks.

"How *did* you get the police?" queried Harry. "We thought Flanagan had you."

"He did," Eleanore revealed. "He had me tied to a chair in his room. I never really found out what he wanted."

"Bait for me, no doubt. The jackal," grumbled Beatrice.

"How did you get away?" asked Harry.

Eleanore dove into the tale, explaining how she'd escaped her bonds and climbed down the drainpipe. She ended in the diner, leaving Beatrice and Harry in stunned silence.

"Boy," Beatrice marveled. "When I said get some moxie, you really went for it!"

The three of them burst into laughter as the waiter came by with two extra waters and asked what the newcomers would like. Beatrice ordered a sandwich, and Eleanore decided on soup. Beatrice imagined her cousin still felt a little off after her jaunt in the rain. Her gaze was drawn thoughtfully to the window as the waiter departed, and she was captivated by the swirls of sunlight and the glow of its rays against the earth. It was like hope incarnate.

"Feels like a whole new world, doesn't it?" mused Beatrice, her eyes fixed on the desert scenery passing by.

"You know, it really does," Harry agreed.

Eleanore asked Harry about his new job, but their voices faded into the background as Beatrice's mind slipped dreamily away. Despite the bruising on her neck and her brushes with danger, Beatrice had never felt more alive than she did in that moment.There were certainly aspects of her job that needed fine tuning, but she could see it all so clearly now. She could turn the library into office space and hire Eleanore as her official secretary and occasional partner. Harry was quite right, Beatrice realized, about her underestimating Eleanore.

When the moment demanded it, her cousin could rise to the occasion, even if she did so with a few complaints. If the Winslow affair hit the papers, clients might roll in, and Beatrice would never be above assisting the police. In her mind, it all seemed so picture-perfect, and the thought made her smile.

The rest of the afternoon passed pleasantly, all events from the night before serving to have brought them all together. Eleanore managed to find a pack of playing cards after lunch, and they spent a few hours beating one another at Mau-Mau, all the world's troubles nothing more than a bad dream.

Night fell as the train rattled on, and sometime after eight, it pulled into the station. The three friends gathered their carry-ons and departed the train together. The sight of the station's polished floors and vaulted ceilings filled Beatrice with a sense of homecoming. While she adored a good adventure, there was something magical about returning home afterward. Loved ones were reunited all around them, whistles sounded, steam billowed, and conversation filled in the refrain. The girls were laughing at something Harry had said while they set off for their baggage, when the crowd suddenly parted ahead of them, and there stood a refined gentleman with dark hair slicked back with pomade, a groomed mustache, and a ritzy suit. He was holding a bouquet of roses.

"Patrick!" Beatrice exclaimed in astonishment. "What on earth are you doing here?"

"Surprising my best girl," he replied confidently, kissing her cheek as she approached and handing her the roses. "Your mother told me what happened. I thought you and Ellie could use a ride."

"That'd be swell!" Eleanore enthused.

Harry stood awkwardly by, shoving his hands into his pockets.

Patrick shortly noticed his presence. "And who is this fine fellow?"

"Oh!" Beatrice cried, realizing introductions were in order. "Pat, this is Dr. Harry Riley. We met in Winslow. He's moved here from New York to take up a post at the hospital."

Patrick stuck out a hand in cordial greeting. "Patrick Hollister," he introduced himself. "Welcome to Los Angeles."

Harry shook Patrick's hand, seemingly starstruck. "As in . . . the film producer Patrick Hollister?" he asked.

"One and the same," Patrick proclaimed proudly. He reclaimed his hand, settling it on the small of Beatrice's back. "Say, we better get a move on, honey. Your mother was in hysterics when I left."

"When is she not?" sighed Beatrice. She adjusted her flowers so she could shake Harry's hand one last time, feeling a sinking feeling she didn't completely understand. "I'll be in touch," she promised.

"Looking forward to it," Harry replied.

Despite her gloves, Beatrice's hand burned when Harry reclaimed his, and she fleetly reaffirmed her grip on her roses as if it would help. Patrick steered her toward the baggage claim, but her gaze lingered behind her. She couldn't help thinking that Harry looked like he'd just lost all his dough betting on the wrong horse.

"He'll be fine, honey," Patrick assured her.

A moment later, they were swallowed by the crowd, and Harry was lost from view. Patrick tipped a porter to see to their bags, leaving Eleanore and Beatrice alone for a moment.

"What's wrong?" Eleanore sang in a tone that suggested she knew the look on Beatrice's face all too well.

"What? Nothing is wrong," defended Beatrice.

"You look like someone just gave you a sockdolager," mused Eleanore. "Don't worry. We'll see him again."

"Oh, I'm not worried about that," said Beatrice, though she certainly could be if she let herself. In earnest, the last two days had been such a whirlwind.

"Then cheer up, sweetie," Eleanore said, touching a hand to her cousin's arm. "Patrick is watching, and you know how he feels about your post-case moods."

Beatrice nodded and plastered a well-practiced smile on her face that could fool the world's brightest flashbulbs.

"What are you chicks chattering about?" Patrick called, standing near the cart with the porter. "Let's go. I've got a meeting early in the morning."

"Just jabbering, darling," Beatrice assured him, looping arms with her cousin. "We're coming."

As they ventured behind Patrick and the struggling porter in the direction of the car, Beatrice couldn't help thinking that the best thing in the world would be more sleep. This thought prompted her to insist Eleanore stay the night rather than worry about a cab and the long drive back to Pasadena. Eleanore readily agreed.

The ride home in Patrick's souped-up roadster was an interesting one. Patrick acted as though Beatrice should have been the damsel in distress through the whole of the Winslow employment, voicing concern over the risks she'd taken, and once more stating his dislike for her chosen profession, again expressing that he could get her an acting gig anytime she decided. Beatrice took all his usual complaints in stride, laughing in good fun at his childishness. She'd never held much stock in his opinions and was too stout of heart to let him sway her decisions. By the time they'd pulled up to the Adams estate, they'd exhausted nearly all topics of conversation.

The moment the car parked in the roundabout driveway, at the center of which gurgled an exquisite fountain, the butler exited the house and approached the vehicle.

"Welcome home, Miss Adams," he greeted as he opened the passenger door. "Miss Hughes."

He handed them each out of the car in turn.

"Owens, old boy," Patrick addressed as he let himself out of the driver's side. "Mind fetching us a brandy after you've seen to the bags?"

"Not at all, sir," replied Owens.

Beatrice leaned in and murmured to the butler, "How's mother?"

Owens's face took on the more casual expression of a trusted friend as he answered, "Same as ever, I'm afraid. There'll be no scotch left soon enough."

Beatrice sighed in worry. "Well, I'm glad she's had you here to look after her."

The butler smiled and dipped his head as if to say it was his pleasure.

Beatrice turned for the house, but Owens's voice stopped her in her tracks.

"Oh, there's a telegram for you, miss. Came this afternoon. I've left it on the hall table for you."

"Thank you, Owens," Beatrice replied over her shoulder.

Unlike some who had the privilege of servants, Beatrice viewed Owens as part of the family. She treated him with the utmost respect, and he was exceedingly loyal in return.

Patrick and Eleanore had disappeared inside already, and Beatrice followed suit, leaving Owens to the bags. Beatrice was little surprised to find her cousin already at the top of the curved grand staircase with its glorious Art Deco handrails. Patrick had made himself comfortable in the parlor just off the foyer, perusing a nearby newspaper. Beatrice removed her gloves as she approached the round marble table at the center of the entry hall. Owens always kept fresh flowers in the vase here. Today they were brightly colored orchids. A telegram envelope was perched against the vase. Beatrice snatched it up curiously and opened it to read:

Flanagan dead. I suspect foul play. I will call when I know more. Be careful.
—Joe Mason

It felt like someone had slapped her. Beatrice stood, dumbfounded, reading the telegram over and over as if the words might change by her diligence. They remained as cutting as ever.

"Something the matter, darling?" Patrick called from the parlor, noting her expression.

Beatrice startled. "What—oh, no. Just a thank-you card," she lied, tucking the telegram into her handbag. "I think I might head to bed too. I'm beat." She crossed into the parlor and kissed his cheek. "Don't stay too late."

"Sure, honey," he promised. "We'll chat tomorrow."

Beatrice dashed up the stairs with a little more haste than necessary for someone on her way to bed, but she couldn't contain herself. She was so intent on her mission to find Eleanore that she nearly flattened her mother in the upstairs hall.

"Where's the fire, darling?" Virginia laughed, her voice deep and a hint scratchy but no less affectionate. She wore an extravagant silk robe in peacock blue with a turquoise feathered fringe, and her hair was done up in curlers.

CHAPTER SEVENTEEN

"Hello, mother," Beatrice said, embracing the older but no less beautiful redhead. "Not heading down for a nightcap, I hope."

"Oh, don't be silly," Virginia said with a dramatic wave of her hand. "Warm milk, honey. Only warm milk."

Beatrice quirked an eyebrow, her eyes boring through her mother with loving ferocity. "Bed. No nightcap for you. Come on now." She gently shoved her mother away from the stairs. "We've talked about this."

"You're right. You're right," Virginia sighed. "I'm better off without it. Besides, you're home now. A mother can rest easy. Did you solve the case, my pet?"

Beatrice couldn't help smiling. Of all the people in her life, her mother was the most supportive of Beatrice's choices. While she knew her mother would probably support a career in larceny with equal fervor, Beatrice never took her mother's love for granted. "Mostly," she answered. "I still have a few puzzle pieces that need finding."

"Excellent. Excellent," cooed her mother.

They arrived outside the white and gold door of the master bedroom, and Beatrice pushed her mother eagerly through it. "Bed," she ordered. "I'll tell you all about it over breakfast. I promise."

Virginia sighed. "All right. Goodnight, my darling."

She patted Beatrice's cheek, and Beatrice smiled fondly, closing the door once her mother had retreated through it. Beatrice had no doubt her mother was listening at the door, waiting for her to leave, but at least now her voice would be in her mother's head. She waited until her mother's shadow left the crack of light beneath the door before she continued down the open, railed hall toward the guest room. A large waterfall chandelier of fine crystal glittered in the triangular opening between the staircase and the upper hall, aided in lighting the upstairs by beautiful gold wall sconces. An elaborate carpet runner quieted her footsteps as she picked up the pace and knocked urgently on the guest room door.

"Come in," said Eleanore.

Beatrice burst into the room to find Eleanore sitting at the vanity running a bristle brush through her blonde hair. Eleanore caught sight of her cousin's expression in the vanity mirror. She turned immediately toward Beatrice, the brush in her hand forgotten.

"What's happened?" Eleanore demanded.

Beatrice yanked the telegram from her handbag and held it out. "I just received this from Detective Mason. He must have sent it a mere hour after getting the evidence from the hotel."

Eleanore opened the envelope swiftly and read the telegram, her countenance falling. "But if Flanagan is dead, then—"

"Then our case is falling apart!" cried Beatrice, flinging herself dramatically on the double bed. "Oh Ellie, how could I be so *stupid* as to think this would all be easy?"

Eleanore fixed her soft blue eyes pointedly on her cousin. "Beatrice Darlene Adams, you are not stupid!"

"Then I'm a fool," muttered Beatrice.

"Malarkey!" snapped Eleanore. "You're human. This isn't some dime novel. You're not Sherlock Holmes, for goodness' sake. What you are is a stubborn, indignant, good-hearted girl who can't stop until the puzzle is solved. Detective Mason said he would call you, didn't he?"

"Yes," sighed Beatrice.

"Then get to bed, missy. It'll all be jake tomorrow."

It dawned on Beatrice that their roles had seemingly reversed, and she sat up with a curious expression. "When did you get so tenacious?"

"When a mobster tied me to a chair," mused Eleanore, a soft smile crossing her lips. "Now go. You still have a mystery to solve. You need the sleep."

Beatrice gave an appreciative smile in return. "Thanks, Ellie." She rose and kissed her cousin on the cheek. "Goodnight, darling!"

"Sweet dreams," wished Eleanore.

Beatrice crossed the room to leave, but Owens appeared at the door with Eleanore's bags in hand before she could exit. "Your bags, Miss Hughes," he said.

Beatrice stepped aside to let him in.

"Thank you, Owens. Just put them at the end of the bed," said Eleanore.

The butler did as requested and then turned to Beatrice. "I've already returned yours to your room," he said to Beatrice.

"Thanks, honey," replied Beatrice.

"Can I do anything else for you?" he asked.

"That will be all, Owens. Has Patrick left yet?" she wondered.

"Yes ma'am. I saw him out myself," the butler assured her.

"Good. I'm off to bed, then. Lock up and get some rest yourself."

She patted his arm and left the guest room, heading for her own with a mind newly burdened. Four bodies. Four *murders*. There had to be something she'd missed. How had she let this happen? Realizing there would be no new leads until morning, Beatrice resigned herself to sleep. She could take a look at the puzzle again after Detective Mason called . . . if he called.

CHAPTER EIGHTEEN

An Unexpected Package

A long, agonizing week passed without a single call from Detective Mason. Every time Beatrice passed the rotary phone in the hall, she eyed it desperately, willing it to ring. When it did, it was usually something trivial: an invite to a party, Patrick asking about auditions that Beatrice didn't want, or someone trying to reach her mother. Beatrice hung up after each of these feeling dejected and exasperated. No amount of soothing from her mother or Eleanore could placate her growing anxiety, and Patrick was unsympathetic to her worry. It was his view that the events in Winslow should be a deterrent to further detective work, and any time Beatrice tried to argue, he'd point out the greening bruises she still hid beneath colored scarves.

Eleanore was a shining light through it all. She quickly recognized the growing melancholy setting in and elected to prolong her stay in an attempt to lift Beatrice's spirits. On the morning of the eighth day, the pair of them sat on the terrace for a late breakfast, Beatrice in a pair of maroon sailor trousers with a navy-blue knit shirt and Eleanore in a dress of blue floral print. Eleanore was in the middle of buttering her toast when Beatrice, skimming the newspaper, ejected, "Well . . . I'll be damned!"

Eleanore paused and looked up curiously. When Beatrice gave no explanation, she asked, "What is it? Some newfangled doodad hitting the market you feel the need to throw money at?"

Beatrice cast her cousin a pointed look over the top of her paper. "No. The paper has done a write-up on the murders."

"Did they forget to include you?" Eleanore teased, returning to buttering her toast.

"Do you want me to say or not?"

Eleanore waved with her knife for Beatrice to elaborate and bit carefully into the buttered bread so as not to smudge her lipstick.

"They pay homage to Tiffany, of course—she was one of theirs—but when they mention Mrs. Vickeridge . . ." Beatrice trailed off.

Eleanore swallowed her toast. "Well, are you going to leave me in suspense? Or do you want me to guess?"

"It looks like her entire fortune went to her son," said Beatrice, laying down the paper. "It's no wonder Mr. Vickeridge was so torn up by her death. He's penniless."

"Only if the son refuses to share. I can't imagine a child not looking out for their out-of-luck parents."

"Don't be such a boob, Ellie," said Beatrice. "If he thought for one moment that his son would look out for him, he would only be half as torn up as he was. He didn't love Martha. I'd wager their marriage died long ago. No, he was too distraught. I'll bet you anything he and his son don't get along."

"Would you eat something?" Eleanore prodded. "I feel like a cow over here. You haven't even touched your eggs."

Beatrice huffed and shoveled a forkful of eggs into her mouth to appease her cousin, prompting Eleanore to cast her a sympathetic look.

"Still no call?" Eleanore pried.

"Not even one from Mr. Riley," said Beatrice, deciding on toast. A few crumbs littered her shirt when she bit into it. She brushed them away.

"Maybe he's just busy," suggested Eleanore.

Beatrice shrugged. "I thought he'd call when he was settled to at least let us know how to reach him."

"It's only been a week, darling," Eleanore pointed out. "Give the man some time. You did sort of spring Patrick on him at the last moment. I'm sure his head is reeling."

Beatrice looked incredulous. "Whatever do you mean?"

Eleanore set her fork down deliberately as if her next words needed the full force of her attention. "I love you, Bea, but sometimes you can be a real lamebrain."

"Says you!" Beatrice exclaimed.

"Would you let me finish?" said Eleanore.

Beatrice closed her mouth begrudgingly.

"I don't think you realize just how much you dazzle people," Eleanore continued. "It's going to get you into trouble one of these days."

"Dazzle people?" Beatrice repeated.

"Harry Riley is positively smitten with you, and he looked like someone had given him a sockdolager when Patrick showed up at the station. I thought for sure you'd at least *mentioned* Patrick, but honestly, Bea . . ."

"Oh, don't '*Honestly, Bea*' me," snapped Beatrice. "You make me out to be some sort of minx! I was only being myself. You know what men are like."

"Actually, I don't," mused Eleanore. "It's usually you they fawn over. Not that I'm complaining. From the bleachers, it looks like too much to juggle."

Beatrice was flabbergasted. She gaped at her cousin as if Eleanore had accused her of adultery and murder all in the same charge. "It's not like I *dazzle* people on purpose," she sizzled.

"That is precisely my *point*," replied Eleanore. "Be careful. That's all I'm saying." And with an innocent shrug, she returned to her toast.

It was just as well. Owens stepped outside a breath later clearly bearing news.

"Yes, Owens. What is it?" asked Beatrice, her tone sharper than she'd meant to be.

"A telephone call for you, miss," said Owens, unbothered by her abruptness, "from a Mr. Mason."

Beatrice nearly overturned the table in her haste to get up, knocking over the salt but thankfully nothing else.

"Careful, honey!" Eleanore complained, but Beatrice hardly heard her.

She dashed through the French doors that led into the parlor and sped for the foyer and the hall phone, which sat on its little table in the curve of the stairs with the receiver set gently beside it. She fleetly pressed the phone to her ear.

"This is Beatrice," she greeted politely, trying not to sound too out of breath.

"Hello, Miss Adams," came Detective Mason's gruff voice over the line. "I hope I haven't disturbed you."

"Not at all," Beatrice said eagerly.

"Good. Good," he said. "I don't have much time, so I suppose I'll get right down to business. I take it you received my telegram."

"Oh, boy, did I ever," said Beatrice. "You gonna fill me in, ace? Or do I have to shake it out of you?"

Mason chuckled. "It's been a real mess here since you left. I would have called sooner, but I didn't want to drag you back into this unless I had to."

"As if I mind," mused Beatrice. "What's the scoop?"

"Flanagan was found dead in his hospital bed the morning after the accident—asphyxiation," said Mason. "From the looks of things, someone held a pillow over his face. As many broken bones as he had, there was no way he could have fended off his attacker."

"Jeepers," breathed Beatrice.

"You sure you want to stay tangled up in this, kid?" asked Mason. "People around this case seem to end up dead."

"That's precisely why I intend to solve it," said Beatrice. "Did anyone see or hear anything?"

"No. But the night nurse could have been paid off."

"Didn't you have guards posted or something?"

"Of course," Mason replied. "No one but the hospital staff went in or out of that room all night."

"The assassin was dressed as one of them, then," Beatrice reasoned. "It's the only explanation."

"I was starting to think very much the same thing. I've got the boys writing down every detail they can remember, but I don't expect we'll catch a break."

"What about the evidence?" asked Beatrice. "Is it safe?"

"That's the other thing I wanted to call about. I've mailed it to you with further instructions. It should be arriving today."

Beatrice breathed a sigh of relief. She'd take any shred of good news she could get.

"I'll keep an eye out for it," she promised.

"Be careful, Miss Adams," Mason requested with sincerity. "Whoever bumped off Flanagan may come after you next."

"I will. Call me if anything changes."

"Yep."

They said their goodbyes, and Beatrice hung up the phone lost in thought, Detective Mason's words repeating themselves over and over as if she'd spot a pattern by their repetition. No matter how many times she went through it, one detail bothered her: How had the killer known about Flanagan's arrest so quickly?

"Is everything all right, Miss Adams?" asked Owens. He stood in the doorway to the parlor, watching her with the concern of a loved one who'd known her since she was small. Beatrice would forever praise the day her grandparents had appointed Owens to the family.

"Yes," she answered. Owens didn't seem convinced, so she added, "Just some new puzzle pieces, that's all. There's an important package arriving today. Can you keep an eye out for the courier?"

"Of course, miss," Owens assured her. "Shall I clear the table?"

Beatrice thought on it before replying, "Not yet. I think I'll have another cup of coffee."

"Very good," Owens said with a smile. He departed for the kitchen to instruct the cook, a warm and rotund woman named Anna, to warm up another pot.

Beatrice returned to the terrace at a far slower pace than she had before, and Eleanore looked up eagerly at her cousin's return.

CHAPTER EIGHTEEN

"Well," pressed Eleanore, "what did he say?"

Beatrice reclaimed her seat and took a thoughtful bite of cold toast. "Someone smothered Flanagan in his sleep," she answered once she'd swallowed. "But who would be bold enough to pose as a nurse? And how did they know?"

"How did they know what?" asked Eleanore.

"Where Flanagan was. That he'd been arrested," supplied Beatrice. "Donavan's mob is here in Los Angeles. Even if word had gotten back here, it would have taken time to send someone. The train ride alone is at least twelve hours."

"Unless someone was already there," said Eleanore, pushing her polished plate away.

Beatrice perked up. "Say that again."

"I said unless someone was already there."

"Yes," Beatrice agreed, "someone who was keeping an eye on things from a distance. But who?"

Owens came outside then with fresh coffee, which he set on the table between them.

"Thank you, darling," Beatrice said absentmindedly. She practically stared a hole through the table as if the answer would be revealed, etched into the glass. Owens departed.

Eleanore fixed Beatrice's coffee and pushed it toward her with a quiet "Bea."

"Hmm? Oh, thank you," Beatrice murmured, taking up her cup and marking it with red lipstick on her first sip.

Her mind was a maze of information, and the more she combed through the facts, the more clouded the answers became. The assassin could be anyone at the hotel or even someone who'd been on the police force, loathe though she was to think it. If Harry hadn't been with them on the train all day, sneaking into a hospital with ease might have made her suspicious of him all over again.

"How do you feel about some minor detective work?" she asked her cousin after a length of silence.

"It depends on the work," mused Eleanore. "I'm quite content having things back to normal."

"We need to find Harry. Hospitals are his area of expertise, and he might have noticed something we missed."

"Are you sure he *wants* to see you?" chimed Eleanore.

"Oh, don't start that again," huffed Beatrice.

Eleanore hid a smile behind her own sip of coffee, and the two fell into a companionable silence. Beatrice didn't want to admit it, but she was rather afraid Harry might not want to see her. Perhaps she had been a little too charismatic. She could never tell. Patrick seemed quite immune, but then he was surrounded by Hollywood elites on a daily basis. It seemed all they did was argue these days, which her mother swore was a sign of affection. Whatever the case, Beatrice wanted to set it straight. Harry's company was a breath of fresh air, and his mind was a valuable asset. She doubted she'd find another doctor in the whole of Los Angeles County who would willingly assist her if she asked. Even with the blessing of former-Detective-now-Captain Raglan, the district coroner still didn't like her. Harry's countenance and expertise could be a help in opening those otherwise stuck doors.

With this determination foremost in her mind, Beatrice tucked her newly batteried flashlight, driver's license, coin purse, and some business cards into a navy-blue handbag and then telephoned for a cab, lamenting the absence of her Lincoln roadster—that was the last time she'd agree to a street race. Hopefully it would be out of the shop soon. Eleanore squeezed into the cab beside her when it arrived, and Beatrice rattled off the address for Los Angeles County Hospital. The half-hour drive was made in silence. Beatrice spent the majority of it staring out the window and contemplating what she would say when she saw Harry. Nothing seemed adequate.

They exited the cab curbside when it pulled up outside the edifice, and Beatrice handed the appropriate cash plus tip through the driver's window, adding a cheery "Thanks!" Car horns honked in the distance mingled with the squeal of bus brakes as motor vehicles big and small navigated the street blocks around the hospital. People crowded the sidewalk around them in a steady stream left and right, making a straight path to the door impossible. Beatrice took her cousin's hand, and they made a zigzag through the throng of city dwellers. It was a relief to yank open the hospital door and enter the small foyer. An exiting gentleman held the next door open for them, and Beatrice beamed with a hearty "Thank you" as they passed through, Eleanore mimicking her sentiment. The hospital's reception area had beautiful polished floors, decorative high ceilings, and warm wall sconces that made it feel like a nice place to stay a while.

A kindly woman sat behind the reception desk with her blonde hair pulled back in a perfect bun. Not a single wrinkle could be found in her uniform. When Beatrice and Eleanore approached, she greeted them with a warm smile.

"Can I help you?" she offered.

"Yes," Beatrice replied, leaning against the counter. "We're looking for Dr. Harry Riley. You wouldn't happen to know where we could find him, would you?"

"Let me check the directory," the receptionist said, pulling a book from a slot in front of her.

It took all of Beatrice's strength not to tap her foot impatiently as the woman flipped page by page through the book.

She shook her head. "I don't see a Dr. Riley on the register."

Beatrice was about to open her mouth when Eleanore's hand on her arm cut off the redhead mid-breath.

"He would only have been here a week," said Eleanore in a gentle tone that could get her through any door.

"Then it's possible he wouldn't be in the book yet," the receptionist reasoned.

"Can you page him?" asked Beatrice, trying with all her might not to sound too eager.

The receptionist gave a sugary smile as if she'd like nothing more than for Beatrice to leave. "Of course," she said, lifting the intercom receiver in front of her from its perch. The speakers crackled around the hospital, and the blonde's perfect pronunciation announced, "Paging Dr. Riley. Please come to reception. Paging Dr. Riley. Please come to reception."

She hung up the phone-like device and smiled up at the cousins. "Will that be all?"

"Yes," said Eleanore. "Thank you."

She tugged Beatrice gently away from the reception desk, and it was only then that Beatrice realized a small queue had begun to form behind them.

"Well," huffed Beatrice, "she was cheery."

"Oh, stuff it," said Eleanore. "You've never had to work a job like that in your life."

"And you have?" Beatrice accused.

"I volunteered two summers at the library," said Eleanore. "Remember?"

"Oh, yes . . . you wore that horrible sweater," teased Beatrice.

"Wasn't it yours?" quipped Eleanore in return.

They shared a smile, nearly laughing.

"Relax, darling," Eleanore continued. "I'm sure there's a reason he didn't leave us an address, and I'll bet it has nothing to do with anything *you* did."

Beatrice didn't know how her cousin could possibly have known her innermost fear, but then she supposed they were as good as siblings. She doubted there was another in the whole of the world who knew her as well as Eleanore Hughes.

Their patience paid off a few minutes later when, dressed in a suit with a doctor's white coat over the top, Harry Riley came striding their way across the lobby. A heart-stopping smile crossed his face at the sight of them, and Beatrice felt relief wash over her. That was hardly the smile of a man who didn't want to see her.

"Well, this is a pleasant surprise," he mused. "I didn't expect to hear from you so soon."

"Nor did I," admitted Beatrice. "Something has come up . . . and you didn't leave an address for me to reach you at. I figured I'd bump into you here . . . sooner or later."

"Is everything all right?" asked Harry, countenance one of immediate concern.

Beatrice smiled at his expression. "I tell you something has come up, and you're already worried."

"Well . . . it is *you*," he reasoned.

"He has a point," said Eleanore.

Beatrice waved a hand as if to bat away their points and plunged on. "We need to talk somewhere we can't be overheard. Can you come by the house for dinner?"

Harry fidgeted uncomfortably. "You sure your fella won't mind?"

"Mind? Why should he?" asked Beatrice.

Harry took a moment to fish for an answer, but Eleanore beat him to it.

"Patrick had words with you, didn't he?"

Harry scratched his neck. "He might have stopped by and told me to lay off."

"He did *what*?" cried Beatrice. Her voice echoed in the vaulted room, and every eye turned their way. She quieted. "Oh, he'll get an earful from me. It's none of his business who I befriend. It's not as if he doesn't work with other women."

Beatrice's reply brought an easy smile to Harry's lips, and all the tension seemed to melt away at her disregard for Patrick's opinion.

"My shift isn't over until seven," said Harry.

"Perfect," replied Beatrice, beaming. "I'll tell Anna to have dinner ready by seven thirty."

"Sounds swell."

"Do you need the address?"

"I've still got your card," he assured her. "I better get back to work. It's a madhouse upstairs."

"It was lovely to see you again," chimed Eleanore.

"You too," he assured her.

With a final smile and farewell to them both, Harry departed for the elevator to get back to his duties. Beatrice and Eleanore retreated through the main door and stood on the curb to hail a cab, the former fuming.

"The nerve of Patrick!" Beatrice ejected. "What does he think he's going to do? Lock me in a room?"

"I'm sure if it wasn't frowned upon, he would," mused Eleanore. "You don't have to put up with him, you know."

"Oh, fiddle-faddle," said Beatrice. "He just needs reminding that

I'm not a doll."

A vacant cab finally drove up the street and, via eye contact, a wave, and a surprising whistle, Beatrice managed to flag it down. She climbed into the backseat with her cousin and gave her home address. She was still fuming as the cab pulled away, but she kept it internal. Beatrice knew well enough the quiet argument that would follow. Eleanore would again tell her she could leave Patrick any time she pleased, and Beatrice would counter that she was perfectly content. Patrick had been good to her family, unafraid to share his wealth when, for a brief moment, Beatrice's grandparents—namely her grandmother—had refused to bail her mother out of a hole Virginia's drinking habits had caused. Beatrice would never forget that kindness, and life was too unpredictable in the current climate to risk losing such an ally.

Beatrice promptly paid the cab driver when he parked in the circle drive outside her home. It was quieter in Bel Air than in the middle of the city, the gurgling fountain and the occasional singing bird the only noticeable soundtrack. Owens, ever on top of things, opened the front door before Beatrice could even knock. She beamed at him.

"Thank you, Owens."

"Of course, miss," he said, dipping his head.

"Let Anna know we'll have a guest for dinner around seven thirty," said Beatrice as Owens closed the door behind them.

"Yes, ma'am. Oh, that package arrived for you. I placed it in your room for security's sake."

Beatrice's whole world seemed to jolt with electricity. "Thank you!" she enthused, kissing his cheek and tearing up the staircase at top speed.

"Good heavens," Owens chuckled, rubbing the lipstick stain away.

"Wait for me!" cried Eleanore, trying but failing to keep up with Beatrice, who was far better than she at running in heels.

Beatrice burst through her bedroom door into a room of resplendent coral and gold. The package in question, which sat on her double bed, was a small rectangular parcel tied with twine and postmarked from Winslow. She snatched it up and tugged anxiously at the twine as she sat on the end of her bed. Eleanore came into the room, huffing and puffing, and sat herself on the vanity stool. When Beatrice managed to get the wrappings open, she tilted not only Tiffany's notebook from the box but also an unmarked key and a small luggage claim ticket for the La Grande Station. Her brow wrinkled. She'd only been expecting the notebook.

A letter addressed to Beatrice had also fallen out of the box. She fleetly opened it to read a handwritten note from Detective Mason.

Miss Adams,

I think your theory about the Donavan mob may be true. Ever since you left, strange things have been happening here. Your case notes, the ones you were meant to leave me, they weren't there when I arrived to collect them despite the clerk swearing you'd dropped them off. Then I get to the station to find out Flanagan's dead—killed in his sleep. I immediately secreted all the evidence out of the station, which proved a good idea. Someone tried to break into evidence not half an hour later. It feels like I'm being watched at every turn. Someone is trying desperately to bury this case. I'm mailing everything of interest I've found to you. This goes entirely against protocol, and I could lose everything if this goes pear-shaped, so get out there and solve this thing. *After what you've already pulled, I have no doubt you can.*

I'm sure I don't need to tell you to check out the La Grande Station. You're a clever dame. Cleverer than any I've met before. Find out what that luggage tag is for, and maybe you'll figure out what that key goes to. I doubt we'll pin one on Nikki Donavan through all this, but do me a favor, kid—put a heck of a dent in his armor.

Stay safe out there.

Joe Mason

Beatrice felt elated and burdened all at once. That Detective Mason was placing his entire career in her hands was a massive gesture of faith. She picked up the key and turned it between her fingers thoughtfully.

"Well, what did it say?" demanded Eleanore.

Beatrice was jolted from her thoughts, nearly having forgotten her cousin's presence. She held the letter out to Eleanore to read for herself. Eleanore did so swiftly, her eyes moving back and forth across the paper as if she were watching a race. Her face held the emotion of disbelief with such grace that she almost looked like a painting.

"This is madness," she finally said.

Beatrice nodded. "I quite agree, but what puzzle isn't?"

Again, she eyed the key, pondering all the things it could possibly belong to. The obvious answer was a trunk, but Beatrice would almost be disappointed if it were that easy. Almost. The thought of bodies piling up was a cause for worry. If someone else tied to the case and to the Donavan mob was still lurking about, then everyone close to Beatrice was in danger. She needed to solve this with all due haste, or the next dead body might be someone she couldn't bear to lose.

CHAPTER NINETEEN
THE DINNER PARTY

It was seven forty before the doorbell rang, announcing Harry's arrival for dinner. Beatrice and Eleanore sat in the parlor, the former nursing a coffee and the latter a cup of tea with milk. Both looked up expectantly at the ring. Owens passed by the open parlor arch, crossed the foyer, and opened the door Though she couldn't see Harry from her perch, Beatrice could hear him, and a smile quirked on her lips. He wasn't the least bit fazed at the door being answered by a butler, and she couldn't help wondering just how much opulence he'd left behind for his new life.

"I'm here to see Miss Adams," said Harry.

"Of course, sir," replied Owens. "Right this way. Shall I take your hat and coat?"

"Yes, thank you."

A moment later, Owens strode into the parlor and announced Harry's arrival. "Mr. Riley for you, miss. Shall I instruct the cook to serve dinner?"

"That'd be aces," Beatrice said to Owens, rising to shake Harry's hand. "I see you found the place all right."

"Sure did," said Harry. "Sorry I'm late. The traffic was terrible."

"Oh, pishposh," said Beatrice with a dismissive wave of her hand.

Harry turned to Eleanore next, cordially shaking her hand. Eleanore smiled. "It's lovely to see you again," she greeted.

He returned her sentiments.

"Would you like a cocktail or a coffee before dinner?" offered Beatrice.

"Oh, no. I'm fine, thanks."

Beatrice returned to her seat, and Harry perched in the vacant armchair, elbows resting casually on his knees. "You gonna tell me what happened?"

"I'd make you guess, but I'm afraid I'm all out of door prizes," teased Beatrice. "Flanagan is dead."

"You're kidding!" Harry exclaimed.

"Not even a little," chimed Eleanore.

Beatrice shook her head. "Detective Mason telegrammed the day we left to let me know, and he's sent all the evidence here. He thinks someone is trying to bury the case."

"Does anyone know he sent the evidence here?" asked Harry.

Beatrice sipped her coffee with a shrug. "I'm not sure. This whole case has been a sporadic game of cat and mouse."

"You better be careful. Whoever killed Flanagan could come after you next."

"Oh, I didn't even think of that," groaned Eleanore. Newfound courage did not equal newfound sense of adventure, it seemed.

"Don't worry, Ellie," said Beatrice. "I'm sending you home in the morning."

Eleanore looked torn between wanting to stay and wanting to flee, but even if she did protest, Beatrice was adamant on sending her cousin home If any goons came poking about the house, Beatrice would feel better knowing Eleanore wasn't around to get caught in the middle.

"What did you need my help with?" asked Harry.

"Well, Flanagan was killed in his hospital bed, and there were guards posted at the door," said Beatrice. "I have a theory that the killer posed as a member of staff to get inside, but I wondered if that would be possible. You have a mind for hospitals more than I do."

"Sure, it could be possible," said Harry. "It'd take a cool personality, though. And they'd have to get their hands on a uniform. Sometimes high-profile patients have a list of staff members who are the only people allowed in the room. Your killer would have either bribed his way onto it or paid someone to look the other way."

"Given the times, I've a feeling it's the latter," sighed Beatrice.

That seemed to be the way with this case: payoffs and bump-offs.

Virginia Adams entered the parlor then, dressed for dinner in an extravagant dress of deep blue.

"Darling! You didn't tell me we were having a guest for dinner," she said, extending a hand to greet Harry. "Virginia Adams."

Harry stood at her presence and accepted her hand, kissing it respectfully. "Harry Riley. It's a pleasure."

"And so polite too," mused Virginia, looking Harry over in appraisal. "Beatrice has told me all about you, of course. I suppose I owe you thanks."

Beatrice suppressed a smile. For all his good breeding, Harry was clearly starstruck. There once was a time when her mother had graced the silver screens frequently.

"Oh, it was . . . my pleasure," he assured her. "Your daughter is well worth the price of a shiner."

At that Beatrice colored, Harry's fading black eye less noticeable but still present. Owens thankfully entered then.

"Dinner is served," the butler said.

"Oh, splendid, Owens. Splendid!" said Virginia.

The older redhead departed the parlor and retreated down the lavishly decorated hall with a certain swagger. Eleanore and Beatrice set their drinks aside and stood in unison. Harry gestured politely for them to go ahead of him, and all together, they made their way to the dining room, where another grand chandelier presided over a rounded and polished table of ash with six curved chairs around it, all cushioned in white. Owens held out the chair at the head of the table for Virginia. Beatrice and Eleanore sat themselves, though Harry seemed about to offer to hold out chairs for them. He sat to one side of Virginia, and

Beatrice sat across from him on the other. Eleanore sat beside her cousin. The dishes on the table were an expensive blue and white china paired with lovely crystal wine glasses in which Owens now poured a measure of Spanish wine for each of them.

"Brought it home from my last trip to Spain," said Virginia as if worried Harry would think ill of her for serving wine at dinner.

"My parents would approve of your taste," he replied graciously.

"And who are your parents, dear?" asked Virginia. "Would I know them?"

"I don't believe you would," said Harry. "They're in the railroad racket up in New York."

"Oh, how charming," Virginia enthused, sipping her wine.

Beatrice helped herself to mashed potatoes while they chattered, passing them to her cousin when she'd finished. Roast and green beans were passed around next. Soon everyone had steaming hot food on their plates, and the conversation dulled as the scraping of forks on plates ensued. With everyone settled, Owens disappeared through the kitchen door to have his own meal with Anna. The tradition of making the staff eat at separate times wasn't one upheld in the Adams household. Anna and Owens were just as much part of the family as anyone else. Beatrice imagined this came from her mother's upbringing. Beatrice's grandmother was what some might call old money, and she'd run a strict Victorian household. Virginia, the story went, had always striven to do the opposite of what her mother expected, and for that Beatrice was glad. Being a live wire herself, she much preferred having a mother who wasn't constricting.

Virginia turned her attention to Beatrice after a length of silence. "So, darling, have you worked out what's next in your thrilling murder case?"

Beatrice couldn't contain her smile as she met her mother's equally blue gaze. "I'm off to La Grande Station tomorrow morning to do some more digging."

"La Grande? What for?" asked Harry.

"There was a luggage claim ticket for the station in the evidence Detective Mason sent me," she explained. "Along with a key. And you're going straight home," she added, pointing her fork in Eleanore's direction.

Eleanore looked indignant at being told what to do. "Now, hang on just a minute," she complained. "I may be a bunny, but someone has to watch your back. Like you said, I'm the one who gets us *out* of trouble when you get us into it."

"She makes a fair point," said Harry. "You shouldn't go alone. This jack-o'-lantern could figure you've got the evidence and come looking for you."

"All the more reason *to* go alone," said Beatrice, sipping her wine.

"It'd make me feel better if I tagged along," Harry offered. "I can find someone to cover my shift."

"I couldn't ask you to do that," Beatrice replied, though her heart leapt at the offer.

"You didn't ask," he mused with a smile. "Eleanore can go home like you want, and you'll still get to do your job."

"I think that's a marvelous idea," Virginia cut in with a devious smile. "Let the nice doctor go with you, Bea. For my poor nerves."

Beatrice cast her mother a look of awe. "You really are something, you know that?" she said.

"I do," replied Virginia, giving her daughter a wink.

"Fine," agreed Beatrice, her attention back on Harry. "You can come, but only because you're good in a scrap."

Harry laughed, and the sound of it made Beatrice's heart glow in a way that she didn't understand.

"Swell. That's settled, then," said Virginia, leaving Beatrice to feel as if the whole room had ganged up on her. "What are you hoping to find at the station, my pet?"

Beatrice, mid-sip of her wine, took a moment to swallow what she'd swigged and set her glass aside. "I'm not sure, really. I suspect a piece of luggage. I haven't had a chance to go through Tiffany's notebook."

"We should do that after dinner," suggested Eleanore.

"I wouldn't mind having a look," added Harry.

Beatrice beamed. "Three heads are better than one, I suppose," she agreed.

"You always were such a sharp young thing," said Virginia, reaching over to pat her daughter's hand.

Her wine glass by now was empty, and she reached for the nearby bottle to refill it.

"Oh, no, let me," offered Harry.

Beatrice pressed her lips together to keep from smiling again as Harry hopped up and refilled her mother's glass. He may have left what she lovingly referred to as New York royalty, but Harry Riley came from good breeding, and there was no hiding that.

"Anyone else?" he offered, holding up the bottle.

"I'm fine," said Eleanore, who rarely had more than one glass of anything.

"I'll take a top-off," said Beatrice.

She rested her chin in her hand and held out her half-empty glass to him. Harry walked around the table to refill it, careful not to spatter any. When he was through, they shared a smile and he returned to his seat, setting the wine bottle back in the center of the table.

The rest of dinner was a casual affair. Virginia asked after Patrick, which turned out to be a sore subject at the moment. Being the sort to never keep anything from her mother, Beatrice explained her beau's ridiculous threats to Harry and expressed her intention to have words with him once this business with the Harvey House murders was all wrapped up. She had no intention of telling Patrick that she was still investigating either. He would only attempt to stop her, and Beatrice wouldn't have that. Harry seemed amused at the fire with which she spoke, but if he had an opinion on the matter, he kept it to himself. Virginia asked after Eleanore's father next. Eleanore said Uncle Theo was doing well, but he was eager for her return after what he'd read in the papers. All the more reason to send her cousin home, Beatrice thought.

Dinner concluded before Virginia could pry Harry about his family, much to Beatrice's relief. It was a subject he tried to avoid, or so she gathered from their brief conversation on the topic. It was a life he'd left behind for a reason, and that was a mystery she could delve into at a later date, preferably when he trusted her a little more. Virginia retreated to the library after dinner under the guise of finding a book. Beatrice knew full well she kept a stock of brandy hidden in there, but as her mother had only two glasses of wine at dinner, she decided not to press the issue in front of Harry.

Eleanore and Harry took up residence in the parlor while Beatrice raced upstairs to grab the evidence. The box it had come in was re-sealed with twine and entirely empty, sitting on the footstool of her reading chair as if begging to be stolen. The evidence was safely hidden in a hollowed-out copy of *Moby Dick* that sat on Beatrice's personal bookshelf. It was a trick she'd employed since childhood whenever she'd wanted to hide things. Only Eleanore knew about it. She took only the notebook from this secret treasure trove and replaced the leather volume to the shelf before skipping back down the curved stairs Eleanore and Harry were whispering about something, but at the sight of Beatrice crossing the parlor, they quieted.

"What are you two gabbing about?" Beatrice asked in a teasing tone.

"Nothing," they both said in unison.

At any other time, Beatrice might have been suspicious, but presently she was far too wrapped up in the mystery at hand to worry about it. She sat herself in one of the armchairs. Eleanore and Harry sat on the loveseat, eyes expectantly on Beatrice. She thumbed through the notebook again until she reached the part about Donavan's gang, where she'd been rudely interrupted by Flanagan. She read a little past this before releasing a hum of interest.

"What is it?" asked Eleanore.

"Pages are missing. Torn out," said Beatrice, holding it out to her cousin.

Eleanore looked for herself before passing it Harry's way.

"Were they gone before?" asked Harry, accepting the notebook absentmindedly. The pages that had been ripped out were followed by blank pages that Tiffany had never gotten to.

"Maybe," sighed Beatrice. Her disappointment poisoned her countenance, and a heavy silence ensued.

Beatrice had been so sure an answer, or at least a lead, would be hidden in those pages. Had Flanagan torn out the pages? Why not destroy the whole book? Harry interrupted her swirling thoughts.

"You don't need what was in here to solve this," he encouraged.

Beatrice met his eye with a curious expression. He went on.

"Whatever Tiffany found out she discovered by investigating. You're a regular gumshoe, Adams. We'll just have to find some new clues."

Beatrice beamed at that, her disappointment fading. It was exhausting, hitting so many brick walls, but Harry was right: They simply needed stronger evidence.

"Well, even if we can't prove it, Flanagan admitted to working for Donavan," said Beatrice. "I just wish I knew what else Tiffany had been thinking. How did she figure it out?"

"Someone must have made a slipup," supplied Eleanore.

Something Mr. Morrow had said suddenly sparked in Beatrice's memory. "She went Nellie Bly on the whole thing," Beatrice repeated.

"Sorry?" said Harry.

She met his gaze. "What Mr. Morrow said when we were interviewing him. He said Tiffany discovered the juice ring and went Nellie Bly on the whole thing. Nellie Bly was notorious for going undercover to investigate things. I assumed Morrow meant her acting undercover as a Harvey Girl. What if I was wrong? What if she actually tried to *join* the operation?"

"That could be how she found out who M was," Harry mused.

"And how she knew where to find David," added Beatrice. "If she was in the inner circle, she would have known where the hooch was hidden for him to find it."

"But Flanagan told Morrow and David to 'take care of it,'" Eleanore pointed out. "Why would he do that if Tiffany was part of the operation?"

Beatrice fell quiet for a moment. A brilliant fire suddenly burgeoned in her eyes, and she shot up as the puzzle pieces rearranged themselves in her mind. "Because she'd confessed to Mr. Morrow that she was a reporter," Beatrice enthused. "When he told Flanagan what he'd learned, Flanagan told them to stop her from nosing about."

"Which David took to mean murder," Harry interjected.

"Yes," Beatrice agreed. "And it threw a wrench in the whole operation by drawing attention to them. She could have gleaned all sorts of useful information before Mary pointed a jealous finger her way in an attempt to get her fired."

"Ugh. My brain hurts," uttered Eleanore.

The hall clock chimed ten, and Beatrice turned to glance at it as if hoping the face would read differently.

"Say, I'd better get going," said Harry, rising to his feet. "What time should I meet you at the station?"

"Does eight work for you?" asked Beatrice.

"Sure does," he said with a winning smile. "Don't let her stay up too late," he added jokingly to Eleanore.

"As if I've any say," mused Eleanore with a smirk. "But I'll do my best."

Beatrice pressed a buzzer on the wall, and Owens appeared a moment later. "Yes, miss?"

"Could you show Mr. Riley out?" she asked.

Owens dipped his head. "Of course. I'll fetch his things."

He left the parlor to retrieve Harry's coat and hat from the hall closet.

"Oh, before I forget," Harry said as he reached into his suit coat. He extracted a small slip of paper and held it out to Beatrice. "Now you can't say I forgot to give it to you."

Beatrice glanced at the slip of paper to read his name, address, and telephone number written in his messy doctor's scrawl. She smiled. "I'll add it to my address book," she promised.

With a final nod to Eleanore, Harry left the parlor and met Owens in the hall to share pleasantries before receiving his things. Eleanore came to stand beside her cousin, watching Harry leave through the parlor arch. Whatever she wanted to say seemed barred at the end of her tongue.

"Spit it out," encouraged Beatrice, giving her full attention to the blonde.

"Oh . . . nothing," said Eleanore. "Only . . . say, do you mind terribly if I sleep in your room tonight?"

Beatrice laughed. "Don't tell me you're a scaredy-cat now too," she teased. "Of course I don't mind."

If she was honest, Beatrice would be glad of the company. As the pair of them made their way up the grand staircase leaving the closing up of the house to Owens, Beatrice had a sneaking suspicion that asking to sleep in her room hadn't been what Eleanore wanted to say at all.

CHAPTER TWENTY

LA GRANDE STATION

Beatrice awoke the following morning to a thrill of excitement at the prospect of further adventures. The thought of enjoying those adventures with Harry Riley only made Beatrice look forward to them all the more. He was one of very few men who encouraged her outrageous endeavors, and his easygoing temperament made him an agreeable companion. Patrick trying to stifle such a friendship was still a cause for argument. The remembrance of it threw a surge of anger atop Beatrice's excitement as she lay in her bed staring at the ceiling. She hadn't talked to Patrick in two days. It was perhaps not the maturest of ways to signal her discontent with his behavior, but the cold shoulder had worked in her favor too many times before to not employ it now. Besides, she didn't want to talk to Patrick until she'd put this case behind her.

Eleanore rolled over on the opposite side of the bed, pulling Beatrice from her swirling thoughts. It was just as well. A glance at the clock on her nightstand informed her it was half past six in the morning. The drive into town would take at least half an hour, and that was if traffic behaved. There was hardly time left to get ready.

"Come on, Ellie," Beatrice murmured, shaking her snoring cousin.

"We'd better get a move on."

Eleanore groaned in protest. She was in no way a morning person.

Beatrice propped up on her elbow and cast her cousin a pointed look, though Eleanore couldn't see it. "Don't make me come back with a pitcher of water. I surely will," she threatened.

With another groan of malcontent, Eleanore threw back the covers in a huff. "I'm up," she grumbled.

Beatrice grinned victoriously as Eleanore edged toward the side of the bed and rolled into a sitting position. Eleanore would sleep until nine if Beatrice allowed it, but there was too much to do for such lazy summer habits. After a much-needed stretch, Beatrice too climbed out of bed and threw on a silk robe before starting the hunt for coffee. Owens was already opening the house for the day when she descended the staircase. He presently stood in the parlor in the process of throwing back the long parlor curtains.

"Good morning, Owens," Beatrice greeted.

"Good morning, Miss Adams," he replied, turning to smile in her direction. "I believe Miss Thomas has put on a fresh pot of coffee."

Beatrice beamed. "Aces. Everything jake down here?"

"Oh, yes," he assured her. "I've checked all the doors and windows per your request. No signs of attempted break-in during the night."

"Wonderful," Beatrice said. "Is Mother up?"

"Not yet. I'm afraid she had rather a late night," he divulged.

Beatrice hummed thoughtfully to herself. Drinking she didn't mind, but it was why her mother drank that bothered her. She needed to find a distraction for her mother—and soon.

"Keep an eye on her today," Beatrice requested. "And don't let anyone in the house you don't know. I'm not sure where this ghostly assassin has gone."

"Of course, miss," he promised.

Beatrice continued on her path to the kitchen, entering through the main arch off the hall. A swinging door led from the kitchen into the dining room, where they'd eaten the night before. Short, plump, and agreeable Anna stood before the stove, her graying dark hair piled in a bun on her head. She'd been widowed in her mid-thirties and, having no children or source of income, had sought work doing the one thing she loved most: cooking. She'd come highly recommended by an old family friend and had served the Adamses for ten years. Much like Owens, Beatrice viewed Anna as a part of the family.

"Morning, Anna!" Beatrice chirped, heading straight for the coffee.

"Good heavens," said Anna, looking Beatrice up and down. "I thought you'd be dressed by now."

The smell of fresh eggs and bacon filled Beatrice's nose and made her stomach rumble. She lamented not making time to eat despite not favoring an early breakfast. She snagged a piece of toast as she poured her coffee. "I couldn't sleep," she said through a mouthful of toast. "Ellie kept tossing and turning, and my mind was busier than a hive of angry bees."

"I'm not surprised," Anna replied, scooping the eggs into a serving bowl. "You be careful out there. I don't want the next murder I hear about to be your own."

She pointed her wooded spoon at Beatrice for emphasis, and the redhead grinned, kissing Anna on the cheek.

"I will," she vowed. "Don't worry. Mr. Riley is tagging along. I'm sure everything will be jake."

"Will you be home in time for dinner?" Anna asked as Beatrice made for the hall, coffee and toast in hand.

Beatrice paused in the entry. "Should be. One never knows. I suppose it depends on what we find."

Anna nodded in understanding and turned back to fixing breakfast, no doubt recalling the last time Beatrice had been on a case. Beatrice had gone undercover as a showgirl, and the hours had been monstrous, at least according to Anna. The cook, while motherly and kind, liked things just so, and not having a head count for dinner was one of the few things that put a real bee in her bonnet. Anna disliked wasting food.

Beatrice returned upstairs, finishing her toast along the way, and found her room devoid of Eleanore, who was probably getting dressed in the guest room across the hall. The girls had decided the night before that it would be best to take the same cab, as Beatrice's stop was more or less on the way to Pasadena. Really Beatrice just wanted to be sure her cousin was well and clear of the house before Beatrice stirred up more trouble. She'd already asked too much of Eleanore. With Owens to look after Anna and her mother, Beatrice was less concerned for the rest of the household. Reginald Owens had been a boxing champion in his youth, and though he was now middle-aged, he was no less fit for it.

Having consoled herself that everything was in order, Beatrice turned her attention on dressing for the day, deciding on a deep navy-blue dress and heels. Blue was an exceptionally good color to wear when she wanted to go unnoticed. Blue stood out less in a crowd. She was just filling a handbag to match when Eleanore entered sporting a floral dress.

"Ready?" she asked. "Owens called a cab. It should be here any minute."

"Just about," uttered Beatrice distractedly. She was running through a list in her head, trying to plan for every eventuality. She had the evidence, a flashlight with spare batteries, and extra pins for picking locks. Her eyes roamed thoughtfully to her side table, and she pulled open the drawer to extract an engraved silver lighter.

"Whatever do you need that for?" asked Eleanore as Beatrice tucked the lighter into her bag.

"You never know when you'll need one," Beatrice mused. "Let's ankle, honey. I feel like we're running late."

The taxi arrived at precisely seven thirty, and once Eleanore's things were safely in the trunk, they were on their way to La Grande Station. The drive was held in silence. It wasn't lost on Beatrice that Donavan could have ears everywhere, and Beatrice couldn't exactly talk about the evidence sitting in her purse with the cab driver present. Eleanore seemed to share Beatrice's sentiments, not even daring to make small talk with the driver, which was against Eleanore's fundamental socialite nature. When the cab pulled up to the curb outside the train station, Eleanore yanked Beatrice into a bone-crushing hug and whispered, "Be careful" in her cousin's ear.

Beatrice smiled. "I will," she whispered back.

They said nothing else. Beatrice paid the driver her half of the fare and stepped out of the taxi. It pulled away the moment she shut the door.

La Grande Station lived up to its name. The brick and stone structure towered over Beatrice, its most prominent feature the curved central dome set amid castle-like conical roofs. Passengers and station employees alike milled about, numerous voices molding together in a general hubbub. It was only now as Beatrice joined the throng that she realized she hadn't specified *where* to meet Harry at the station. She moved inside the grand building, hoping to remain inconspicuous until he arrived. It was a hopeless endeavor. Her presence, as always, drew the gaze of many passersby, some wearing expressions as if trying to place how they knew her. Normally, Beatrice didn't mind the attention, but with no idea who this assassin was, Beatrice felt the heat of every gaze with the cautious air of a doe being hunted.

Beatrice took up a position beneath the clock at the center of the bustling station lobby. It was only ten after eight, she consoled herself, but still she worried. When the clock reached fifteen after, Beatrice had half a mind to investigate on her own. The longer she waited, the more chance there was of something going wrong. Just as she was about to give up on him, the crowd parted and she spotted Harry Riley striding toward her in a brown tweed suit with a sharp red tie and fedora.

"This place is a madhouse," he said when he was in earshot.

The very sight of him made Beatrice smile. "I thought you'd gotten lost," she teased.

"New city. New bearings," he said. "Eleanore get off okay?"

Beatrice nodded that she had, the stares of passersby no longer feeling so threatening. "I should warn you: I have no idea what we're about to find."

"All the more fun," Harry mused.

Beatrice grinned wider, Harry's effortless nature a breath of fresh air among all the opposing forces she usually faced. She signaled for him to follow, and they melted into the crowd, heading in the direction of the baggage claim. The clerk was mid-argument with a thin, irritable woman when they arrived.

"I'm sorry, madam," he said for what Beatrice was sure must be the hundredth time. "No luggage claim, no luggage."

"This is outrageous!" the woman cried, turning and storming off, shoving between Harry and Beatrice with extreme force. Beatrice scowled after her, rubbing her shoulder, which stung in protest.

Harry's attention was fixed on the expectant clerk. "We're here to pick up a case left on hold for us."

"Name?" asked the clerk.

"Flanagan," Harry replied.

Beatrice was impressed at the speed with which he lied.

"Do you have your ticket?" the clerk asked.

"Oh, yes," said Beatrice, rifling for it in her handbag. She shortly handed it over.

The clerk examined the ticket extensively, and for a moment, Beatrice thought they were about to be found out. But then the clerk adjusted his hat and said, "Give me a moment to find it."

"Take your time," Beatrice replied, flashing her best smile.

The clerk was affected immediately, again adjusting his hat. He soon remembered how to breathe and departed to the long-term storage room to search for the luggage.

Harry chuckled the moment the clerk was gone.

Beatrice looked over curiously. "What's so funny?"

"You," he teased. "You're a regular Aphrodite, you know that."

Beatrice felt her cheeks warm. "I am not!" she returned. "All I did was smile."

"Sometimes that's all it takes."

Their eyes met, and Beatrice couldn't help but notice the flecks of gold in his irises.

"You seem perfectly immune," she mused.

He half-laughed and tilted his fedora a little farther back. "Maybe I'm just not intimidated by beautiful women."

A teasing reply perched on Beatrice's lips, but before she could give it, the clerk returned lugging a suitcase. He set it on the counter.

"You'll have to sign for it, Mr. Flanagan," the clerk said, trying to avoid looking in Beatrice's general direction.

"Sure," said Harry, and Beatrice was doubly glad she'd brought him along. She hadn't thought of Flanagan's name being attached to the bag.

The clerk thrust a clipboard and pen Harry's way, which Harry pulled closer and signed with confident grace. Beatrice peered over Harry's arm to see a convincing "D. Flanagan" scrawled across the signature line. She could only hope they didn't keep a record of Flanagan's actual signature on file, but given that the clerk didn't recognize Harry as an impostor, she doubted they did.

Beatrice moved to lift the case, but Harry's hand met hers on the handle, his other sliding the clipboard back to the clerk.

"I'll get that, honey," he said.

Beatrice retracted her hand with a delicate smile and a quiet "Thanks."

Harry scooped up the case from the counter and tipped his hat to the clerk. Beatrice gave a polite wave of farewell, falling into step beside Harry and taking his arm to solidify their being together in case questions were asked. Her hand burned where his had touched hers, reminding her that she'd quite forgotten gloves. They were halfway down the station when Harry leaned over and said, "So, what now?"

"Now we need to find somewhere to open it," she reasoned, casting her eyes around them for a room to duck in to. Their only option seemed to be the ladies' room.

Harry followed her gaze, shortly coming to the same conclusion. "It'll be too conspicuous if I follow you in there. Not to mention the scandal."

"I quite agree," said Beatrice.

Harry handed her the suitcase. "I'll wait outside and keep watch. You can tell me what you find."

Beatrice nodded resolutely and left his side to join the queue forming outside the restroom. The woman ahead of her, a middle-aged brunette in bright green, glanced back at Beatrice's approach, and they swapped polite but disinterested smiles, neither in the mood for conversation. Beatrice looked back over her shoulder in search of Harry. He'd taken up residence on a bench across the way. He held up his hand, and Beatrice mimicked the motion, smiling to herself. From her vantage point, it was impossible not to notice how handsome he was.

She wasn't the only girl to notice. The young blonde behind her asked almost conspiratorially, "Is he yours?"

Beatrice was caught off guard, but only for a moment. "Oh, yes. Newly engaged. Traveling to meet the in-laws."

The girl, who looked to be younger than Beatrice by a few years, grinned excitedly. "Say, that's fabulous! You're one lucky gal!"

"Don't I know it," replied Beatrice.

The line had moved into the bathroom by now, and Beatrice fidgeted impatiently. Answers or more questions could lay in that case. She longed to know which. That the case was lighter than anticipated piqued her curiosity all the more, and she peered around the woman in front of her to take stock of the situation. There were three women ahead of her awaiting use of the toilets. The long decorative-tiled space in which they queued was set up as a sort of lounge, complete with a loveseat, rows of mirrors, a reading table, and even a station for writing. Had the restroom not been crowded with women powdering their noses and chattering excitedly about their travels, Beatrice would have plopped the case down here to open it. While rummaging through a case in the ladies' room at a train station was nothing sensational, Beatrice had no idea what was inside. She'd rather not create undue panic. She settled both hands around the handle, resolved to wait, and tried not to count the seconds. Thankfully the girl behind her was jabbering with her companion, a sister by the looks of it, leaving Beatrice to her thoughts.

The next stall opened, and Beatrice took a step forward as the line moved ahead. She grew more and more anxious with each passing moment.

"Are you all right, duck?" the woman ahead of her asked, having noticed Beatrice's increased fussing.

"Oh, yes," Beatrice assured her. "I'm just worried I might miss my train, that's all."

"You can go ahead of me if you'd like," the woman offered. "I've just arrived, and I'm in no hurry."

"Really?" Beatrice replied in a tone of polite gratitude. "That'd be aces!"

The older brunette nodded and swapped places with Beatrice.

"Thanks ever so!" chimed the redhead.

"You just be sure and catch your train."

"I will," Beatrice promised.

The line moved another pace forward as a stall opened up. Beatrice was next. Her heart hammered with excitement. She glanced down at the brown case, noting the keyhole. Would it really be that simple?

A toilet flushed, the next stall opened, and Beatrice rushed forward, catching the wooden door before it even had a chance to swing shut. As the station was built in the late 1800s, the stall was rather large to accommodate the ridiculous Victorian garb that Beatrice's grandmother frequently bemoaned the loss of. It worked in Beatrice's favor that day. She fleetly latched the door, set down the suitcase, and slipped her handbag from her arm. Detective Mason's entire career rested on whatever was in that case, and depending on the outcome, hers might as well. Beatrice took the key from her bag and knelt in front of the case, heart thudding like a jazz room snare drum. She placed the key in the lock. It was a perfect fit. She suppressed a triumphant laugh as she turned it to hear the lock click. She pushed the lid open eagerly.

Nothing.

The case was empty.

Disappointment and denial fell like a stone. Beatrice stared at the empty case as if the evidence could only be seen if you looked at it just right. Unsurprisingly, nothing materialized. Had the assassin arrived before them to empty the case? Why was the case there in the first place? Flanagan surely didn't have the *only* key. There would have to be another in case something like this happened. After all, they didn't call it organized crime for nothing.

A knock on the stall door made her jump.

"Are you all right in there?" asked a woman's concerned voice.

Beatrice realized she'd lingered longer than the usual amount of time one spent in a stall.

"Fine," she called back. "Just a run in my stockings."

Her tale satisfied the knocker, who pried no further. With a heavy sigh, Beatrice closed and locked the case, wishing she had more to go on. Maybe Harry would have a thought. Beatrice flushed the toilet via the pull chain before she left the stall and made a show of washing her hands at the sinks. An occasional glance her way was the only attention paid her by the other women in the restroom. She left the heavily scented space without another word said.

The station was even busier than before when she reached the lobby. The loud cacophony of jabber and footsteps echoed off the vaulted and domed ceiling. Beatrice couldn't see the bench where Harry sat for all the people. She shouldered through the crowd, murmuring an occasional apology when she bumped someone a little harder than intended. It was like fighting against a river's strongest flow, and she was quite out of breath when she finally reached the benches and the small pocket of freedom from chaos they provided. Her expectant smile faded, and for a moment, she thought she'd gone the wrong way. A quick recalculation of her position in the room told her otherwise. This was where she'd left Harry, but Harry wasn't there.

Perhaps he actually needed to use the facilities, she thought to herself.

A scream shattered the hubbub from the other end of the station. Beatrice whirled toward it to see the crowd parting fearfully to get out of a massive goon's way, a limp figure slung over his shoulder like a rag doll. Beatrice gasped.

It was Harry!

She surged forward to make chase, but another hand on the case handle jerked her back, the momentum bringing her face to face with another thug. He smiled grotesquely, and there was no escaping his foul breath when he said, "You're comin' with me, sweetheart."

Beatrice only had a moment to react. His hand on the case had brought him into close proximity. With all her might, Beatrice stamped on his instep with the heel of her shoe. The goon howled in pain, instinctively releasing the case, which Beatrice flung upward. It crashed into the thug's face, breaking his nose and sending him sprawling backward into the throng of shrieking onlookers. Beatrice bolted toward the station exit and the goon carrying Harry. It wasn't perhaps the wisest decision, running *toward* the bad guys, but Beatrice couldn't let them take Harry.

The crowd parted like the Red Sea, now cognizant that something was amiss. No one seemed eager to get flattened, and from the cries of protest behind her, Beatrice was certain her pursuer was back at her heels. It dawned on her as she burst into daylight that, short of getting kidnapped alongside Harry, she had no hope of stopping these goons. Her theory proved correct when she spotted an unconscious Harry being shoved into the back of an unmarked delivery truck.

"There! Grab her!" a third goon shouted, pointing a stubby finger at Beatrice.

Beatrice gasped and took off running in the opposite direction. The loading and unloading area in front of the station was a madhouse. She flattened some poor woman who'd stepped out of her car at the wrong moment. Beatrice felt bad, but there was no time for apologies now. A quick glance over her shoulder showed all three goons after her, the one with the broken nose gaining at incredible speed. As luck would have it, a cabbie was just climbing into the driver's seat of his cab at the end of the row, having finished helping his previous passengers unload. Beatrice dove into the back of his cab and slammed the door, keeping a hand firmly on the handle as the broken-nosed goon caught up with her, his ugly bleeding face filling the window. The cabbie, in the middle of counting his fare, stared at her in surprise.

"Open the door!" growled the goon as he tugged on the handle. Beatrice held it shut with everything she had in her and locked eyes with the cab driver.

"Fifty dollars if you squeal tires *now!*" she offered.

The driver's eyebrows shot up. "You got it, lady," he said, dropping the cash onto the seat.

He mashed on the gas pedal, peeling away from the curb and momentarily dragging the goon along with them. Beatrice turned to look out the rear window as the goon fell into the street behind them, adding a few more bruises to the injuries she'd already caused. Tires screeched as oncoming traffic halted to avoid hitting the man, the forward Model T nearly clipping him. His friends ran into the road to help him up, growing smaller all the time as Beatrice's cab progressed down the road.

Beatrice breathed in relief, resting back against the seat. "Thanks a million, mister," she uttered. "My goose was almost cooked."

"You in some sort of trouble, lady?" he asked, sounding sincerely concerned.

"Almost always," mused Beatrice. "Just keep driving, and make sure we aren't followed. There's an extra sawbuck in it for you."

"Gee, thanks, lady," the driver praised.

An extra ten bucks went a long way these days. Beatrice rested the suitcase in her lap, wondering why so trivial an object had caused so much trouble. Surely they wouldn't have wasted all that effort for an empty case. Decidedly, Beatrice began to inspect the case a little closer, running her hands over the rough fabric in search of hidden latches or grooves. This led her to extract the key and open the case again, a new thought giving her fresh eyes. There was something unique about that case. Something those apes didn't want her to see.

Beatrice ran her fingers over the fabric of the interior, finding nothing out of place in the base. A closer inspection of the lid, however, made Beatrice pause. Something small and sharp pricked her finger. She jerked it back in surprise and leaned closer. There, cleverly concealed at the top of the lining, was a small sewing pin. Beatrice carefully tugged this out. The lining fell loose. She dipped her hand hopefully into this hidden pocket and felt around. The cabbie noted her in the rear mirror.

"Everything all right?" he asked.

Beatrice's fingers closed around a piece of folded parchment. She pulled it out and unfurled it, a heart-stopping smile crossing her lips.

"Everything is aces," she said. "I have an address."

"Lay it on me, sweetheart," he replied. It was all an honest fare to him.

"The university, please. I need to see an old friend."

"You got it," chirped the cab driver.

He signaled to change lanes, turning at the next corner. Beatrice stared at the paper in her hand. It was an invoice written by hand instructing Flanagan which hooch to move next and which shipments they were in. Wherever it had come from was likely where those thugs had gone, which gave Beatrice a wild idea.

CHAPTER TWENTY-ONE
SUPPLY AND DEMAND

The crime lab for the Los Angeles Police Department was currently housed in the sciences building at the University of California. A relatively new division of the police force, it only had three employees, the youngest of whom Beatrice sought now. She crossed the campus at a brisk pace, ignoring the catcalls and jeers of the more immature male students. Her heels clicked against the decorative walk with every step, fingers clutched tightly around the case from the train station. Beautiful brick buildings loomed on both sides of the path, promising wisdom and knowledge to all who entered their sacred doors. She finally reached the building she'd come for and smiled in thanks when an exiting professor held the door open for her.

The lab was located on the first floor and had a frosted glass door that read Crime Lab in gold drop-shadowed letters. Beatrice knocked eagerly on it. The sound of breaking glass came from the other side, followed by muffled cursing. A moment later, the door was jerked open by a sandy-haired man of no more than twenty-eight. He wore silver wire-rimmed glasses and a tweed vest with white sleeves rolled up to the elbows. The instant his olive eyes found Beatrice in the hall, his countenance shifted to one of annoyance.

"Oh. It's you," he huffed.

Beatrice smiled. "Hello, Greenie."

Daniel Green bristled at the nickname, but his expression made it clear that he'd ceased asking people to stop long ago.

"I'm busy," he said to the younger redhead. "Can't you go bother some other department for a change?"

"Don't be a boob," replied Beatrice as she brushed past him with a roll of her eyes. She spotted the smashed beaker on the floor. "Thank goodness it was empty."

"Yeah, yeah," muttered Daniel, closing the door.

Beatrice wandered through the rows of lab tables, peering curiously at projects with only a mild understanding of the science behind them. "Where are Pinker and Morris?" she wondered as she inspected an assembly of bullet casings that sat next to a microscope.

"Testing a ballistics theory," said Daniel, gently pulling her away from the lab table by the arm. "Don't touch anything."

Beatrice pursed her lips and met his eye defiantly. "I wasn't going to," she insisted.

Daniel gave her a look that said he knew she would if he gave her the chance, but he said nothing more about it. After a careful breath to calm himself, he released her and asked, "What do you want?"

Beatrice pulled the scrap of paper from her bag and held it out to him between two fingers. "Can you check for trace evidence on this? I need to know where it came from."

Daniel stared at the parchment, debating. His eyes betrayed his inner struggle.

"Oh, come on," Beatrice urged. "A friend of mine has been kidnapped, and it's my only lead! Don't you want to do something real? Or are you too busy cleaning the equipment?"

Her eyes once again focused on the broken beaker to make her point.

Daniel groaned and snatched the invoice from her hand. "Fine. But only because Captain Raglan likes you."

Beatrice grinned. "Oh, hush. You like helping."

"No, I don't," he countered unconvincingly as he moved to the appropriate lab table. "You're going to get me fired one of these days. I'm only a junior analyst, and it was damn hard to even get that respect."

Beatrice pulled up a stool and perched atop it, setting the case on the floor beside her. She watched curiously as Daniel set the paper in a tray and started pulling on gloves.

"I don't know why you give me such a hard time," she mused. "I see your worth more than they do, you know."

Daniel fell silent, his back to her. Beatrice knew that behind all his complaining, he enjoyed the challenges she brought him. If she truly thought otherwise, she wouldn't keep coming back.

After a length of silence, Daniel asked, "Do you have a copy of this?"

Beatrice shook her head.

"Better write it down, then," he said, "in case it smudges."

He left the lab table and moved to an overflowing desk to grab a paper and pencil. Despite ignoring her comment, he seemed to move with new diligence as if to prove her faith wasn't misplaced. Beatrice knew it wasn't. He had a brilliant scientific mind, and he had since he was very young. Age, unfortunately, made his colleagues underestimate him. Some of his techniques were experimental and out of the box, but he got results, and Beatrice trusted his work more than that of Pinker or Morris. Daniel might get annoyed with her, but he never disrespected her. He treated her as a fellow intelligent human being, and he gave the work she brought him his full attention.

"If your friend was kidnapped, shouldn't you call the police?" Daniel asked while he copied the invoice in his tight scrawl.

"If I called the boys in blue for every little problem, what sort of detective would I be?" Beatrice mused. "Besides, I don't even know what we're up against yet. Better to go in quietly."

Daniel shrugged. "It's your operation."

Silence fell after that as he focused on the task at hand. The job was trickier with paper but not impossible. He tested small slivers of the parchment over a flame, in different solutions, beneath a microscope—no stone was left unturned. The process took several hours, and by mid-afternoon, Beatrice's stomach growled with hunger. She didn't realize she'd nodded off until Daniel was shaking her awake. Her eyes met his expectantly.

"Trace amounts of iron ore, limestone, and aluminum," he supplied, excited. "On their own, nothing extraordinary, but together?"

Beatrice arched an eyebrow. "Together?"

Daniel smiled. "Your note came from a steel mill."

"You don't say," Beatrice enthused, sitting up taller. "Could you tell which?"

"I called R and I while you were dozing," he replied, smiling wider as he held out a fresh slip of paper. "There's only one steel mill in a hundred miles that's been completely abandoned. I got you an address."

Beatrice jolted to her feet. "Oh, I could kiss you!"

Before he could protest, she did exactly that, leaving a red lipstick stain on his cheek. Daniel colored.

"Just doing my job," he uttered, a little dazed.

"Well, you're a crackerjack!" she praised, looking at the case on the floor. "Any chance you could put these with evidence?"

"They're not part of an official investigation," he replied. "You know the rules."

"Then open a file for one," she said. "Tell Raglan it's for me. I'll explain later."

Beatrice was already halfway to the door.

"Where are *you* going?" Daniel called after her.

Beatrice paused at the door, flashing him another million-dollar smile. "To close this case."

She disappeared into the hall, leaving a disgruntled analyst behind her.

The abandoned steel mill stood dilapidated and crumbling against the bright afternoon sky. Large, rusting spires were all that remained of the once-smoking furnaces, and mammoth exhaust pipes stretching along the chinked brick building looked like they might fall over at any moment. Forgotten railroad tracks lined the edge of the property, many sections missing ties altogether. Beatrice imagined they'd been looted by desperate scavengers to be sold or melted into something else. As she approached the scene on foot, gravel crunching beneath her shoes with every step, Beatrice was glad she'd asked the cab driver to drop her a few blocks away. It'd have looked terribly suspicious to walk across this expanse with an audience. Someone might think she was up to no good.

Beatrice crossed the broken tracks and paused to survey her surroundings. Other than the location, discovered so quickly due to Daniel's foresight to call Records and Information, Beatrice had no idea what she was looking for or how many goons waited inside. The mystery both thrilled and alarmed her, and, not for the first time, she contemplated getting a small pistol to keep in her bag for such occasions. From her position, there were no signs of life that she could see—no smoke or lights. The place looked as abandoned as ever. Beatrice knew better than to judge anything by its appearance, especially where mobsters were concerned. She ambled forward a few more paces, suddenly wishing she'd waited for the cover of darkness. She felt exposed in the afternoon sunlight with naught but a wisp of clouds for shadow. But then, Harry might be dead, she reasoned. Time was of the essence, and that thought spurred her on at a lively pace.

Beatrice edged along the side of the rotting brick building, keeping her eyes peeled for anything out of the ordinary. The summer sun was a cruel mistress in such a dust bowl, but Beatrice was too focused to care about the sweat beading on her brow. She dabbed it absently away with the back of her hand, the movement drawing her eyes to the dirt around the old factory. There, freshly imprinted in the soil, were tire tracks. Judging by the width of the wheel base and the depth of the impression, it *could* be the delivery truck the goons had been driving earlier. Beatrice followed these hopefully, soon coming around the side of the building. She fleetly ducked back and peeked around the corner. The tire tracks led to an open air shed where tools and supplies were likely once stored to protect them from the sun and the rare drop of rain.

Parked beneath it was the delivery truck, its back doors open and waiting like a hungry maw. Two strong thugs walked back and forth from the delivery doors of the mill, each carrying heavy crates that clinked with every step—smuggled liquor, no doubt. They loaded them into the back of the truck, then went back for more. Fortuitously for Beatrice, they were in deep conversation, which left the entrance unwatched as they walked side by side to the truck to deposit the load. Beatrice waited until they were halfway to the truck before she scurried on tiptoe around the corner and into the factory doors. She took refuge behind a nearby stack of old pallets.

Voices neared as the goons walked back inside to grab more crates from the stack near the door.

"I still don't understand why the boss is keepin' him around," a gruff voice said. "He doesn't have the case or the order."

"Nah," the other replied, sounding as though talking through a cold. "The broad who has it'll come to us. We just have to wait. I wouldn't mind a little revenge for breaking my damn nose."

Beatrice tightened her lips to keep from laughing. It was only now she realized he'd been the poor fool who'd tried to nab her at the station. From the sound of his voice, she'd done a good job of busting his nose.

"How will she find us?" the gruff voice asked.

"Hell if I know," the broken-nosed goon said. "I just work here. Now get that outside."

Their voices faded again, giving Beatrice time to peer around the corner and assess her situation. The factory was just as derelict on the interior. Rusting furnaces sat unused along one wall, and broken conveyor belts were scattered around the room. A large portion of the ceiling had caved in, piling in a long-forgotten mound of brick and wood on the factory floor. Beatrice wondered if it had happened before or after the steel mill's closing. Her eyes next found stairs that were surprisingly intact, possibly rebuilt, at the far end of the building. They disappeared into an office with square-paned glass windows, many panes of which were missing altogether. Beatrice reasoned this must once have been the foreman's office.

Beatrice ducked low as the goons returned and each grabbed another crate. Their conversation had shifted to lady troubles, which Beatrice felt no inclination to tune in to. She cast her eyes toward the stairs once more. Harry was presumably the "*him*" mentioned, and if he was being held here, the foreman's office seemed the most promising place to keep him. The long, rectangular room was presently devoid of any other mobsters. Beatrice reasoned this was just a warehouse for them rather than headquarters—an in-between place to hide their supplies until they got orders, which must have been what that note she'd found was. The bottles David Phillips emptied hadn't come from a *local* supplier like Beatrice initially thought; they were brought in via courier just like the perfume bottles.

Beatrice glanced at the diminishing crates of booze. The goons only had a few left. They might check on Harry when they were through. She'd have to be quick. Once the goons departed with two more clinking deliveries, Beatrice tiptoed down the debris-littered factory floor, pausing now and then to duck behind cover. She was hiding behind a large rusted and overturned ladle when her eyes were drawn to a gaping hole in the floor. The circumference of the hole was jagged and clearly manmade. Loose bricks were piled beside it, and a ladder protruded from the opening. Beatrice imagined the massive upturned crate nearby was used to cover the hole when the mobsters left. Voices echoed from below, indiscernible but audible. At least three more goons if Beatrice had to guess. She gave the area a wide berth and spirited toward the stairs. They were definitely newer than the rest of the building. When Beatrice placed her foot on the first step, it didn't creak as she expected, nor did the next. Emboldened, she ascended the stairs swiftly, careful not to touch the railing lest she get a splinter. She held her breath on the way up, afraid she might be spotted, but no cry of warning came. She burst through the office door, coughing a little as dust was stirred up.

The only light in the small room came from the grimy window overlooking the factory interior, but it was enough for Beatrice to take in the discarded crates, scattered papers, and overturned desk. In the far corner, a figure sat hunched in a chair with their head drooped over their chest.

Beatrice lurched forward and gasped, "Harry!"

He didn't stir. She knelt in front of him and gingerly lifted his head, horrified. He bore a bloody nose, split lip, and another flowering shiner. Beatrice couldn't shake the sinking feeling that his injuries were her fault. She should have insisted on going to the station alone.

"Harry," she whispered, gently stroking his non-bruised cheek.

He roused steadily, blinking uncertainly against the sudden light. Her face came into focus. "Bea?" he whispered.

She smiled in relief. "I think that's the first time you've called me that," she murmured.

"Is it?" He tried to smile but winced instead.

"What were they after?" she asked, moving behind his chair to untie him.

"The case," Harry breathed. "And you. They thought you'd told me what was in it. Used chloroform judging by the ether-like smell on the rag. Dragged me off before I knew what was happening."

Beatrice started working on the knots around Harry's wrists, struggling against the scratchy ropes and feeling guiltier by the minute. "They didn't say anything else?"

"No," he assured her. "Just that they were waiting for someone before they decided what to do with me."

"Me, no doubt," Beatrice mused. She huffed in aggravation. "These knots are impossible."

"Then leave me here," suggested Harry. "Come back with the police."

"And return to your corpse?" replied Beatrice incredulously. "I think not. You're leaving with me. We can get the police together."

As she spoke, Beatrice slipped her handbag from her shoulder and started rummaging through it. She pulled out the lighter.

"What are you doing?" asked Harry, an edge of panic to his voice.

"You're not gonna like it, skipper," she admitted. "Just hold still."

Harry sighed. "I'm going to regret meeting you, aren't I?"

Beatrice smirked. "It's very likely."

Without further ceremony, Beatrice flicked open the decorative lid and activated the lighter's flame.

"When I tell you to, give your wrists a good yank," she instructed.

Harry nodded, clearly steeling himself for more pain.

Beatrice knelt and held the fire to the topmost piece of rope in an attempt to keep from burning Harry. It took a moment for the flame to catch, but when it did, it bloomed rapidly.

"Now!" Beatrice cried when the rope visibly weakened.

Wincing, Harry jerked his wrists apart, and the rope audibly snapped. Beatrice stamped the fire out while Harry rubbed his chaffed and slightly singed wrists. Beatrice stowed her lighter and came around his chair to help him to his feet.

"Come on," she urged. "Let's jet before those meatheads come back."

"You're not going anywhere," said a cool voice from across the room.

Both Harry and Beatrice whirled.

There, standing in the doorway casually pointing a gun at them, was none other than Henry Morrow.

CHAPTER TWENTY-TWO

A SHOCKING HEADLINE

He'd shaved his pencil mustache, and his fidgety personality had been replaced by a tall, confident model, but there was no mistaking. The man in the door was Morrow.

"But," stuttered Beatrice, "I checked your handwriting. It wasn't a match."

"It's amazing how different a man's left-hand writing can be from his right," Morrow mused, his voice even sounding different than before. "People never think to check."

"Care to fill a half-concussed guy in?" asked Harry.

"He's been M all along," Beatrice explained. "Flanagan was a scapegoat. He was never more than a courier."

"Oh . . . great," said Harry with a measure of sarcasm.

"Enough with the chitchat," said Morrow, moving into the room. "Hands where I can see them."

Beatrice and Harry raised their hands steadily in unison. Given that he hadn't shot them on sight, Beatrice reasoned he had other plans for their demise. Morrow waggled his gun for the pair of them to walk ahead of him.

"If you've been M this whole time, why did you put me in the room with Tiffany's body?" wondered Beatrice.

"That was all Phillips," growled Morrow. "I was going to pay off the broad, three times what she would have made selling the story. There was even a steady paycheck in it if she agreed to be a mole for Donavan at the paper, but I never got to make the deal. Phillips killed her and panicked in the aftermath, which almost cost us the entire operation. Once I've gotten rid of you and the evidence, there will be nothing left to keep us from starting over."

Harry and Beatrice had reached the door by now, and Harry gestured for Beatrice to go first, both being a gentleman and keeping himself between her and the gun. Beatrice took the steps as slowly as she dared, hoping to buy more time to think of a way out.

"Pick it up, sweetheart!" Morrow barked. "I have other stops to make today."

Despite his insistence, Beatrice made no effort to alter her pace.

"So, your wife? The personality? It was all theatrics?" said Beatrice.

"All," Morrow confirmed, more than happy to gloat about how amazing he was. "My job was to set up the way stations and leave once they were secure and the couriers well-recognized."

"All the while letting everyone think the couriers were in charge," said Harry. "So you could easily disappear and do it all again."

"Give the doctor a medal," patronized Morrow.

In the lead, Beatrice processed it all, trying to calculate how she'd missed this little detail. At one point, she had suspected Morrow. He was organized, manically so, and he had seemed to be reluctant at her desire to investigate. But all the evidence argued against him as time went on. It was a valuable lesson for the young sleuth: Sometimes the evidence lied.

Beatrice's silence unnerved Morrow, who promptly spat, "Don't get any ideas, little miss detective. I won't hesitate to shoot either of you if you don't cooperate."

"Oh," Beatrice half-laughed, "don't mind me. I was just admiring your work."

This comment caught Morrow off guard, which had entirely been Beatrice's intention. She paused at the base of the stairs, looking back and cherishing the look of absolute confusion on his face.

"Not many actors are good enough to fool me," she went on. "But you played me for a sap with well-rehearsed ease. If you ever want to change professions, I'm sure I could put in a good word with some friends of mine."

Morrow didn't seem to know if this was a compliment or an insult. Either way, it made him hesitate. Harry took the opportunity to whirl and knock the gun out of Morrow's hand. Beatrice made a break for it, nearly running into another gun, this one aimed at her face.

It was the two thugs who'd been loading the truck, and the one with the weapon was the very same man whose nose she'd broken earlier. He looked a little too pleased to be holding her at gunpoint.

"And just where do you think you're going?" he said, clicking the hammer back.

"Matinee," quipped Beatrice. "And I'm very late."

"Gee, that's too bad," said the other man, his gun aimed at Harry. "Looks like you and your pal here are gonna miss the first act."

Harry again raised his hands and moved toward Beatrice as Morrow angrily collected his gun from the floor.

"What was that fancy word you used before?" asked Harry when they were back to back and completely surrounded.

"Jimmy-jacked," Beatrice supplied.

"Yep . . . we are definitely that," he mused.

They were outgunned and outnumbered. Three more mobsters climbed up the ladder from the secret tunnel below. They looked at the scene unfolding on the cluttered factory floor, confused at first, but they shortly imitated their comrades and drew their weapons. Beatrice couldn't remember ever being in so tight a jam, but her hope didn't waver, nor did her bravado.

"So, what happens now?" she asked Morrow. "We befriend the fishes? Sport concrete shoes?"

"Given the circumstances," chimed Morrow, "I was thinking of something a little more *dramatic*." He looked to the largest of the goons and barked, "Fetch a crate!"

The ape lumbered off to do so without argument. A bad feeling crept up Beatrice's spine.

"Have you ever been sauced, Miss Adams?" Morrow asked sinisterly.

She stiffened, jaw taught and eyes stubbornly fierce. "You don't expect a lady to answer that, do you?"

When Morrow smiled, he resembled a cobra, and new respect came to Beatrice for her enemy. She'd underestimated him every bit as much as he had underestimated her.

"I'm sure Dr. Riley is well aware of the symptoms brought on by intoxication . . . and even more so with those associated with poisoning."

"Leave her alone!" Harry growled, lurching angrily forward as Morrow's plan dawned on him.

Morrow shot at the ground next to Harry's foot, and the doctor froze.

"I never miss," Morrow said. "I suggest you save yourself a little pain."

Harry glowered at Morrow with a ferocity Beatrice didn't think possible for so handsome a man.

"Ladies first?" Morrow suggested, and before Beatrice could protest or come up with a good quip, she was grabbed by the broken-nosed goon and held flush against his disgusting body, the cold tip of his gun touching her head.

"Get your meathooks offa me!" she shrieked.

Struggle though she did, she shortly realized it was futile. Not only was this smelly ape stronger, but the hammer of his gun was still cocked. One wrong move and he'd blow her head off. In the interim, another goon had grabbed Harry. The large one who'd left returned with a crate full of booze and set it at Morrow's feet.

"Force it down their throats," Morrow ordered. "When they're good and sloshed, dump them on the side of the road. Their bodies will do the rest. It'll be the scandal of the year."

"Where are you going?" asked Broken Nose.

"To deal with her cousin," Morrow said simply. "I don't like loose ends."

His words hit Beatrice with the full force of sledgehammer, and for a moment, she felt like she couldn't breathe. "No!" she screamed, her throat aching in protest.

Her agony only made Morrow smile.

"Finish them off," he said, stowing his gun. Satisfied that everything was under control, he turned and headed down the long factory building for the exit, every step taking him closer to Eleanore.

Beatrice fought against her captor with every ounce of energy she had, no longer caring about the gun. Angry and desperate tears leaked from her eyes, and the shrieks emitted from her mouth were inhuman. In the tussle, her head snapped back, slamming into her captor's already-broken nose. He jolted back, swearing loudly, the motion setting off his gun. Miraculously, the bullet struck Harry's captor. Harry dove for his downed captor's dropped weapon. Beatrice, meanwhile, bolted after Morrow and launched onto his back with a feral snarl, arms wrapped like a boa constrictor around his throat. She squeezed with as much strength as she could muster, gunfire erupting behind her. For a moment, Morrow was surprised and gasping for air. Then he regained his faculties. He threw Beatrice to the ground like a rag doll and whipped out his pistol with militant precision.

BANG!

Beatrice gasped.

She watched in a stupor as Morrow froze, a curious expression on his face as if feeling pain and surprise all at once. Then, he keeled over and collapsed on the floor, giving Beatrice full view of Harry standing across the room holding a smoking gun. The other goons were all dead too. For a moment, all Harry and Beatrice could do was stare at one another, questioning if it was really over. Harry lowered his gun. Beatrice slowly rose to her feet. Then, the fog seemed to clear and they raced into each other's arms, sirens blaring in the distance. Neither was aware of the police milling into the building as they embraced, Beatrice gladly burying her face in his shirt. They were safe. Eleanore was safe. Beatrice couldn't ask for anything more.

"Where in the world did you learn to shoot like that?" she asked, pulling back to stare into his eyes with wonder.

"On the back lawn at my parents' estate," he replied with a smile. "Clay pigeons are a little different than live targets, but I managed."

Beatrice laughed in relief. "I'll say. Maybe you can teach me."

"I'd be glad to."

It wasn't until a familiar voice called out her name that Beatrice finally registered the presence of other people.

"Miss Adams!"

She whirled to see Captain Raglan standing there, surveying the bodies and broken liquor bottles with a team of mystified officers.

"I expect yeh've a damn good explanation," the captain went on, his Irish accent unmistakable.

Beatrice smiled innocently. "You bet I do," she replied.

Harry seemed reluctant to let her go when she stepped away, an expression of curiosity on her face.

"How did you know to come?" she asked.

"Greenie," Raglan replied. "He brought the evidence to us along with an address. Said yeh might be in some sorta trouble."

"You didn't have to come in person," said Beatrice, appreciation in every syllable.

"For Beatrice Adams, I do," he replied. "Now . . . why don't you two walk me through it."

The headlines the following morning all said much the same: Beatrice Adams had foiled an organized mob operation with style and grace befitting the daughter of Virginia Adams and Thomas Hughes. She hadn't quite escaped her parents' names, but at least now they weren't the only reason she was famous. Not a single word was mentioned in the paper about Donavan for fear of retribution, but in Los Angeles, it was usually a safe bet as to which mob was involved. All liquor left at the steel mill was promptly confiscated, and the building was roped off and placed under guard until it could properly be demolished. Further research turned up an owner for the property, but this quickly turned into a dead end—literally. It turned out Richard Mathis had died some years before, and his identity had been stolen and used to purchase the steel mill. Though the name was flagged to bar continued use, Beatrice had a feeling Donavan would only use others. The man was about as untouchable as the moon.

The headlines, of course, didn't go unnoticed by Patrick, who expeditiously interrupted Beatrice's late breakfast on the patio the following morning to plop a newspaper atop her plate, sending the salt shaker toppling.

"Oh, Pat, really," she complained, righting the salt and brushing the remnants off the table. It was lucky she wasn't superstitious.

"What the devil is this?" he demanded. "You didn't call me! You didn't so much as leave a note!"

"Would you have come?" she rebutted, arching an eyebrow.

"That's beside the point," said Patrick defiantly. "You called *him*!" He jabbed a finger at Harry's name, which had also made it into the paper.

"Yes," she admitted guiltlessly. She took a casual sip of coffee and set it aside. "Which reminds me . . . we need to have a little talk."

"Oh, do we?" he said, hands on his hips.

"Yes. We do." Beatrice adjusted to face him and crossed her legs, an arm draped over the back of her chair. Her electric blue eyes were so pointed, it was a wonder he didn't back away. "Harry Riley is my partner," she said firmly, "and my friend. You have no right to tell him he can't see me, just like you have no right to tell me I can't investigate. Are we clear?"

Patrick stumbled for words.

"I thought so," said Beatrice, turning back to her breakfast. "Now, sit down and have some breakfast or get out. I have work to do."

"Work?" he repeated incredulously.

"I'm reorganizing the study to use as an office space. I already have another client lined up and nowhere to properly conduct interviews."

"A client?"

"Yes, dear. Weren't you listening?"

Patrick seemed about to lose his temper, then at a loss for words.

Finally, he accepted his fate and snatched up the newspaper.

"I need something stronger than coffee," he grumbled, retreating into the house and calling for Owens.

Beatrice took a triumphant sip of coffee and smiled to herself. That was one less thing on her to-do list. All she had left to do now was celebrate, and she had elaborate plans for that.

Evening came on swift wings, and Beatrice donned a gown of exquisite coral with matching clutch and white gloves. She met her mother in the foyer, who was dressed in equal splendor, sporting a gown of blue.

"You sure clean up nice, kiddo," her mother praised as Beatrice descended the curving marble stairs.

Beatrice smiled. "I have good genes. Shall we?"

She offered her mother an arm.

Virginia beamed and linked arms with her daughter. "We shall!"

Together they made their way to Beatrice's newly refurbished Lincoln, the top of which was up to keep the drive from ruining their hair before they arrived at their destination. Virginia chatted the whole way downtown about the latest Hollywood gossip, including the recent rising star Jean Harlow, whom Beatrice knew her mother was insanely jealous of.

"You could have been like her, you know," Virginia was saying as Beatrice pulled up outside the Brown Derby on Hollywood and Vine.

"Yes, but I didn't want to be," said Beatrice.

A valet opened her door, and Beatrice exited with grace and style, pulling a few bills from her clutch for a tip, giving an earnest thanks before following her mother inside the beautiful edifice. The interior of the Brown Derby was the epitome of class with polished floors, white tablecloths, and an elegant brown and gold color scheme. Large half-circle booths made a row at the center of the high-ceilinged dining room, many of which were already brimming with dinner guests. Delightful caricatures donned the walls of famous guests who'd dined there in the last year. Her face was up there somewhere, as were her parents'. The formal attire and general glamour quickly made it a favorite haunt of Beatrice's, which is why when she had to think of a way to celebrate the success of her case, dinner at the Brown Derby was the first thing that came to mind.

When the maître d' showed them to their table, Harry and Eleanore were already sitting there. Beatrice was nearly floored at the sight of Harry in a tuxedo, but she let it roll off, matching his smile with confident ease.

"There you are," he said. "We were starting to get worried."

"I like to be early, and my mother likes to be fashionably late," mused Beatrice, sliding into the booth beside Eleanore. Her mother sat on the end.

"Where's Patrick?" asked Eleanore.

"I invited him, and he elected not to come," said Beatrice.

"Which is social suicide if you ask me," mused Virginia. "I mean, really. Who turns down an invitation to the Derby?"

Harry seemed uncomfortable. "You sure it's okay that I'm here?"

"Of course it is," said Beatrice. "Patrick being a boob has nothing to do with you. I can't very well celebrate success without my partners, now, can I?"

"Partners, huh?" repeated Harry with an earnest smile.

Beatrice raised her water glass. "Partners."

Eleanore and Harry lifted their water glasses as well, and the three friends clinked them together while Virginia Adams looked on with a proud smile.

That's what they were now: partners. Beatrice couldn't imagine taking on another case without Eleanore and Harry at her side, and she had a feeling there was another one waiting just around the corner. If the Harvey House murders could be credited with one thing, it was how they had brought them together.

If only Beatrice had realized then how violently Nikki Donavan intended to rip them apart.

ACKNOWLEDGMENTS

No book is ever a solitary act, and this novel has been no exception. From the very birth of this story idea to the end, I had encouragement and support from so many people, it's hard to know who to thank first. I guess the best place to start is always the beginning.

First, I owe an enormous thanks to my dad for satiating my need for adventure on a road trip down historic Route 66. It was on that excursion that we found the La Posada hotel in Winslow, Arizona. The basic building blocks for "Murder at the Harvey House" came together while I wandered the empty halls at one o'clock in the morning, and the story kept bugging me for two years until I finally wrote it down. Massive, massive thanks to you, dad. Your support means more than you will ever know.

My family as a whole deserves the biggest thanks for participating in what I liked to call "Sunday Murder Madness." I needed to get Beatrice's story out of my head, but I was working on another project at the time, and I knew I'd never finish the story without some incentive. I also had never really tried to write a mystery like this before and wasn't sure if I could do it well, so I decided to write a chapter a week and release it to my family every Sunday like an episode on a radio show. My family made a game of trying to guess the killer, and their reactions each week kept me writing until the story was done. So, to my grandmother, my mom, my sisters Kaitlynn and Christina, my cousins

Roxanne, Samantha, Candi, Courtney, and Wes, my Aunt Sherry and Uncle Bryan, Aunt Ellen and Auntie Kaye: THANK YOU. You were all such a big part of this story development, and you never discouraged my dreams. This book is for you!

Jaimie—fearless bestie and the strong, feisty redhead in my life—you were such a major cheerleader of this project. You kept me positive when I doubted I could do it, and you read every line I stuck under your nose. Thank you for being there for me!

Dearest Ashley, artist extraordinaire and the best friend I can always turn to with my crazy, creative ventures. When I came to you with my mad, Walt Disney-sized plan to start my own company, not only were you supportive, you immediately asked what you could do to help. Collaborating on book design and layouts together has been such a fun adventure, and I owe such a huge thank you to you for how beautiful this project turned out. You never questioned my desire to do things bigger and better, and you always exceeded my expectations. I look forward to future projects together!

To my editors, Jon and Amy: I have no idea what I would have done without you, truly. I knew what I was trying to say, but you both helped me say it better. I'm grateful for your feedback, your support, and especially your patience! Sometimes writers just need a good cheerleader in their corner, and you guys really made me believe this dream was possible. You guys are the real MVPs.

To my cover illustrator, Sydney Bowling…girl, you are talented! I hope you keep drawing and improving your talent. You were an absolute joy to work with, and I can't wait to see the beautiful art you create as your career goes on.

And lastly, but never least, I must thank God for opening all the doors that were closed to me on this journey, and for giving me a passion for stories in the first place. It feels so good to finally be doing what I was created to do.

About the Author

Ari Ryder is a Mystery, Science Fiction, and Fantasy writer who revels in the thrill of a good adventure. When she isn't writing, she can usually be found studying forensic science, traveling on research trips, and solving impossible puzzles. Ari has a Masters in Publishing from The George Washington University which has forever deepened her love and appreciation of books. Ari currently lives in Virginia with her sister and her stubborn Siberian Husky where she's currently working on her next novel.

CPSIA information can be obtained
at www.ICGtesting.com
Printed in the USA
BVHW071200071021
618420BV00002B/214